SAVING SEYMOUR

L.N. Loch

SAVING SEYMOUR

First paperback edition June 2021

Cover design and illustrations by Tricia Reeks

ISBN 978-1-7361741-2-8 (hardcover)
ISBN 978-1-7361741-1-1 (paperback)
ISBN 978-1-7361741-0-4 (ebook)

lnloch.wordpress.com

For every Ivan

1

The day Ivan Notte ruined his life, he forgot his umbrella. This didn't prove to be a problem as far as weather went, but it did make it harder, when he reached his building, to keep the usual protesters at arm's length. The cologne at his collar was no match for the breath of one particularly foul individual, and by the time he collapsed at his desk, resigned to the lingering smell on the starched cotton, he found himself actually wishing for rain.

Around the office, nearly every chair was cloaked with a waterproof jacket or a change of clothes. Ivan's was one of the few left bare. He refused to assimilate into Seattle's backwards culture in even the smallest way, and that meant refusing to trade his umbrella for a raincoat. The only justification he needed for his resistance was written across Galaxsea Entertainment Inc.'s front windows in bold, spraypainted letters that always reappeared as soon as they were rained or scrubbed away. Maybe the locals wouldn't have such a conniption every time they saw an umbrella if so much of the sidewalk wasn't taken up by sheltered, jobless brats in Northface jackets shouting for animal rights and other things they didn't take the slightest bit of time to ponder the logistics behind before they criticized others for failing to match their righteous outrage.

When he didn't have to think about rushing to the drycleaners after work to make sure his only remaining fitted suit didn't smell like civil disobedience for longer than it had to, Ivan's irritation usually faded with the protesters' shouts. At least, until he was insulted in some other way, and Galaxsea never failed to deliver on that front. That damn "documentary" (a sensationalist amalgamation of shaky performance footage, cherry-picked interviews, and soulful cello that had gotten a whopping 81% on Rotten Tomatoes, because of course it had) had left Galaxsea with the turnover rate of a poorly-managed McDonald's, which certainly didn't make anyone, including Ivan, more inclined to politeness. So it was that, on the day he ruined his life, Ivan didn't bother hiding the flock of cubes overflowing the margins of his legal pad as he stood to leave the conference room, sparse as they made his actual notes appear.

He gave a quick glance out the window and let a few little interns shuffle past him to network with his sister. A heavy fog was drifting in over Puget Sound, and it didn't look like any significant crowd had built throughout the day. In fact, he couldn't see anyone.

His sigh of relief was abruptly cut short.

"See? They'll find something new to be outraged over."

Ivan turned to look at Mike Swan, Director of Digital Communication, a tall man with a wide face Ivan still thought was handsome, in spite of the fact that they'd broken up years ago, and Ivan was irritated with him just now.

"Oh, you know what I meant," Mike said, reading his expression. "*My* father loves theme parks. Of course he would enjoy this."

Weary, Ivan tried to slip past him. It wasn't like there was much of a point in maintaining civility around here, anyway. The entire floor had just spent the past two hours agreeing with their CEO, Robert Cass, that it was a wonderful idea to throw a Father's Day celebration despite the fact that their turnout for Christmas had been nothing short of abysmal, and besides, they could barely afford to feed the mopey sea lions in their parks anymore, let alone a Mylar balloon or whatever the hell they were planning to decorate with.

Finding his path blocked by the suits still draining from the room, Ivan muttered, "You can't think this is a good idea."

With his hair gelled high and tight, Mike was just a bit taller than him. He also weighed about double.

"Well, no offense," Mike said, in a tone which indicated he was about to say something extremely offensive, "but you don't exactly have that much experience looking at things long term."

"Neither does Allison." Ivan's sister.

"Oh, I know!" Mike insisted. "It's just, Cass is where he is for a reason." That particular reason, of course, was that if the board voted him out they would need to find someone else to become the new face of whale torture. "I don't mean to offend. Really," Mike insisted, and Ivan hoped his expression was as cool as what he was trying to project, because he felt more like taking the sunglasses the bastard carried like a talisman and tossing them down twenty stories than he felt like having this conversation. Allison's eyes were burning holes into his back.

"There are more productive things," Ivan said, "to be offended about."

Mike laughed—an all-American cackle that belonged in a cereal commercial—and left Ivan standing in a cloud of cologne.

As the glass doors swung shut behind him, one of Allison's schmoozers made a quip about the sunglasses that made Ivan want to go out and buy the biggest umbrella he could find and start carrying it everywhere, rain or shine, just to wait and see if the reactions were similar. If you were Mike, not belonging was endearing, not embarrassing.

In the hopes of avoiding further conversation and the swell in protesters that would come when the few old enough to work clocked out, Ivan hastened out of the building. When he stepped outside, the air was thick enough to swim in, but the morning crowd had completely vaporized, evidently without anyone to take the next shift. Behind him, the revolving doors birthed another faceless manager. She wore gym shoes over her hosiery and was in the process of pulling on a raincoat. Most people passing by had already donned theirs.

Ivan looked at the sky and swore under his breath. The thought of sitting in a filthy taxi and making small talk was almost enough to reduce him to tears.

He set off by foot and was sweating within minutes. Ivan had managed to convince himself by about midday that the smell on his collar had faded, and that it was only the memory of it that he caught whenever he moved, but now he realized it was very much still present, and his current state wasn't doing anything to help it. It ought to have been a law you couldn't get within a certain distance of people if you drank coffee without brushing your teeth after.

It soon felt like his entire person was saturated with moisture. The only part of him that held even a hope of presentability was his hair (since moving here, he'd redirected his sunscreen fund towards gel), which more or less shielded his ego enough that he managed to walk as though he half-deserved to. That is, until the unmistakable shape of a lofted picket sign caught his eye.

Ivan's heart skipped a beat. A modest crowd had planted themselves at the corner half a block from his apartment. Paint was slathered on the brick building behind them.

Ivan approached and read:

Safety for Seers

So that's where they all went. The evening Seymour crowd had redirected their vandalistic abilities towards the campaign to install colored street signs all over Seattle. Yes, he even believed he could recognize a few pierced faces. You'd think all of the anti-discrimination legislation would have been enough, but no. Ivan was astounded when he considered the amount of entitlement necessary to believe an entire city ought to be redecorated to make driving easier for two percent of people. It wasn't as though Seeing color rendered you incapable of recognizing a damn stop sign.

Yes, Ivan thought, as his shoulder was hit by an ominous drop of rain, *shout on the street corners. Vandalize. That'll get people to think you deserve handouts.* He had only taken one handout in his entire life, and look where that had gotten him. A pariah in a company that was America's pariah. Maybe if Allison hadn't come to Galaxsea things would have been different. But because she had, it was no longer a dead father; it was a dead father, a handout, and a conflict of interest.

Anyway, the entire Seer movement was moronic and always had been. In fact, one of the rare instances in which Ivan had found himself in agreement with Robert Cass and Mike had been when one of their former interns suggested they use colored paint to accent the park's murals to be more inclusive. They'd laughed her out of the room.

A raindrop hit his face.

Better-off-blind. Instead of being cathartic, the thought of the slur only heated his blood further. As a few more droplets fell, Ivan quickened his walk so ferociously he could have outpaced a slow jogger. He wasn't about to let these people make him get caught in the rain and punish him for being a contributing member of society. Christ, they weren't even chanting or anything! Ivan's ire only heightened when one of them who didn't look older than fifteen laughed at a joke a bearded man told her while continuing to stand in Ivan's way.

Some people really had no damn clue, did they? Ivan was fed up within less than ten seconds, when he indiscriminately started to shove the people too stupid to move. He just knew every member of this crowd was full to bursting with the same kind of self-aggrandizing righteousness that made Allison so unbearable. Damned Seers, inventing a new color every day of the week, shouting off the rooftops how difficult it was to See the world differently than normal people, and how hard it was to have a *Mate* and a *Bond* instead of the respectable, normal relationships that most people settled for.

Ivan's anger got him into trouble often, but no bruised ego, suspended license, or hospital visit compared in scale to the chain of events it would set in motion that day. Unaware that he was about to upend the order of his life rather than set it right, Ivan charged past a lamp-post of a man with a "watch it!" that was nothing less than vicious. His arm was still throbbing from the contact when he stumbled free of the densest part of the crowd, and when he finally emerged on the other side, his ears were ringing too loudly to recognize the word a deep female voice hollered after him as "scab."

A raindrop hit him on the nose, then another on the hand. The locks to his building's heavy doors had barely buzzed open when a cascade of early-summer rain began to fall, darkening the pavement and the clothes of anyone unlucky enough to be caught on the streets without protection.

When he finally reached his apartment, Ivan flicked on every light switch he could find. The large windows in the main sitting room would ordinarily have let in a decent amount of sun, but currently they were as good as a stretch of wall. He threw his things down onto the kitchen table, and himself into a chair, resigned to the evening ahead. Massive raindrops pattered against the windows, and he pictured the protesters stuck in a sideways downpour.

Welcome to the real world, Ivan thought, imagining their slogan melting down the vandalized wall. Imagine having nowhere better to be than standing on the streets of Seattle in a rainstorm. Walking damn clichés. Actually, the rain would probably do them more than a little bit of good, if the smell of the man from this morning was any indication of their hygienic state.

On that note, Ivan dragged himself off to the shower, where he spent a good forty minutes thinking of all the cruel and just things he could have said as he'd pushed through the crowd, and why he hadn't said them. He went to bed with a headache, but chalked it up to stress.

2

By the time Katie bellowed her thanks to everyone for coming out, the rain had found its way through their waterproof jackets. Winston was grateful it wasn't cold, but where shivers didn't hold them back, the wind did. Tonight's rain was an uncommon one, with gusts straight to their faces that rendered their hoods useless and sent several picket signs flying out of sight. Winston squinted through the storm and eventually spotted Katie's guitar, which was sitting useless (and hopefully dry) in its case.

Its owner met his eyes. At least, he assumed she did. It was very hard to see.

"Time to call it?" Winston hollered over both the downpour and those of the crowd who, bless them, were still chanting.

Rather than answer him, Katie cupped her hands over her mouth and yelled, "Stop!"

This quieted about three-fourths of the crowd, but a remaining few were still stumbling through "Keep us Alive, Redo the Signs," when she reiterated, "Go home! Get dry! Disperse!"

"And thank you!" Winston added, though at least half of the group had dashed for cover before the last syllable of "disperse," and were already too far away to hear.

The wind began to still, but the rain remained so heavy that it was nearly impossible to see anything. He and Katie splashed their way to the nearest building, whose security kicked them out of its lobby after about half a minute (which was enough for the water running off them to form small lakes on the marble tile), and then braved the elements again until the next unlocked door, a block and a half away, which led to a brightly-lit little waffle store the size of a closet.

A few other protesters were there, but Winston and Katie still managed to snag two swivel chairs at a table. Katie did her best to keep her guitar out of peoples' way, and carefully avoided the eyes of the waitress as she maneuvered around the tiny space.

A drop of water rolled down Winston's nose and landed on the aluminum table. It was tempting to wring his hair out and get it over with, but he really didn't want to push their luck, since he wasn't sure they could afford anything here, and he doubted a place with a menu item called the "Stars and Strawberries" waffle was likely to stick its neck out in solidarity with Seers. Not many people in general were, or would be in the future, if their protests kept going like this.

It was possible a few people had seen their signs, but it had only taken a few minutes in the rain for the array of posters reading **Street Signs Save Lives**, **Safety for Seers**, and **We See Your Apathy** to be reduced to a collective pulp, drooping on their pickets and eventually falling off. Winston hadn't really been able to see the wall they'd painted, but the wind had been blowing straight at it, so he assumed the rain had washed away any evidence that the brick and mortar had ever been anything but pristine. Of all the days to get a disruptive rain, it had to be the one when they were using their expensive, colored spray paint to make a statement.

Winston tried to cross his legs and loudly knocked their tiny metal table. Katie slammed her palms down to steady it, which made such a loud noise that the waitress, who was crossing the room with a plate of what must have been waffles under a tower of banana and whipped cream, nearly dropped the precious cargo. She, the table waiting for her and, inspiringly, a few of the protesters, shot them dirty looks.

"Do you have any cash?" Katie muttered.

Winston did, from a recent commission, but he wasn't sure he wanted to spend it here, no matter how many foul looks they got. Though they were, upon closer inspection, within budget, every item on the menu had some awful pun in the name, save for the single plain waffle with maple syrup, which was called what it was, and which Winston assumed was its own special kind of degrading to order.

His shoulder throbbed, a reminder of another of today's specific miseries. He rubbed it absentmindedly.

Katie didn't miss this. "You should have broken his arm."

Winston grinned. "Doubt I could've caught him." The bastard had looked like he'd slicked his hair back with an entire tub of Crisco. Winston bet the rest of him was equally as slimy; the crosswalk had been right there.

The rain might have been slowing. If Winston squinted. He sighed and ran a hand through his hair, which was starting to curl. "Today sucked."

"Might have been out last protest together."

"Don't say that."

Katie lowered her voice, and Winston immediately knew what she was going to bring up. "You won't be able to show your face anywhere, even if you pull this off."

"I know," he said, because there was nothing else to say. He knew she saw it as a suicide mission, but if he relieved her of her grief and let Seymour die in captivity, he'd never get to prove to her and the world that it could be done.

"They might still do it themselves."

"Seattle won't even paint their street signs to be Seer-safe, and you think Galaxsea will get behind freeing everyone's favorite dying cetacean?"

Katie smirked and gave a nasal iteration of: "Where am I supposed to take my family on weekends now?"

"It's so much harder to see it if it's in the ocean," Winston imitated her tone, then switched back to normal. "I mean, not See-see."

She gave him a knowing look. "I promise you, the Rezzies look just the same in the ocean as on land." Just then, her phone lit up. "Speaking of the Rezzies, Barney says he saw K pod up by Samish." Barney was their mutual friend who worked in the logging industry.

"Pictures?"

"Not yet."

Winston rolled his eyes. Barney would think his left foot was a killer whale after enough beer. He stood. "C'mon. I'm tired of being here."

Katie headed straight for the door, but Winston held back and pretended he wasn't bothered by the familiar judgement in the waitress's eyes as she rang them up a box of chocolate-covered waffles. He ultimately decided to give her the benefit of the doubt and assume her eyes were locked on the rain, not on Katie, whom in the small space could easily have been overheard identifying herself as a Seer. Winston stuffed a five-dollar bill in the tip jar, on principle, and Katie gave him well-deserved grief for it all the way back to his apartment.

❧

The pair stepped inside Winston's mother's bakery only slightly wetter than when they'd left the protest. The rain had slowed to a gentle shower, probably the last one of the early summer, and the winds had calmed. *Takes the Cake* was promisingly quiet, and he and Katie had almost made it halfway up the stairs when the witch herself came rushing out of the back room to unleash a tirade upon Winston that concluded with what he suspected was a mild hex. Katie, who had allowed him to bear the verbal lashing alone, smirked at him when he plodded the rest of the way up to the landing.

"Better be careful," she said. "One day she'll make good on her threats."

Winston rolled his eyes, unlocking the door. He'd take his chances with the witchcraft, but if his mother ever actually started charging him for the food he "borrowed" from the kitchens, he might be in trouble. The threat seemed distant enough, however, that it was more irritating than worrisome.

"Not even a 'how'd the protest go?'" he muttered. "Straight to 'don't buy from my competitors.'"

Katie patted him with her free hand and set her guitar down. "That for Seymour?" she asked, fiddling with the clasps on the case.

The change in subject brought little relief. Winston didn't need to look at Katie to know her nose was wrinkled. His fridge was full of salmon so much of the time that the entire apartment now permanently smelled like a fishing harbor. The salinity didn't bother him that much, but combined with the fumes from his paints, it gave her headaches.

Shrugging off his jacket, he draped it over a chair to dry and began fiddling with the patterned tape on their box of waffles. There was a tap at his shoulder, and he stepped aside wordlessly to let Katie handle it. Her guitar must have been dry inside its case. Small miracle, too, as in the time he'd been standing at the kitchen counter he'd managed to form a small pool of rainwater on the tile.

While Winston was prying his boots off, the smell of melted chocolate and cinnamon filled the air. The springs of his couch creaked when Katie migrated to the living room sofa.

"Hey, hey, wait for—" The room wavered when Winston stood upright again. He leaned against the counter.

"You okay?" Katie asked. Winston's vision cleared as soon as she finished the question, and he saw she had already taken her first bite.

"I just stood up too fast," he said, though the window behind Katie was still shifting in a way disturbingly reminiscent of the time he and Barney had tried shrooms.

Winston took a seat next to Katie and flicked a hidden switch on the deep-sea diving suit in the corner of the room, illuminating the glass behind its helmet. He wordlessly took a waffle from the box, the couch springs offering commentary.

"She was probably wondering about it," Katie said, speaking of his mother again.

17

Winston knew Katie was right. It was actions that mattered, not words, and his mother certainly didn't have to give him food from downstairs free of charge. But he wasn't sure the occasional botched cupcake, delivered with an endless onslaught of irony, equated to love. He'd been surer as a kid. When he looked at Katie, he knew he was quite lucky to have grown up in such a laissez-faire household. But then, most households would have been better than hers.

The melted chocolate was thick in his mouth. When he checked the window, it was still shifting. The mess of easels, paints, and plants in front of it was completely stationary.

He stood, still chewing, and narrowed his eyes, but it didn't help any noticeable amount. Had they ordered edibles without knowing? Maybe that was why the waitress had looked at them so strangely. In all the years they'd known each other, he and Katie had never gotten high together. Maybe this would be an interesting evening.

"Do these taste off to you?"

"No, why?"

Winston started to answer her, but before he could speak, something changed beyond the window. His stomach plummeted, and without thinking, he dashed to the sill, stumbling over an aluminum can filled with drying paintbrushes.

What the hell?

At first, it was impossible to tell if he was hallucinating, or perhaps even dreaming. Had he seen a humpback whale swimming among the stars, he would have reacted with more composure. At least there were words to describe a whale.

It wasn't the window; it was the sky. There, beyond the lingering wisps of clouds, was a fresh infinity.

"Are you okay?" Temporarily abandoning the waffles, Katie raised a hand to Winston's forehead.

He brushed her away, heart hammering. "Do you not see that?" It was kind of beautiful. Beautiful and terrifying. "Here!" Winston threw the window open, sending cool, humid air rushing into the room. Any other day, he would have panicked and hidden his paintings, but today, his desperation was reserved for observing the sky, frantically trying to imprint what he was seeing upon his memory.

"Jesus, Jinx." Katie wrapped her arms around him, and before Winston knew it, he was being dragged back inside his apartment. He'd been hanging half out the window.

"Where the hell is my phone?" Detaching himself from Katie, Winston dropped to his hands and knees and began digging through papers and canvas.

"Winston."

He glanced back at the sky to make sure it still looked like *that* before going back to his desperate shuffling. Katie may as well have spoken his name underwater.

"Winston."

The commission that had paid for their waffles toppled a stack of paperbacks as Winston tossed it aside. Shortly after, he pulled his phone out from under a corner of the filthy cloth tarp he kept under his workspace and triumphantly stood, only to find Katie blocking his view.

"Winston."

Her voice was so uncharacteristically quiet that he responded as though she had screamed. "*What?*"

"What part of the sky is different?"

He pointed. Just beyond the clouds, it rippled around the moon, which was as unchanged as a rock thrown into a lake. His head was still swimming with nausea, but it was a different kind of nausea, the kind that came when one ran into a large change a bit too quickly. Winston had a hunch as to what this was, but a part of him kept waiting for it to switch back to looking the way it had his entire life. His eyes had never surprised him this much.

"Winston," Katie said, "that's blue."

For a beat, the only thing he could comprehend was the sound of distant traffic. He turned to look at her, and she reiterated, "The color blue. Very dark blue."

It was the sweetest, most understanding kind of devastation. A part of him felt like something had just slid into place, clicking like a cog into a previously-broken machine. Another part of him was remembering the night he'd received a text message from her when they'd been 18, saying that she needed to move out that night, she couldn't take a minute longer in that house. Still another part of him was extremely aware of his aching shoulder.

"That's what I get for leaving a protest for a little rain, huh?" There were tears welling in his eyes, his heart flooded with anguish and relief.

"The ocean's blue, too."

"Seriously?"

Winston looked at the room as though seeing it for the first time. Nothing else had changed so far, but he assumed soon it would be unrecognizable. Most things, even the ones that came from a factory, had some kind of color. Katie had been born a Seer, so she had little clarity to offer on the Bond, but from the time gap between his contact with Crisco and Seeing blue, he assumed it would be gradual.

God, was Crisco his Soulmate, then? Winston was sure he must have touched other people that day. And yet, he was filled with equal, dreadful certainty that if anyone had Bonded with him today, it had been that guy.

"How will I find him?" Winston asked aloud.

Katie was usually frowning in some form or another, but this question prompted one born of true discontent.

"How do you know it's a him?"

"I mean, if I have a Soulmate—"

"Platonic Bonds happen," Katie said. "Besides, just because you're Bonded doesn't mean you have a Soulmate chosen by the universe or God or something. I wish the community had never decided on that word."

"But—"

"It makes it sound like I have no one."

Winston understood her dissatisfaction. For centuries, it had been understood that Seers were a biological function left over from prehistory, evolved to breed offspring with maximum disease resistance, but Katie was an unBonded Seer, an outlier among outliers.

However, he kind of liked the idea of having a Soulmate. Even if it was Crisco. Hell, at least he had the balls to act how he felt. Sure, whoever Winston was Bonded to might not have truly been compatible with him, but it would have still been nice to know what they laughed like, what they looked like...now he'd never even get to paint them. Even if he could, it wouldn't be satisfactory; there was no way colored paints would be in his budget remotely soon, so even the practice required to get to portrait-painting level was far on the horizon. How was he supposed to continue painting skies as he always had when he knew blue, perfect and eternal, existed outside his window?

"It made people stop seeing us as monsters," he said.

She huffed, looking out at their now-shared sky. "So now we're unicorns, not pigs."

"You don't have no one, you have me and Barney," Winston said. "I doubt I'll ever find who it was, anyway."

He'd bumped into a lot of people today, and even if it was Crisco, Seattle was a big city.

"Don't underestimate the magnetism," Katie said. When Winston didn't comment, she continued, "The Bond...well, you'll see." Standing up, she brushed crumbs off herself, adding to the disaster that was his paint tarp. "Oh, and—"

Winston tore his gaze from the window.

"Don't bother trying to get a picture with your phone. They don't design cameras with us in mind."

The world was infinitely more beautiful than he'd ever imagined, and he couldn't even photograph or paint it. What if one day color was lost to time? Centuries of oppression had already nearly bred the ability to Bond out of the world population. When this reached its final stage, and they were completely obsolete, how would they be remembered without photographs or artwork? How would blue be remembered?

"I'll give you time to process," Katie said, picking up her guitar by the door. "Thanks for the waffles, Jinx, and welcome to the club."

Winston echoed a goodbye, not entirely happy to be left alone. The room was an odd mix of smells, cool petrichor, sharp fish, warm cinnamon. He closed the window and the box of waffles, in that order, already regretting subjecting his paintings to so much humidity.

He could feel the change in the sky behind him like eyes on his back, and when he turned back around to stare at it, his heart broke quietly. Van Gogh had painted Starry Night looking at a sky that was no longer his own. Winston had always taken for granted that he woke to the same sky each morning. Now in its place was an alien cosmos that, apparently, had been there all along. He felt blind, almost cheated. He was a newborn again, having never before seen a sunset or a flower or his mother's face. The world had grown infinitely in size for him within the course of one day, and his only real complaint was that he would likely never meet whoever he had to thank for it. This was a voyage he was doomed to undertake alone. He prayed the ocean would still be a home to him after it.

3

Ivan resisted the urge to tap his foot as the barista started the order of the person two places in front of him; evidently it was more important she share a laugh with a coworker than do her goddamn job. Instead, he fiddled with the handle of his umbrella, sliding it up and down while casting periodic glances at the street to check that hoods weren't being pulled up. When he left, croissant in one hand and coffee in the other, the pavement was still dry, but a cluster headache was already growing at his temple.

He imagined he looked ridiculous, switching his breakfast between hands as he walked, but it was only because the drink was so hot it was nearly burning him through the cardboard protector around it. He nearly dropped it several times, but the closest came when he thought he saw Allison pass him in her car, her dark hair pulled into its usual severe bun and the steering wheel in an easy, one-handed grip. As uncannily as the stranger (as he realized, upon closer inspection, she was) resembled her, it was only when his gaze traveled from her car to the stop sign in front of it that his coffee actually slipped out of his grip.

Ivan stopped in his tracks. There was a ringing in his ears, a drop in his stomach like he'd skipped a stair, a scalding pain in his leg.

Swearing, Ivan stumbled back from the spreading, dark puddle, but his eyes remained locked on the stop sign, which looked different from any other he had seen in his life. Some part of his mind was aware of a bicycle gliding by him, a few distracted glances from other foot traffic. The growling of his stomach.

Its shape was the same as any other stop sign, and the letters were clear as ever, but the fill of it was so unlike anything Ivan had ever seen that he questioned whether he was hallucinating or dreaming. He blinked repeatedly, but each time he opened his eyes again, its deformity was just as pronounced, and some part of him knew the anomaly was too large to be the product of his unconscious, although its surface and the area just around it was shifting like ocean waves. After a minute of staring, he began to feel dizzy.

Suddenly self-conscious, Ivan collected himself enough to pick up the empty coffee cup and throw it away with the rest of his breakfast. A passing woman gave his soaked ankle a piteous glance, but resumed ambivalence when she caught sight of his umbrella, probably thinking he was a tourist. Ivan watched her near the sign, but she didn't spare it a second glance.

Heart pounding, Ivan returned to the site of the anomaly and reached up, as discreetly as he could, to touch it. A chill ran down his spine; where the surface appeared to be shifting, it felt solid and smooth.

Oh, God, he was losing his mind. Late-onset schizophrenia, maybe. To his knowledge, the Nottes didn't have a family history, but he wouldn't be surprised if his mother's side had covered something up. Or, maybe one of the protesters he'd had to push past in the last few days had exposed him to a drug that had triggered it. Though he tried, Ivan also couldn't fully deny the possibility that this was his fault. When he'd been in court, they'd talked about managing his stress. Maybe this was what happened when you didn't do that. If he'd never had his license revoked, he wouldn't have had to shove past this many protesters in the first place.

I don't want to see you, Ivan thought. *When I open my eyes, everything will be back to normal.*

Taking a deep breath, he closed his eyes, and opened them again.

Fuck.

It was still there, still alien, still wrong, **STOP** sitting surrounded by a ring of abnormality, all resting atop a tiny print at the bottom that made his blood run cold.

THIS RED-COLORED STOP SIGN WAS APPROVED BY THE CITY OF SEATTLE ON BEHALF OF THE SEE SIGNS, SAVE LIVES CAMPAIGN.

Ivan read the inscription again, and then a third time, but in spite of his current visual uncertainties, it remained the same, and he was left with no choice but to face the apocalyptic implications of his situation.

Somehow, they had found a way to force everyone to See it.

He'd thought it was impossible for Seers to bring this upon regular people without a Bond, but apparently that was no longer the case. Ivan knew full well he wasn't Bonded, that much was common sense. People at Galaxsea barely wanted anything to do with him, so it wasn't like handshakes and casual touches came often, and in terms of romance, he'd barely even thought of dating since he and Mike had broken up. What was more likely was that all the extra exposure to color through these damn signs had affected his vision. Probably something in the paints, he might have heard something on the news about that. Oh, God, maybe this was where all the unBonded Seers were coming from. He sure as hell didn't remember there being this many five years ago.

Blinking back tears of shock and rage, Ivan drew out his phone and dialed Galaxsea's reception desk, starting off for the nearest hospital at a pace that could have matched a particularly lethargic biker. He gave as few details on the phone as he could get away with. The less the receptionist knew, the less Allison knew, the less Mike and Cass and everyone else knew. If Mom somehow got wind before this was all straightened out (and it *would* be straightened out), it would be the end of Ivan. He'd have to leave town, have to leave the job his father fucking died for and let Allison take all the clout for herself, and that was not what he'd made himself miserable all these years for. In the event he wasn't hallucinating, Ivan hoped Street Signs Save Lives enjoyed their final hours before the lawsuit of their lives hit them.

The pressing feeling that a great red monster was lurking behind him intensified with every flash of color Ivan glimpsed in his periphery. He arrived at the hospital quickly, but when the building's doors parted for him, he experienced a fresh surge of panic that halted him in his tracks. This was in part because he was faced with what was unmistakably a second color, and in part because it was atop someone's head.

A willowy man with the wildest mop of curls Ivan had ever seen was arguing with an apathetic-looking nurse at the reception counter. Even if the man hadn't been crowned with the second sign that Ivan's life was officially spinning out of control, everything else he wore was enough to warrant hatred. He dressed like a college student. Or an artist. Or, God forbid, both.

A father with a snot-nosed toddler in tow shoved past Ivan, throwing a dirty look over his shoulder. Ivan closed his gaping mouth in a hurry, stepping out of the way without taking his eyes off Artist Boy.

Ivan blinked a few times and was disappointed but not surprised when the hair remained the same vibrant color. It was crystal clear, unlike the stop sign. He supposed it was almost beautiful, in a poisonous way.

"I'm telling you, I think they're dead!" Artist Boy said, oblivious to Ivan's stare.

"Sir, calm down," the nurse deadpanned.

"How can I calm down? I was Seeing yesterday."

Ivan's stomach flipped at the word.

"And today, it's gone."

"Yes! I think my Soulmate is dead, and I'd just like some reassurance—"

He sounded genuinely distressed, though Ivan couldn't comprehend why. Waking up to find everything back to normal sounded like a dream.

"You know, there are people here who are actually sick."

"I know what I Saw!" AB exclaimed. Ivan was beginning to question whether that statement applied to him as well when, with a sigh audible all the way across the waiting room, another nurse took up the computer next to her coworker.

"I can help who's next," she called, making eye contact with Ivan, who closed the space between himself and the counter without bothering to see if anyone else was waiting.

"Hi." Ivan felt a bit like he was on trial. "I've burned myself, and I need treatment."

"How did you burn yourself?"

Ivan told her. They could go over the whole hallucination thing when he had a private room with a real doctor.

"Do you have blisters?"

Ivan knelt down to check, and he didn't, though there was a waviness in his vision whenever he focused on the burnt area that couldn't mean anything good.

"Well, your local drugstore should have a variety of topical anesthetics to choose from. If the pain doesn't go away within a week, feel free to come back in."

"I'm hallucinating."

The nurse stared at him. "Can you elaborate?"

Shame welled up in Ivan like tar. For a moment he stood paralyzed, uncertain if it was more horrifying to turn and run or voice what he knew to be true. Ultimately, he chose the latter.

"I think I might be Seeing color."

The nurse looked up at him. "Oh, you're Seeing?" Her voice was unbearably loud.

Ivan pinched the bridge of his nose. "No, of course not." He should have run. Maybe then he'd have had a chance at denial. Now, after facing off with his reflection in her glasses for several more seconds, he had no choice but to break. "Yes, I think I'm Seeing."

This couldn't be real. How could such a normal morning preclude such a waking nightmare? Somewhere there had been a brushing of a hand, a shove, an accidental closeness that would have started the...Bond. Like catching a cold on the subway. And because of it, he would never, ever measure up to Allison.

His fate was sealed now, his coffin nailed shut. He could do great things, sure, but he would still See what he was never meant to See, and they would all know it. Mike had a particular talent for it; he'd used to point them out at the other tables for fun, when he and Ivan had gone out for dinner, how they picked at their food, studied things in the flickering candlelight. Ivan supposed there was a dark sort of humor in the fact that his driver's license had already been taken away. Once he had it back, he would get to experience firsthand what it was like trying to focus on uncolored street signs amidst a colored world. How helpless would he become, trying to navigate the city? Perhaps in a year, he'd be on the picket lines.

This was all so embarrassing. Animals mated, humans found partners based on mutual relationship benefits and, above all, logic. What did it say about Ivan that he was a member of the former group?

Truly, he thought bitterly, *better-off-blind*.

"Oh." The nurse's tone was cool. "We have some pamphlets on the process of becoming a Seer. I'm assuming the contact happened recently?"

"I don't know," Ivan said miserably, trying not to think of *pamphlets*. Suddenly, an idea occurred to him. "Is it too late to stop it?"

She regarded him with utter derision, and he repeated the question.

After a beat of silence, the nurse, goddamn her to hell, said, "That's not possible. What have you Seen so far?"

Whatever tiny glimmer of hope had begun to quicken inside of him was immediately annihilated with that sentence. Fantastic. Fan-fucking-tastic, this was probably for forever.

"A stop sign painted especially for Seers, and," he glanced over at the still arguing (albeit quieter) Artist Boy next to him, "someone's hair."

As soon as Ivan's eyes left AB, he felt AB's land on him.

Ivan swallowed, scowling deeply. Something was nagging at the corner of his mind. He might have brushed it off as the discomfort of being stared at, had it not so distinctly reeked of familiarity.

"Are you alright?" the nurse asked.

"I'm in a hospital," Ivan snapped.

"Your eyes are darting around, like you're nervous."

Ivan was about to ask, given that he had just told her he was having hallucinations, if this was to be expected, and where the hell had she gotten trained, he wanted to speak to her supervisor, when another voice, easy and smooth, addressed him directly.

"You watching out for someone?"

Ivan's heart skipped and he turned to AB, who was watching him with the look of someone who had just finished making a joke. Yes, there was definitely something familiarly irritating about him. Maybe he had gotten Ivan's coffee order wrong on a Monday. Then again, Ivan didn't know how likely he would be to accept food or drink from someone whose hair looked like it hadn't been brushed in its entire life. At this point, he doubted it would respond to any kind of discipline.

Despite his earlier distress, AB didn't seem to mind Ivan's silent appraisal. In fact, he now looked calmer than Ivan had felt within the past decade of his life. Leaning against the counter with curiosity in his eyes, everything about his person exuded tolerance and ease.

Well, that settled it. Ivan definitely hated him.

"I—" Ivan replied brilliantly, suddenly unable to form sentences.

For a moment, the four strangers stood in complete silence. Or, rather, he and Artist Boy stood, and the nurses sat on their asses offering zero help or excuses for Ivan to escape.

"You bumped into me at the protest yesterday," AB said. "Still got the bruise to prove it."

Ivan's face went hot, but he quickly replaced his shame with annoyance. Imagine. Here he was, having a private medical conversation, and a stranger decides to butt in and make it look like *he* was in the wrong.

"You must," he said icily, "have me confused with someone else."

"You just started Seeing color." AB turned his lanky body towards Ivan, who now felt socially obligated to listen. "I did, too. Around the time I got home afterwards."

Ivan didn't like the realization that was creeping into his voice. He swallowed, unable to stop his eyes from drifting back to the man's hair. "You must have bumped into a lot of people that day."

"But did you?"

A sigh from the nurses. "If you two are finished—"

Despite the fact that he was quite afraid of The Hair, Ivan found a completely insane part of him almost wanted to lace his fingers through it. The stop sign had proved solid to the touch, but maybe this was different. Maybe he could still snap out of it.

"Are you staring at my hair because you can See it?"

Ivan's eyes flicked to AB's face, which wore a crooked smile.

"Yeah." Ivan's heart pounded so loudly it nearly drowned out his voice. "Yeah, I noticed when I walked in."

AB's smile broadened. Ivan didn't think he'd ever seen anyone look so happy in his life, and certainly not to see him. He hoped he wasn't thinking about that word he'd used earlier: "Soulmates." He'd heard the term used before for pairs of Seers, but of course, there was no scientific stock in it. It was nothing more than the PC way of saying you were Bonded. People Ivan liked just called it like it was and said "Mated." If there was one thing he didn't believe in, it was self-delusion.

When AB spoke again, it was with a sense of calm resolution Ivan really didn't like. "Well, that settles it, doesn't it?"

Ivan was feeling sick in both the terrible and the wonderful sense. "What's settled?"

"You can See my hair because it's me you bumped into. Our contact must have set off the reaction." Mercifully, he lowered his voice. "I think we're…"

"Don't say it," Ivan interrupted, losing his composure to desperation as usual. This was all getting to be a bit too much. He was just beginning to formulate an escape plan for whatever grandiose speech the damn poet had in mind when something completely unexpected occurred.

Artist Boy held out a hand.

"I'm Winston," he said. "Winston Jinx."

Ivan looked from the hand to its owner. What was he, a Harry Potter character?

"Ivan," he said, readying himself for the weakest handshake of his life. "Ivan Notte. Why were you at a Seer protest before I even bumped into you?"

"Supporting a friend." Winston gave Ivan's hand a squeeze and a firm shake.

Dammit. Ivan wished he didn't look such a mess.

Winston didn't elaborate further, and they sunk into silence. Ivan hadn't realized he'd raised an eyebrow, but when he finally let go of the other man's hand, it was with his face twisted into a slight grimace.

"Right."

"Come on, let me buy you a coffee."

"Oh," Ivan laughed, gentle and detached, "I have a boyfriend, actually."

Winston didn't skip a beat. "Really? What's his name?"

Ivan was truly sweating now. "Tom."

Outrageously, Winston snorted.

Ivan did his best to arrange his face in such a way that made it very clear, to all the hospital goers awaiting bad news around them, that he most certainly had not just said anything funny. Unfortunately, Winston just kept snickering, and by the time he'd raised his head to look at Ivan again, the majority of the latter's ire had melted away into resignation.

"I'm sorry," Winston wiped a tear from his eye, "it's the inflection. I'm sleep deprived."

A laugh of surprise escaped Ivan before he could stop it. "The *inflection?*"

"Yes. And you're not a very good liar."

"I'm not lying," Ivan lied.

"Tom just goes to a different school."

"You know," Ivan said, "frankly, I find this intrusive and insulting."

"Look," Winston said, "fine. You have a boyfriend—"

"No, I don't!" Ivan exploded.

"Fine, you don't or you do," Winston said evenly. "Platonic Bonds exist. I only meant our vision is gonna change completely, and it would be kind of nice to know someone going through the same thing, don't you agree?"

Ivan opened his mouth to say that, no, actually, he wasn't about to make this thing out to be his entire identity, or something, when one of the nurses spoke.

"So will you two be needing any help, then?" She didn't even look up from her phone.

"No, thank you." Winston actually *grabbed* Ivan's hand to pull him away. His skin was rough, and his hands larger than Ivan's.

"Do you want any pamphlets?" a nurse called after them.

"No thanks!" Winston answered, leading them outside. To Ivan, he muttered, "Screw her pamphlets. My unBonded friend, Katie—she's the one I was supporting—can tell us way more."

"Well, that's kind of her." Ivan had an almost masochistic desire to allow the interaction to continue, despite the stares Winston's volume was already drawing from pedestrians. If he omitted the details about his own condition (the Seeing, not the burn), this could make a good story for Mike tomorrow, and besides, from the way Winston faltered when he turned his eyes to the sky, it was still possible they weren't Bonded at all. Though Ivan was flattered enough by his enthusiasm, he knew the feeling would pale in comparison to witnessing the look on Winston's face when he broke the terrible news.

4

Winston was surprised at his own disappointment when they stepped outside and the sky still appeared drained of color—the prospect of not being Bonded with Crisco ought to have been a relief, but it only reanimated the previous night's weariness.

Seattle was a big city, but it was possible they'd both Bonded to different people and run into each other by coincidence. That was for the best, probably. Ivan might have been fun to argue with for a few minutes, but Winston imagined it would get old quickly.

Ivan cleared his throat, his strong brow emphasized by the scowl that had dominated his face since their first interaction. Winston was so taken aback by the intensity of his expression that it took him several seconds to realize they were still holding hands.

"Shit, sorry." He let go, and his eyes traveled down to the dark stain at the bottom of Ivan's left pant leg. "Bad day?" Or maybe bad week, if his demeanor was any indication.

"You have no idea."

"Moronic nurses don't make it much better. I can't believe how uneducated they're allowed to be on this stuff."

"It's probably difficult to keep up, with new colors being invented every day of the week."

Winston studied his face, but he couldn't find a trace of irony. God, Ivan didn't actually believe that, did he? The idea that Seers made up new colors for attention wasn't exactly an unpopular one, but if Ivan was bigoted enough to believe it, Winston wasn't sure he wanted to keep him around, Bond or no Bond. By the second, it seemed less likely they would ever meet with Katie.

"Red is the only one I know," Ivan continued. "Your hair is different, but I don't know what it's called."

The temptation to tell Ivan he didn't have to talk about color like one talked about crystal meth faded to make way for worry. It seemed like Ivan's Bond was more developed than his, if he was Seeing two colors already. God, what if they were Soulmates, but something was wrong with Winston's vision, or his Bond had fractured? Moreover, why the hell hadn't Katie mentioned his hair was colored? Winston wondered if he would ever be able to See it for himself, or if color would leave his world as soon as it had entered it; if he didn't find the person he'd Bonded with soon, his vision would return to greyscale.

Winston opened his mouth to respond with his own experience, but he'd hardly done that much before Ivan violently pulled him to the ground.

"*Ow!*"

Ivan shushed him in response, and Winston bristled. "Excuse me?"

"Shut up." Ivan was on his knees, peering over the decorative hedge shading them.

Winston was flabbergasted. "This is the second time you've—"

Ivan rounded on him. "I said, shut up!" He turned back to the hedge and hissed, "That's Robert Cass."

Winston's jaw dropped. "The Galaxsea CEO?"

The familiar, self-assured boom traveling over the hedge was enough of an answer. Winston wasn't sure if Robert Cass was as close to them as he sounded, or if his voice was just as loud in real life as on television. Winston smiled as it formed the words "character assassination," though he pitied whoever was on the other end of the phone call.

Ivan didn't answer, and after a few tense seconds lowered himself so they sat side by side. A few strands of his hair had broken free of their gelled bonds, falling into his face.

"Do they have you on file?" Winston whispered. After the documentary had dropped, Galaxsea had decided the most efficient way to smooth things over was to call the cops on anyone that showed up on the picket lines more than once. Apparently that was more feasible than removing animal torture from their business model.

"What?" Ivan was still looking over his shoulder.

Winston rephrased in the hopes of making a broader determination. "I mean, do you hate Cass too?"

"He's an ass."

Winston let out a breath and leaned back against the wall, watching the sky. "Ain't that the truth." Maybe there was more to Ivan than met the eye.

Cass's shouting eventually faded, and the two of them sat in silence for a moment before Ivan hissed, "Go check if he's still there."

"Why me?" Winston was almost positive Cass was more likely to recognize him than Ivan. The bastard wasn't known for his involvement in company affairs, and probably had no clue which activists Galaxsea had record of, but Winston couldn't risk any more run-ins with police.

Ivan looked at him like he was a moron. "Because I asked you to."

Winston huffed. "Is that an order?"

"Please, if you would be so kind, Winston Jinx, check if he's gone."

Winston was beginning to think Ivan's personality was just as obnoxious as his cologne. Nonetheless, he obeyed. When he lowered himself again, Ivan remained deep in thought, seemingly oblivious to Winston's irritation, which actually bothered Winston more than his bossiness had.

"Well, it looks like he left," Winston said. Then, because he couldn't stop himself, "Don't know why you don't wanna see him. Seems like you two would get along great."

The ghost of a sneer crossed Ivan's face. "At least I have common sense."

"Having 'common sense' doesn't exempt you from cruelty."

Ivan's jaw dropped at the last word, finally awarding Winston his full attention. "Cruel world you live in, where kindness isn't common sense."

"And that's your personal philosophy, is it?"

"How do you know it isn't?"

"I mean, you're kind of a jerk."

"You don't know that! You don't know anything about me!"

"Every interaction I've had with you, you've been rude," Winston said, a bit of anger flickering in his chest.

"All two interactions. You're making assumptions."

39

"I'm making observa—"

It was halfway through this statement that Winston realized they were being watched. A trembling old man had parked his walker in front of them, and was watching them with a raised brow. This may have been enough to shut Ivan up, but Winston's temperament was such that nothing less than the man's cloudy *blue* eyes could have halted his verbal onslaught.

Only after he was certain he had their full attention did the old man remark, "Young love," before hobbling on his way, as if he hadn't mollified them enough already by eavesdropping. It must have been a solid minute before he was out of view, and that was when Winston allowed for the way his last word stretched the seconds like taffy. Like taffy if it could be blue. Imagine that. Colored candy.

Now he understood why Ivan had seemed so transfixed by his hair. It was miraculous slowly waking to a parallel world of color, but it was nothing short of transcendent to See color on people. He felt a bit like he'd Seen into that man's soul, and, if his tone was any indication, like the man had Seen into his, as well.

When Winston turned to Ivan again, sobered with the knowledge that the latter had Seen him in the same way, he was jolted to find he was being scrutinized like a difficult math problem.

"Your face." Ivan, unbelievably, leaned closer. "It's red."

Winston's heart skipped a beat. "What?"

Ivan faltered and blinked a few times, as one waking from a particularly disconcerting dream, and stood promptly. He brushed off his pants and the front of his suit, and Winston found it endearing, if a little bit weird, that he even bothered, what with the coffee stain.

"Nevermind. I'm so sorry about all this."

Winston couldn't complain about the change in tone, but he felt it still amounted to a pretty poor apology.

"I just can't believe we ran into Cass." Winston stood. He was taller than Ivan, but it didn't make the chilly way Ivan nodded and cleared his throat, allowing the silence to file in afterwards, any less intimidating.

"Well," Winston started, and never finished. He didn't know if it was worse for him or Ivan to say what they were thinking. He didn't know *what* he was thinking.

It was Ivan who ended up taking the plunge. "Clearly," he said, "we aren't Soulmates." The way he looked at his feet irritated Winston all over again.

"Right."

"It was interesting meeting you."

"You too." What the *fuck?*

"Hearing your opinions."

Fine. As long as they were being petty.

"Yours as well."

"I truly wish you the best."

"And you and…" Just as the fake-boyfriend's name, Tom, came to Winston, something caught his eye. "You're bleeding."

In fact, Ivan was bleeding a lot. Winston had been so preoccupied with the resurfacing of blue that he hadn't noticed the dark, colorless blood streaming from dozens of cuts on Ivan's palms. When the sun emerged from behind a cloud, it illuminated the fine pricks of glass responsible for the carnage. There were dark handprints on the ground where Ivan's had rested, and Winston had no doubt anyone passing by later that day would think they'd stumbled onto a crime scene.

Winston checked his own hands, but it looked like Ivan was the only one who had nearly sat in the shards of what was hopefully a broken bottle and not some kind of biohazard. His misfortune was compounded by the fact that, in the process of brushing himself down, he'd spread a fair amount of blood down his front.

Winston glanced from Ivan to the hedge and back again, which was suddenly wavering in a familiar sort of fog.

It's us. Oh my God, it's definitely us.

He knew it as surely as he knew Seymour belonged in the ocean. Katie—hell, a lot of people—wanted proof, but Winston, Winston knew there were some things, higher things, that didn't lend themselves well to proving. They had to be felt, touched, Seen.

Unfortunately, as much as Winston wanted to deal with the implications of his instincts, there were other pressing matters at hand.

"Shit." He pulled off his hoodie and offered it to Ivan. It was warm enough today that he'd be fine with just a t-shirt. "There must have been glass on the ground."

Ivan recoiled. He was holding his hands out as if they didn't belong to him.

"Let's sit down," Winston said. He was sure he could catch Ivan if he passed out, but better safe than sorry.

Ivan's eyes were wide. "It's red." His voice was barely a whisper. "It's *red*."

Winston's pulse hammered. "Your blood?"

"Jesus, just shut up!" Ivan spat, his eyes slightly feral. "This wasn't supposed to make its way to me, understand?"

Whatever Winston had begun to feel, the words slit through it in a series of short strokes. Nonetheless, he pressed on. "Ivan, you're getting blood everywhere."

"Fuck off with your *Ivans*," he said, appearing on the verge of hyperventilation. "You don't know me, I'm not like you! This is a mistake, and I'll bleed out if that's what it takes to fix me."

Fed up, Winston gave a pointed glance to the hospital doors mere feet to their right, and Ivan's face grew wan.

"Would you rather I help you take care of it?" Winston offered, uncertain if he was doing something supremely stupid.

Ivan seethed, hiding his face from what few passersby had the balls to glance their way. Winston was insulted, though relieved, at the ones who pretended not to notice the situation as the hospital's automatic doors spat them out.

"I have to go," Ivan said suddenly. "I'm sorry to have troubled you."

"You haven't," Winston lied. He took a step closer, holding out the sweatshirt. "Take it. I'm not leaving you bleeding in the street."

Ivan didn't respond, but he also didn't shrink back when Winston approached this time, eventually using the shirt to dab at the edges of a few of the larger cuts, careful not to press any of the glass shards. A morbid part of him wished he could See what it really looked like, but the desire evaporated when he moved the fabric by accident and Ivan gasped.

Winston made up his mind then. He wasn't turning Ivan over to those shitty nurses. Not in this state. Who knew what kind of bullshit they'd tell him?

"Look, I can't force you, but I really think we should get back to my place so I can help you with this. I'm used to patching people up, and I can give you something to wear."

Ivan bit his lip.

"And then we can part ways and forget all this ever happened," Winston added.

Ivan scoffed, then said, mostly to himself, "Forget."

As if that was possible, when your very blood was no longer familiar to you.

"I shouldn't have shouted," Ivan continued, "or pushed you. It's better if you just let me go."

"Okay."

Ivan balked, apparently surprised at his readiness to quit. "Okay?"

Winston shrugged. "I'll see you around, then. Keep the hoodie."

He had taken not one, not two, but three terrifying steps before Ivan called him back. The magnitude of the relief that washed over him in that moment was disconcerting, to say the least. This was a stranger. A stranger, a stranger, a stranger.

"Wait?"

It was posed as a question. Winston considered it almost offensive that Ivan felt the need to ask at all.

When he turned around, the hedge had exploded into full color, dashing any hopes he might have had of keeping his expression neutral, and stealing the breath from his chest. The trees standing sentry outside the automatic doors, the mosses filling the sidewalk cracks, and the lichens crawling up the buildings all metamorphosed into something new and strange in the blink of an eye. With one more, the vines, the grasses, and the eyes of a passing woman joined them.

Ivan asked if he was okay, and Winston forced his eyes away from the new color. He didn't have the faintest idea how to truthfully answer. "Nothing. The uh, the plants."

Ivan looked like he'd just watched a dog get hit by a car, but said nothing. Winston tried to gather his bearings. Although he'd spent his childhood on the line between trees and sea, he was suddenly hyperaware of the wilderness, and couldn't shake the sensation he was being surrounded, stepping down the rabbit hole to someplace unreal and esoteric.

"Come on, my apartment isn't far. Is your burn bad?"

Ivan shook his head, holding the sweatshirt close. Winston let him set their pace, as he was clearly in a lot of pain, not to mention dizzied enough from blood loss that he brushed against Winston's shoulder by mistake. At least, that was what Winston told himself in the moment. The silence had a way of reviving his doubts.

5

They hadn't walked far before Ivan's anger yielded to resignation, which did little to alleviate his misery. During this time, Winston offered little comfort, but Ivan couldn't blame him for that; if their positions had been reversed, he wouldn't have given him the time of day.

Well-worn and pilling, the sweatshirt kept the worst of his thoughts at bay, if only because it brought a different kind of pain. The sharp pangs that came whenever he pressed it between his marred palms were enough to make him see stars. This worked well enough (after all, he would rather see stars than color) until a particularly potent pang caused him to bump into Winston for the second time that week. And although Ivan managed to steady himself fast enough to pass it off as an accident, he was disappointed to find he didn't need to. Evidently, Winston had been too enraptured by the plants to notice the contact.

By the time they reached their destination, a homey little bakery titled *Takes the Cake,* Ivan was a proper wreck. The lingering smell of coffee was not a pleasant companion to the comingling odors of blood and sweat, and while this would have been uncomfortable enough on its own, when married with his

unkempt appearance it sired a shame in Ivan unlike anything
he'd felt in his adult life.

The interior of the bakery was mercifully dim, and the
seemingly unattended candle next to the register cast flickering
light that bounced off the glass jars of herbs and preserves lining
the walls. Some of them were filled with things Ivan could See,
others remained ambiguous. It was the same with the bakery's
actual fares, which Ivan assumed were responsible for the divine
scent of roasting pecans and rising dough that was strong
enough to mask his own. An array of goods sat in the display
case under the candle, but the croissants were what drew Ivan
closer. Gleaming with egg-wash, larger than dinner plates, and
$3.00 a piece, they were better than any he and his father had
ever made, though they'd certainly tried. They were also the first
proper food he'd ever seen in color.

"Ivan?"

Winston's whisper alerted him to how hard he'd been
gripping the shirt again, and he gritted his teeth as he released it
slowly. Winston led him to the base of a wooden staircase,
doubled back, and wiped his sneaker across a few stray drops of
blood. The visual kept Ivan queasy until they arrived at
Winston's apartment, whereupon he was hit so strongly by the
acrid stench of paint that his vertigo cleared.

"Sorry about the smell," Winston apologized, holding the
door. "I paint, obviously, and my fridge is full of fish."

"Fish?" Ivan asked, muttering a thank you as he stepped
over the threshold. Upon reconsideration, he supposed he
caught a bit of it, but it was faint compared to the paint. Then
again, his nose had been through so much today he wouldn't be
surprised if it was just too overwhelmed to detect it fully.

"You should sit down." Winston guided Ivan into a scratched hardwood chair at a table that, like everything else in the apartment, was small.

"You don't have to—" Ivan started a last futile attempt to save his dignity.

"I'll be right back." Winston marched off down a narrow hallway to the left, and it wasn't long before Ivan heard him rummaging through his medicine cabinet.

Ivan allowed himself a small sigh of relief, sinking into the chair with a creak. It felt good to sit down, better to be out of range of judgmental eyes. And he knew, upon closer examination of his living space, that Winston would not be inflicting any judgement today. His apartment was the size of Ivan's closet, but it appeared he owned twice as many things! Every surface was littered with clutter. Interesting clutter (the scuba suit in the corner was actually kind of awesome), but clutter all the same.

Ivan wondered if Winston ever felt claustrophobic. After growing up with a sizeable suburban abode and summer lake house, it had seemed extreme when his mother had downsized to a condominium, but this was something else. Did Winston not know the space would seem bigger if he segregated the brushes from the paperbacks from the…Christ, were those tomato seeds? Ivan didn't share his mother's green-thumb, but he knew those wouldn't grow here—there wasn't nearly enough sun. Although, Winston was clearly having success with everything else in the small jungle underneath his window.

Tension, paint fumes, or a combination of the two was starting to revive his dizziness, and only one of those things was within Ivan's control. However, when he moved to rest one of his hands on the table, his eye was drawn to a small stack of posters in the way.

Seeing is Sin!
In modern America, emotion reigns
supreme. Children are taught in school to
rely on their instincts and "follow their
heart," even if it comes at a detriment to
others or themselves, resulting in a culture
lacking in respect for duty or God.

Ivan couldn't believe what he was reading. Was it possible he and Winston were starting on the same page? He continued:

It seems like the number of self-identified
Seers is growing by the day, despite being
only 2% of the population. In this
groundbreaking conference, Pastor Richard
P— will answer this question and more,
empowering you and other likeminded
individuals to stand up against the tide and
choose marriage over Mating, while offering
hope to Bonded individuals who want out.
Neuroscientist Danielle Y— will present new
scientific proof of color's negative effects on
the eyes—

Ivan made it this far before a drop of blood rolled off his hand, soaking into the paper right next to the curled 'stache someone had drawn over the smiling preacher's lip.

At this point, he gave up hope entirely and left his teeth to their grinding. Winston returned shortly thereafter, toting a small dish, tweezers, gauze, and disinfectant spray, which he set on the table after tossing the posters to the floor. They landed with a wobbly flutter.

"Do you need anything? Water?" Winston dashed off again as he asked it, and Ivan heard him washing his hands in the other room. Small miracle, too; the kitchen sink was so full of paint that his hands would have emerged from it dirtier than when they'd entered. Not, of course, that Ivan was currently in any position to be judging things on their cleanliness.

He was, nonetheless, perplexed when it came to Winston's landfill of a workspace. Ivan grew overwhelmed and disillusioned as soon as he accumulated one too many coffee mugs, but Winston's clutter seemed to add to, not detract from, his art. All his paintings were smudgy and haunting, with the unnerving air of a barely remembered dream, and the chaos of his apartment fed into the frothing waves, leviathan whales, and stormy cliffsides forming impressive horizontal stacks around his threadbare sofa. He seemed to live his life as he painted: cryptically, romantically, and in the spirit of the sea.

"You paint?" Ivan asked when Winston returned and took a seat.

Winston glanced at the easel in the center of his workspace. It depicted a tall, dark fin emerging from smooth water, overlooked by Mount Rainier. A post-it was stuck to the wood with what looked like a date and a few other scribbled words, but Ivan couldn't read them for the life of him.

"I'm just holding those for a friend."

Ivan glared at him.

Snickering, Winston pried the hoodie loose from Ivan's hands. "Are you sure you don't need water or food or anything? If your blood sugar's really low, it'll be harder not to pass out."

"I'll be fine, Doctor," said Ivan. Then, feeling guilty, he added, "Thanks." He ought to have been the one feeling smug, his split-second assumption about Winston's artistic tendencies had proved correct, right down to the potted plants and mismatched furniture. "Have you been in many galleries?"

Winston drew one massacred palm across the table. "We'll do the one that's worse, first," he said, picking up the tweezers. "Don't look if you're squeamish."

"Okay," Ivan said, unable to tear his eyes from his hand in Winston's.

Abandoning all prospects of forewarning Ivan of what lie ahead, Winston set to work. With a little pinprick and a clink, the first piece of glass was removed. "No, I haven't," he answered. "I get commissioned to do portraits sometimes, but otherwise there's a reason for the term, 'starving artist.'"

How Winston seemed perfectly content as he disclosed this information was baffling to Ivan. What right did he have to try to improve society when he refused to even improve himself? His confidence was aggravating.

"It'll get better," Ivan said. He almost added, *if you make it better*, but decided it was better not to be inflammatory while he was being operated on. For the same reason, when Winston in turn asked what he did, he responded vaguely, "I work in corporate."

Winston's only response was the repeated *clink* of glass in the dish. Ivan would have let the conversation die then and there, but his head was starting to swim, and the idea of passing out or vomiting on his apparent Soulmate was not appealing, so he pressed on for purposes of distraction.

"What about your parents?"

"Mom runs the bakery downstairs, Dad studies starfish."

"Starfish?"

"Starfish." Winston punctuated it with another pluck.

Ivan scrutinized the strange creature in front of him. "Is that why all your paintings are of—"

"The ocean?" Winston glanced at his art. "I guess it might have played a role, but I think growing up with the Rezzies was more of a deciding factor. It's easier to love something if it's connected to someone you know."

Ivan must have looked confused, because Winston continued, "Sorry, the Southern Residents." Another pause, then, "The orca pods. Didn't you say you hated Cass, too?"

"Uh," Ivan stammered, "sorry, yeah. It's the blood loss."

Now that Winston mentioned them, Ivan was pretty sure there had been a bit in the documentary about the Southern Resident pods. How Seymour had been taken off the coast of British Columbia as a baby. He didn't remember much more, it may have been about that point in the screening that Cass had slammed a fist on a table and startled an intern into spilling a soy latte into Allison's lap.

"Are you a transplant?" Winston asked it with what sounded like genuine curiosity, but Ivan still bristled. Winston didn't miss this, and gave him a gentle kick, nodding at his bag, which sat at the foot of the table. "Umbrella."

"Oh, please." Ivan rolled his eyes. "That rule is ridiculous."

"I know," Winston said, "it's just a way for me to take your mind off this."

The piece he pulled next made Ivan gasp.

"*Fuck*, you're a butcher." His vision was dark at the edges again, and he tried to focus on Winston's voice.

"Sorry. I promise I'm not enjoying this."

The next shard of glass was equally brutal, and Winston had to wriggle it free of the skin. After it was over, Ivan risked a glance down to find his hand steadily gushing red onto Winston's.

"Have you ever studied anything remotely close to medicine?" he asked.

Winston frowned. "I'm trained, if that's what you're asking."

Did he just not want Ivan to know where he studied? "So where—?"

"Not at college. From other activists."

"Oh." Ivan was skeptical as to how qualified that made him, but from their earlier experience, he doubted it was anything worse than the treatment he'd have received at the hospital, so he didn't press the issue. It did, however, revive an entirely different one. Because Ivan was, apparently, a moron, he inquired, "The rain ruin your protest?"

"It's Seattle."

Ivan's face felt hot.

"I'm glad."

"Me too. Progress is happening; they put up a stop sign in color on Seneca—"

"In red," Ivan blurted.

Winston paused in his glass removal and raised his brows. "Yeah. Red. You'd know better than me."

The painter's voice was cool enough to pass for apathetic, but Ivan discarded that possibility in favor of an alternative he had previously considered impossible: somehow, to Winston, Seeing was not a tragedy.

"Okay," Winston murmured, taking the last microscopic piece of glass out of the pad of Ivan's thumb. He dabbed at the blood with the hood of his soiled sweatshirt before picking up the disinfectant spray. "This'll probably hurt a lot."

Ivan winced at the sting. He stayed very still as Winston wrapped his hand in gauze, his fingers navigating around the cuts with ease. Although Winston's hands were paint-stained and riddled with tiny scars, Ivan welcomed the change from the chalky, pampered hands he'd grown used to shaking.

The hairs on Winston's arms were the same color as those on his head. Ivan watched him cradle his hands and wondered, for a flicker, what color his own hair was.

"The other one doesn't look as bad…" Winston grabbed Ivan's other hand, and Ivan's stomach did a flip.

"What color is your hair?" Ivan asked.

Winston looked up.

"I don't know." He appeared mildly pleased.

Of course he's pleased, Ivan thought, with a touch of mania. *He'd do anything to convert you into an embarrassing protester blinded by entitlement and a vague doctrine of beliefs that will do anything to ignore practicality so everyone can feel a little more comfortable.*

"Katie actually gave me a chart of them. The colors, I mean," Winston continued, vaporizing Ivan's train of thought. "Apparently, it cost a fortune to print, since most places can't even facilitate that kind of thing, but—"

"So there is," Ivan interrupted, "a definite number."

It was Winston's turn to roll his eyes.

"Wait here."

When he returned, he had a sheet of laminated paper in his hand. The circle of red on it instantly drew Ivan's eye. It sat at a two o'clock position in a ring of seven other circles of identical size, most of which he couldn't See. In fact, only one had color currently visible to him, and it matched the hair of the artist standing over him. The unassuming Arial font below it read "orange."

He didn't know if he liked the word. It was a bit too eclectic for him, a collage of sounds forced together like magazine cuttings pasted in a scrapbook.

"Well?" Winston asked. "What is it?"

"It's…" Ivan's heart hammered against his ribs. "It's orange."

"Orange…" Winston murmured. He was a professor having discovered an ancient civilization, a chemist having discovered his perfect ratio, anything but afraid.

With a newly-bandaged hand, Ivan drew the page closer. The colors of the croissants, the pie crusts, and the breads downstairs were nowhere to be found. "Where did you get this?"

"It's Katie's. Not much use to her, since she's been Seeing all her life, but it's so expensive to print in color we keep it around."

"Are you sure this is all of them?" Ivan demanded.

"Look," Winston's voice sharpened, "there's a lot of shades of light and dark, right? It only makes sense that when combined with color, you get an exponential rise in variety."

Ivan knew which conclusion his experience pointed to, but he didn't like it. Was it possible every young Seer he'd ever watched Mike Swan and his companions humiliate had been treated unjustly? That the different shades of color they dismissed as deluded ravings were actually real?

"You don't seriously believe them, though," Ivan said. "I mean, these kids…it's like a new one every day…"

Ivan stood and handed back the paper. Things weren't supposed to be this way.

"Thank you for your hospitality."

Winston frowned. "Your other hand."

"I think I can handle the rest of this by myself." Ivan did his best to straighten out his mess of a suit. "Really, you've been too kind." Way too kind.

"At least let me give you something to wear."

"I'll catch a cab," Ivan said, throwing his bag over his shoulder. He considered offering to wash the bloodied sweatshirt, but that would mean coming back.

"Hey, it's okay."

Ivan felt a hand on his arm as he made for the door. "No." Ignoring his heartbeat, he shrugged it off, not looking back. "It's really not."

6

Winston fanned the canvas with one hand and brushed his teeth with the other as Katie, unmoved by the spectacle, picked her way around projects in progress and candle-lid palettes.

"What an ass. Didn't even offer to wash your sweatshirt," she said, eyeing the bloody mess still lying stiff over the back of his kitchen chair.

Spitting into the nearest cup of paint water, Winston set his (tooth)brush aside and continued fanning and paying Katie as little mind as possible. It wasn't that he didn't appreciate her concern about Ivan—actually, it meant the world—it was just that he knew it was strategically directed. He could have finished this commission before one a.m. if he hadn't been with Seymour half the night.

Katie twanged her guitar. "Tell me more about him. He was at the protest?"

He faltered, and she didn't miss it.

"What?"

"He was the one who bumped into me," Winston admitted, then fanned the painting harder. Maybe some of the breeze would help cool his warming face. He wondered how much of Katie's apparent perceptiveness could be attributed to her ability to See tells more obvious in color.

She inhaled sharply. "That ass who almost pushed you over?"

"Look, can we just talk about this later?"

She snorted. "You think he's your Soulmate?"

Winston bristled, and touched a finger to the paint. His finger didn't come away coated with it, but it wasn't clean, either. He stared at it for a moment, then his eyes were drawn upwards. The sky was a spectacular blue today, feathered with strokes of wispy cloud that made not just the portrait he was working on, but every canvas within his range of sight, feel limited and juvenile. All of Katie's critiques he'd ever ignored came rushing back to him, and his prices suddenly felt not just high, but exorbitant.

"I mean," she continued, "he's clearly a bigot."

"Maybe, but, again, I think right now it's smartest to focus on the issue at hand." In all honesty, the fanning probably wasn't doing much, if anything, to speed along the drying process, but he really needed somewhere to direct his energy. He wished he was in bed. Maybe with Ivan. Just sleeping, though.

"The issue you got yourself into?" She played a little tune to soften the blow, and it might have worked, if not for what she said next. "If you think I'm being harsh about Seymour, I can't imagine what he would say."

"Actually, he hates Galaxsea too."

"*Everyone* hates Galaxsea," Katie said. "That doesn't make him progressive! I mean, what are you expecting? He'll fund your Seymour jailbreak and the two of you will get a mansion up in Anacortes? Don't be stupid."

The last word seemed to lower the room's temperature. When Winston turned to look at her, it was obvious an apology was already on her lips, but he wanted to hurt her back more than he wanted to hear it.

"You sing for change, Class of 2016," he said before returning to his work which, mediocre though it might be, at least allowed him to scrape up a living. Seconds after, he heard the door shut behind her.

"Dammit," he said, already regretting it. He'd hoped the shared experience of Seeing would thin out the Seymour fights, but it appeared they were just as frequent as ever. He knew what she valued, so why the hell did she have such a problem with him finally sticking it to Galaxsea? He and Barney had done plenty of reckless shit for the Rezzies before, sometimes even by her side.

A knock at the door snapped him to attention. It wasn't Katie; she always took longer to cool off. Sending a quick prayer up to the first deity that came to mind, Winston tried the paint and found it mercifully dry. He didn't waste time savoring his relief, however, and instead dashed to the window in the hopes that letting in some fresh air would begin to dissipate the lingering stench of paint and salmon. And God, it was a blue day. Eyes on the sky, he hadn't even finished calling that it was open when Mike Swan let himself inside.

"You didn't answer my texts."

Winston was terrible at that, and it drove everyone, especially clients, mad, but he, frankly, didn't understand where the hell people found the time to be returning texts all hours of the day. Today was one of the many occasions when he wished he could tell a client to their face that if they wanted the commission finished by the date they specified, he would need to actually spend time *painting* it, but the caustic expression he

turned to find on Mike Swan's face indicated that today would
be a bad day to get snippy.

"Beautiful day." Swan nodded at the window.

For the second time that day, Winston's arms prickled,
though this time, it was not from anger. After hesitating what he
realized was just a second too long, he nodded.

"Is it done, then?" Swan asked.

"Do you like it?"

"Well, I don't know," Swan said, with a bit more volume.
"Is it finished?"

Winston moved to examine the canvas, positioning himself
so the toothbrush and water cup he'd spit in were out of Swan's
view.

Now that he was a Seer, he thought the painting needed
something more, but then, now he thought all his paintings
needed something more. If color was out of the equation, and he
had a sneaking suspicion that, for Swan, it was, the portrait was
technically perfect.

"Yes, it's finished." He kept his voice neutral. "Now, I think
we agreed on cash—"

"I'm not paying for this."

A guitar twanged softly from behind them, and Swan
jumped before whirling around. When Winston turned, he was
startled to see Katie was watching them from the kitchen
counter. A pang of guilt hit Winston in the gut, but as soon as
Mike Swan composed himself, it was hurried along by pressing
fear.

"Is this what you do with all your clients?" he asked
Winston. "You rip them off and use your guard dog to bully
them into giving you money?"

Winston's stomach lurched. *Don't call her a dog.*

"I heard raised voices," Katie looked at Winston as she said it.

He hopped once on the balls of his feet and asked Swan outright, "Why don't you like it?"

Mike Swan looked at him like he was the stupidest person alive for not realizing his own insignificance. "It's not very good. I mean, I could have done this."

"But you didn't," Katie said. Winston met her eyes again and did his best to silently communicate an urgent but loving "shut up."

He locked eyes with Swan. "Usually, before people commission, they do a little research on the artist's work. Or at least take the time to give more specific directions." Which, for Swan, had been little more than a price and a request to look good. "I've given you a service, and now you'll give me payment for my time."

Winston regretted the second half of it as soon as it was out of his mouth, but it was too late to take it back. Swan's eyes had already lit up with ire.

"Why should I pay you," he asked, "for a product I don't want?"

"Because it took me time to make it."

"There's no need to shout," Swan lilted, and his calm pushed Winston over the edge.

"Fuck you, I'll shout in my own house if I want to."

Swan was right in his face now, somehow still looking like he was having the time of his life. "Do you have any idea what I could have done to you?"

Winston felt his face get hot again. No, not hot. Red, like Ivan had said. Although there was no way for Mike Swan to perceive that particular change in his countenance, he'd walked in when Winston's eyes had been practically glued to the sky. That alone might have been enough to know.

"Are you threatening me?"

"No," Swan said smoothly, "I'm recommending you act a little politer, if you don't want me thinking you'd be better-off-blind."

Winston's ears were ringing, his mind blank except for the text of a recent headline: **Oregon Seer Mutilated in Hatecrime: Investigation Ongoing.** The woman's eyeless corpse had washed up on a beach miles south from her home, her sockets staring with unfixed horror as the waves stroked her bloated limbs.

Katie stood up suddenly, and Swan raised his voice, stopping her in her tracks.

"You really should do better to cover your face at protests." Then, he turned back to Winston. "Both of you."

Breathing evenly was hard. It was never ideal to have one's face passed around in Swan's circles, but it was especially dangerous given Winston's plans for Seymour. He didn't think Swan was affiliated with Galaxsea in any way, but if it somehow got around to them that he was protesting again…

"We'll call the police," Katie said.

Swan shrugged. "Please do. It smells like a body is decaying in here. You know maybe," he turned back to Winston, "if you did better business, you could afford to take a damn bath once in a while."

In fact, he'd been too busy touching up the painting to shower that morning. The probability that he still smelled like salt water, salmon, and whale was not a small one. And he knew he definitely looked like shit. Though of course, this didn't make him any worse or better than Swan, it was enough that Swan thought it did. Because if he thought Winston was below him, that made him more of a target.

In another world, he would have given Mike Swan a good shove, asserted that if he'd had money to clean himself with, at least he wouldn't be spending his hard-earned cash on portraits of himself. What kind of narcissist did that? He might have shoved the picture at him, refused to take payment for it, and declared that he didn't need any bigot's dirty money.

But dirty money still paid bills, and Winston was afraid of what would happen if this escalated further. He sighed.

"Is there anything I can do to make you like it better?"

"Don't bother. I hadn't realized how crippling Seeing is. I guess it explains why the damn painting is so bad. I hope you've thought about alternate careers for people in your position."

Katie twanged gently from the couch, perched on the very edge of the cushions. "Actually," she interjected, "they make colored paints, now."

"Of course they do." Swan's voice was gently amused as he opened a sleek wallet. "I should probably give you the money. Not as payment, mind, but as charity. God knows you need it."

"People like you don't give charity," Winston said.

"And people like you," Swan smiled, and it didn't even come close to his eyes, "don't contribute to society. Perhaps do everyone a favor: stop wasting our tax money on *special* street signs, and run into traffic."

Winston's mouth hung open as Swan grabbed the painting and retreated, slamming the door behind him.

He let out a breath he hadn't realized he'd been holding, and whispered, barely audible, "What the fuck?"

Katie crossed the room and squeezed his arm. "Are you okay?"

Winston swallowed and nodded. "Are you? He wasn't like this when we first talked, I didn't know—"

"You couldn't have known," she said. "It's good there were two of us."

It was impossible to suppress a shiver. Winston shook his head. "I was stupid."

"No, you aren't," she said. "Just stubborn."

Winston wanted both to hug her and to apologize, but unfortunately, impatience was a close relative of stubbornness, and Katie had been perceptive as usual in pointing out the latter. He counted out Swan's money, angry before he had even confirmed his suspicions.

"He shorted me!" Winston exclaimed. "Designer sunglasses and he doesn't even pay the full fee!"

"The money wasn't payment," she said, "it was an insult." A sigh. "What's really insulting is that he has enough money to spend on insults."

In Winston's world, insults didn't count unless they were free. He stuffed the bills in his wallet and said, mostly to himself, "At least it's going to a good cause."

"Is that cause buying yourself food?"

Winston went to close the window. He knew full well he wouldn't be able to lie, and it irritated him all over again. The latch clicked, hushing the sounds of the city.

"You before the whale, Winst. Please."

"It's not even an option," Winston said. "If I don't get rigorous with his retraining, he'll—"

"Live a few more years in captivity, and then—"

"*Don't.*"

She didn't, only looked at him in a way that said she knew the time for effective intervention had long passed.

"You're not," he said, "my mom."

"Well, you need one."

Winston wished he could have told her to fuck off, that he had a mom, and she was usually only one floor away from him, but he was exhausted and disgusted with himself and knew full well that when Katie of all people said someone's parenting was unhealthy, she probably knew what she was talking about.

But even if Gretchen Jinx had known about the Seymour mission, let alone how dangerous it was, even if she'd shown miraculous concern that he or Barney would get hurt, it wouldn't have been enough to stop him. Somebody had to stand up for that poor tortured animal, and if Winston didn't do it, no one would.

"I'm really sorry, Katie." For past, present, and future.

She ran a hand through her dark hair like a comb, pushing it over her shoulder in a thick curtain. "Will you go hungry tonight?"

"There's some cereal in the cupboard," Winston lied. They both knew she didn't have extra money to feed him with. If his stomach unknotted itself at some point in the day, there was always extra food downstairs. It was really only his pride that stopped him from taking more.

Katie gave him a look, then packed up her guitar and headed for the door. She gave him a rough pat on the shoulder.

"I have a gig."

"Is it good?"

She grinned widely.

Winston was flooded with warmth. "I'm so happy for you."

Singing for change. People like Mike Swan *wished* Katie Hartzog was singing for change.

Hopefully, Winston thought, eyeing his empty easel, *those wishes don't become a reality*. Mike Swan circulating photos of him and Katie around his contemporaries was more than troubling. That Seer in Oregon had only died a few months ago, and it wasn't like either corporate America or the police would be heartbroken if the two of them washed up on a beach somewhere. Even if Swan didn't deign to have them killed, he could still ruin Winston's business. Big art collector like that, he could circulate word in no time about what a dirty, rude, defensive person Winston was, and urge people to buy secondhand.

He wondered what Ivan would have done.

Perhaps if he kept moving, he could outrun thoughts of what might have happened if Katie hadn't come back upstairs. Winston busied himself with errands and chores, but as the afternoon wore on, raw instinct, little by little, reclaimed ground until, when he headed to the farmer's market to fetch Seymour's next meal, it won out entirely, and he found himself flinching from every camera lens, searching for dark eyes in every crowd.

7

That night, Ivan dreamt in color. He couldn't remember the last time he'd had such a vivid dream, and though he couldn't recall every detail, the ones he did made it hard to calm down when he gasped awake, drenched in sweat and ravenous. The skies had been red, and there had been a terrible, shifting hybrid of Winston Jinx and Mike Swan, and food from *Takes the Cake*. So much food. If these were not enough to terrorize him well into his waking hours, his hardwood floors, which he now Saw had color, certainly did. They watched him from the edges of his bed like a creature out of sleep paralysis.

Sitting up, he rested his forehead in a bandaged palm. His alarm went off a moment later, making him flinch. Its shrilling provided a poor backdrop for returning his breathing to normal, but Ivan let it continue, too resigned to universal misery to mitigate his own.

Last night, he'd been close to looking up the science behind the whole Bond thing, but was ultimately too embarrassed to go through with it. Though the curtains had been drawn and his history ready to delete, he'd still felt watched as his hand hovered over the keyboard. This morning he was even more repulsed by the idea of knowing anything about it, even if it was in the effort to stop Seeing. Maybe there were drugs…but the civil rights groups would have made sure those never reached shelves. He didn't need any of that anyway. Willpower was all Allison needed to succeed. Their father had believed in willpower, and that was all Ivan needed to burn this thing out of him like a cancer.

The prospect of putting this into practice made the room seem a lot bigger around him.

Maybe he was just morbidly fascinated with Winston. It really was amazing that he went around living like he did without fear of consequence. Didn't he know what happened to people who did that? Ivan wasn't sure what, but he knew it was bad as surely as he knew Jinx was precisely the type to stand on Galaxsea's front step and scream for that damn whale's release.

As he attempted to berate himself into submission, Ivan carefully ignored the fact that, every time Winston's face came to mind, the chill seemed to disappear from the room. Though of course, this may have been because of how angry Winston made him.

By the time he managed to psych himself up to touch the floors, he was running abysmally late, a predicament compounded when he realized color had seeped into his wardrobe as well. Not only was the one remaining suit that still properly fit him covered in blood, but the threads and fabrics of all the rest were a mottle of confusing new colors, and it was nearly impossible to discern what, to normal people, would look appropriate. Ultimately, he threw his hands up at both this and the fridge, as he decided he'd already had enough surprises for the day, and wasn't eager to See let alone eat whatever freshly-colored horrors sat inside. However, he needn't have bothered, as his bathroom mirror was soon to deliver the most astonishing Sight of the day.

When they'd been young, Allison and Ivan had played a game with each other. They'd taken turns choosing scary movies to watch, which they'd acquired through all manner of mild mischief. Throughout the films and the days following, the two had attempted to catch the other showing any kind of fright. Ivan had never really admitted, to himself or (God forbid) to Allison, that in the long run he'd lost, as to this day he felt a general unease around mirrors. Today, however, when he walked into the bathroom, what he saw in the mirror made him jump as much as any demon.

Skin was one of those things most people took for granted. When one goes to sleep at night, they tend to assume their face will be the same when they wake up in the morning. Usually, this assumption is correct. For Ivan, on this particular day, it was not.

His skin, and therefore his face, was forever changed. For a moment, he was rooted to the spot with the horror of it. It was the primal terror of waking to find one's face covered in bug bites. It was the immediate annihilation of any and all self-esteem built on one's appearance. It was the shame of realizing that your own perception of yourself as a suitably attractive individual was completely and utterly false.

Ivan gasped for air. It seemed he had forgotten to breathe. Somewhere inside his head, he'd known color was going to spread everywhere. After he'd cut his hands, he'd known that included himself, but he'd failed to register what logically followed.

Of course, he immediately threw himself into a full body examination, as it was more convenient to mourn everything at once. This only increased his panic tenfold. The color was closest, he supposed, to some of his clothes, but it changed in darkness or lightness depending on where it was on his body. His arms were a bit darker than his upper thighs, and the entirety of his body was riddled with imperfections he'd never noticed before; he recognized not only the diffused red he'd Seen before on Winston's face, but also an entirely alien color that defined the veins on the undersides of his arms. Even his hair and eyes looked different than they had the previous night.

Ivan would have loved to have a complete breakdown right then on his bathroom floor, but the thought of Cass's wrath compelled him to throw on some clothing and stumble out the door in a haze of hairspray and cologne, unshaven and unfed for the day. Whether or not he took the extra time to put himself together more sufficiently, he still would be subjected to Allison's pity and Mike's usual deprecating efforts to "help" him, so he might as well show up a mess and pray he ended up walking through the door before Cass did. To increase his chances, he hailed a cab, the mosaic of faces passing the window cementing this day, and not the previous, as the worst of his life.

He managed to avoid any particularly repugnant protesters, though that may have been because he knew he already looked a mess, and was less careful carving his way through them. For the first time in his life, Ivan felt a bit relieved when he scanned his badge and stepped inside to the equine noise of heels on marble and the chlorinated aroma of the lobby's fountain.

As soon as the doors opened at the top floor, however, all semblance of familiarity was dropped, and he was thrust back into the uncanny nightmare. How could he not stare, just a little bit, at the skin, the hair, and the clothing, and the people wearing all of them without a damn clue? Mike *hated* Seers, but there he was, wearing clothes in the same mottled fabrics as Ivan.

A kiss-ass looking intern passed him on the way in, and Ivan asked them to bring him a coffee with one cream, one sugar, before he headed towards his office, where he would be exceedingly pleased to See his desk and chair, along with the tips of the dying plant on his desk and the dry soil it sat in, were colored as well. On the way there, however, he was intercepted by Mike Swan, who abandoned his conversation with one of Allison's friends as soon as his eyes met Ivan's. The other colleague didn't even look at Ivan as she walked away. Or, at least, Ivan didn't see her look at him in the brief period it took for Mike to approach him, standing so close his broad shoulders took up his entire frame of vision.

"Ivan! You look awful!" His eyes traveled to the bandages on his hands. "Did you get into a fight? *I* got into a fight today, you wouldn't believe it."

Before Ivan could ask him for advice on how to stay put together and business formal during a fight, Mike backtracked:

"Oh, I didn't mean it like that. I meant you look tired."

"I am a little tired," Ivan said. His heart hammered despite the fact that Mike had no way of knowing he was Bonded.

"I'm glad you're back."

The feeling wasn't mutual, but Ivan kept this to himself.

"Wanna see what my morning consisted of?"

For the first time, Ivan noticed Mike was carrying a large rectangle of canvas, and although he berated himself for thinking immediately of Winston Jinx (Christ, it was Seattle, there was more than one painter), he needn't have. As soon as his eyes fell on the portrait before him, he knew the work could be no one else's. The technique was inimitable, Mike's body broken down into silhouettes and reanimated with streaks of light into scenes

71

like something out of a haunting yet enrapturing dream. If any doubt remained he was looking at Winston's work, it was silenced when he noticed the tiny **Jinx** signed in the bottom corner.

Ivan did his best to keep his face neutral. "What is that?"

"This," Mike Swan said, "is easily the worst piece of art I've ever paid for. I picked it up early hoping to take it home before work, but I ran into trouble with the artist."

Ivan's blood ran cold. "What kind of trouble?"

"You wouldn't believe the way I was treated."

Good, a reason to end it. Winston Jinx would be easier to forget if he was despicable.

"I mean," Mike shook his head in disbelief, "I got there, and, I don't judge based on income, you know I don't."

"Right," Ivan lied.

"Anyway," he continued, "I get there, and his place is a complete disaster. It's tiny, it's filthy, and I can't help but think, 'is there a reason the bastard isn't making any money?'"

Ivan nodded. Winston's apartment was both small and cluttered. Filthy may have been a strong adjective, but he supposed Mike had a point there. He could still recall the acrid smell of paint, the faint salinity of fresh seafood, the smell of bread from his mother's bakery wafting upstairs...

"I ask him, 'Is this the painting?' and he's already taking an attitude with me. I don't understand why some of these people think it's okay to treat their customers like garbage. So I say, 'This isn't what I paid you to do,' at this point obviously concerned about the situation. He *loses* it on me—!"

Ivan did his best to look passably shocked.

"—and he's like, 'you'd better have my *money*.' Never, in all my years of collecting, have I had an experience like this. At this point, I realized he was probably just desperate, never really painted anything in his life. I know it was dangerous, but to me, it was just sad. Oh," he leaned in confidentially, "and you would not believe the woman there with him. Massive thing. Not fat, you know, just built like a gorilla." He laughed. "Looked like she belonged in a mental institution. With the way the other one acted, they probably both belong in one."

"Birds of a feather," Ivan muttered, hating himself.

Mike sighed. "I almost wish you'd been there, just to see that I'm not exaggerating."

"I know you aren't."

Mike smiled. "I appreciate that. He was such a walking stereotype it made me want to move back to Anacortes. I mean," he lowered his voice, "he was even *Mated*."

Ivan's stomach dropped. "Did he tell you that?" *Better-off-blind* echoed in his mind, and to his surprise, he found himself genuinely afraid of hearing it said aloud.

Mike huffed. "Yes. You know they can't resist the urge to tell everyone they meet."

Ivan was suddenly consumed by an overwhelming urge to defend Winston.

"Here, let me see it."

He took the canvas in his hands, and of course the painting wasn't bad. Of course it wasn't. Ivan knew Mike had a habit of seeking out conflict with people who didn't live in ways that aligned with his standards. That much had become especially clear near the end of their relationship. Granted, Ivan still believed that, deep down, Mike only did so out of a desire to help them, but that didn't mean if Winston had given Mike trouble, it hadn't been at least partially provoked.

Yes, Winston had been protesting when they'd first met, but all he'd really been doing was standing around, at least as far as Ivan had seen. He'd been distraught at the hospital, but he had never gotten violent or even verbally aggressive towards the nurses that wouldn't listen to him. Winston had also taken Ivan, a complete and utter stranger, home with him when he'd been hurt, tended to his wounds, and sacrificed a well-loved hoodie, all despite the fact that they'd only met in the first place because Ivan had been rude to him. Ivan had no way of knowing if Winston Jinx was innocent in most respects of his life, but in terms of Mike's accusations, he had no difficulty clearing him of all charges. Plus, facts were facts: the painting was beautiful.

"You know," he said, his head on a tilt, "I really don't think it's that bad."

"I'm sorry?"

You should be, Ivan thought, wondering if Mike had called Winston better-off-blind to his face. The thought seemed to light his insides on fire.

"Yeah," he nodded, turning the painting so they could both look at it. "In fact, I'd almost say it's good."

Mike's mouth dropped open. He leaned back to look at Ivan.

"Well, if you like it so much," he said, "you can keep it."

"That's not necessa—"

Mike shoved the picture back into Ivan's arms. "I insist! I never want to see the thing again, though I hope you can get something from admiring its *finesse.*"

Ivan wasn't sure he would. It was Winston's work, but it was also, unmistakably, his ex-boyfriend's face.

"I'll see what I can do with it."

"I'm sure you'll think of something." Mike started to walk away. "You know, I can't decide if you've got terrible taste in art, or if you're trying to tell me something."

Ivan frowned at Mike's retreating back, unsure what to make of a comment like that. His eyes easily traveled back to the painting, and he gently touched the paint itself, running the tips of his fingers, which peeked out from his bandages, over the razor-edged strokes that shaped the portrait's form. Winston had painted Mike like the edge of a cliff, and the shadows his cheekbones cast might have been just as long. It really was a flattering likeness, moreover one that perfectly encapsulated what being in a room with Mike felt like.

When the intern delivered his coffee, Ivan nearly spit it out, it was so bitter.

8

Throughout his day, Ivan went through the motions of reviewing revenue reports, addressing a string of emails from the morons at their D.C. location (no, he would not personally fly out there to attend a meeting), and wondering whether, if he had another coffee, he would like the taste this time. All the while, Mike Swan's likeness stared at him from Winston's canvas, commencing the formation of a very bad idea.

It was only courtesy that he return the painting.

Of course, Ivan very well could show up on his doorstep only to learn that Winston truly had been the unreasonable one, weeping and outraged at the possibility that anyone could express a less than favorable opinion of his art. Or worse, Ivan could be forced to stand there like a fool while Winston coolly informed him that yes, of course he was fine, and that no, it really hadn't been necessary to return the painting.

The visceral fear of this second reaction was nearly paralyzing enough to stop Ivan considering the visit any further. And Christ, what if Winston could See his skin now, too? If it hadn't been for the correspondent possibility that Ivan might be able to See Winston's, the plan might have shriveled and died like an unwanted lawn dandelion. Instead, it only grew clearer and more tenable, and Ivan found his eyes drifting away from his screen and towards his potted plants, the wood of his desk, and yes, even his skin, wondering how Winston's paleness would translate to color.

When Ivan departed Galaxsea headquarters, the sky was threatening rain. As soon as he stumbled free of the day's smallish mob of picketers (one contorted woman was sitting inside what looked like an oversized goldfish bowl), he automatically started for his apartment. The fear he felt not of Winston, or of Mike, but of himself when he recalled the canvas under his arm was so potent he almost handed it off to Fish Woman and bolted.

But...this ultimately was a favor, nothing more. Maybe it wouldn't hurt.

When he arrived at *Takes the Cake*, Ivan was still wheezing from what he would later identify as a panic attack prompted by the sight of a new color, royal and deep, on a bed of flowers he'd passed a block ago. The pastries, pies, and breads he could See in the shop window were now even more vibrant, and they judged him from behind the glass. All of the progress he had made in catching his breath was immediately undone when he caught sight of his reflection in it; the humidity had frizzed his hair into an unkempt mess, and his face was drawn and tired. He didn't look like the kind of person he would have wanted to be around. What the hell was he doing wasting Winston's time?

Ivan checked himself. He should have been asking the opposite question. Especially when Winston had snuck him so carefully past the bakery's owner, his mother, the last time they'd been here. What was so off-putting about her that he'd felt the need to do something so juvenile? Unless, of course, it was *Ivan* who was the offensive one. Despite his perfect record of parental approval, he couldn't exactly blame Mrs. Jinx if she turned her nose up at him in his current state.

Clutching the painting tighter, Ivan gave his reflection one last look, steadied himself as best he could, and stepped inside.

The smell of toasted almonds and rising bread was intoxicating. He might have been too dizzy to really appreciate it the first time around, but it reminded him a bit of his grandmother's cottage up in Minnesota. The jars of preserves lining the walls, the creaking floors, and the asymmetry of the merchandise gave him the feeling he'd interrupted the preparations for an especially homey Christmas Eve.

Ivan had just taken a forbidden step closer to a pie with a filling the same new color he'd spotted en route when a voice behind him made him jump.

"Gods, I love it when I'm right."

Ivan whirled around to lay eyes on the most utterly *pagan* woman he'd ever seen, smirking at him rather knowingly from behind the counter. Off her tattooed shoulders hung an apron colored similarly to some of Ivan's buttondowns, and off her neck, a delicate metal pentacle. Her face was both flatter than Winston's and smattered with darker freckles, but they had their hair in common.

"They thought," she said, "you wouldn't come. It's Ivan, right?"

"Winston told you about me?" He didn't know whether this premise made his heart pound in a good or a bad way.

"Didn't have to. You're the one he snuck upstairs while I was kneading the pumpernickel."

Ivan tried not to stare at the pentacle, feeling, in spite of himself, a little like Hansel. He hoped to God this woman was a part of one of those cheeky, new-age religions that worshipped dirt and flowers, and not some kind of Satanist. "I guess."

"Nice of you to return that." Her eyes flicked downward, and Ivan, ignoring her words, was momentarily enraged that a woman who looked like her was appraising his clothing before he realized that she was looking at the painting.

"It's nothing," he said. Desperate to fill the ensuing silence, he asked, "Are you Mrs. Jinx, then?"

Her smile was sharp, an almost exact mirror of Winston's. "Gretchen. Who else would I be?"

"I don't know." Ivan shook her freckled hand. "Someone else who works here?"

"Oh, please." She shooed the idea away like a troublesome fly. "I've managed the work by myself since opening day."

"That must be hard." Ivan wondered about Winston's dad.

"Ha. Don't insult me. Now my *son*, he's the one who overstrains himself, and with the stupidest projects, too. That's his word, not mine, and it's all he'll tell me about them anymore, but of course I know. Never brings boys home and hardly eats. He'd be dead if it weren't for my merchandise. Actually," she looked him up and down again, "you look a little peckish, too. Would you like some croissants to take upstairs?"

Ivan sweated. "Actually, I was just stopping by." Why the hell had he thought this was a good idea?

"Mmm hm."

"Really."

"Stalling, are we?"

"I'm not—"

Ivan didn't get to finish before she disappeared into the back room. She called out to him:

"And stop staring at that pie like it's personally offended you!"

He stopped.

Now that he had a witness (and a witch witness, and a *parental* witness), Ivan had no other choice but to direct himself upstairs. He paused halfway, however, when the folksy twang of an acoustic guitar reached his ears. Several distinct voices were also audible; a booming laugh, a haughty snort.

For a moment, he listened, jittery and uncomfortable, and then finished the way up. He could See Winston's door this time around, and while its wood was the same as that of Gretchen's salesfloor, it was more striking, perhaps, to See this particular scene repainted in color.

This doesn't need to happen. You can leave. There's probably nothing for you here. His mother is a Devil worshipper for Christ's sake. And besides, you've already made a bad impression.

Ivan took a big breath, thought *fuck it*, and knocked.

Unfortunately, he was not greeted by Winston. The dark-haired man standing in front of him had to be a good 200 pounds heavier than either the painter or Ivan, as was accentuated by the massive checkered shirt barely containing his mass. He had more facial hair than Ivan, who shaved daily, had probably ever grown in his life, and smelled, Ivan swore, of faint gunpowder.

Well, this was fun. Time to leave.

"I'm sorry," Ivan said, amazed at how steady his voice was, "I must have the wrong address." Of course he had the correct damn address. "I was looking for Winst—"

"*Ivan?*"

The music stopped, and the massive man stepped aside to reveal the speaker. Winston's hands were messy with paint, and his eyes were still uncolored, but Ivan could See the rest of him, pale skin and faint freckles, with a tinge of red in the cheeks that made Ivan's jaw unconsciously loosen.

Winston crossed the room, and Ivan held out the painting.

"The owner proper," Ivan said, "wasn't appreciating it enough. I thought I'd return it home."

"How…?"

"Mike Swan is a coworker of mine. He came straight from you to the office."

The provider of the music, a curvy woman with hair that surrounded her face in curtains, watched Ivan calculatingly from the sofa.

Winston laughed. "I am so sorry."

"Don't be." Ivan meant it.

Something sparked behind Winston's eyes. "What'd he say about me?"

That you're dirty, and you're poor, and you live in a hovel because you rip people off and threaten them with violence to buy your paintings, which you have no talent for creating.

"Nothing much."

"You fucking *liar!*"

Winston gave Ivan a shove that made him a little dizzy. He felt it even harder to resist the smile tugging at his lips when he felt the eyes of the musician and the large, plaid-clad man on him.

"The bastard threatened me," Winston said. "Can't imagine he said anything good."

Threatened? That didn't sound like Mike. Maybe some of what he said could constitute threats, but he never really meant it.

"Do your clients do that often?"

Winston looked at him sharply. "Here and there. Usually it's more legal stuff. One lady was worried about chemicals in the paint, but I've never had one like Swan before. I don't want to worry you, but he said some kind of scary stuff about Seers."

Their eyes both lowered to the painting, and Ivan said, "You don't have to worry, he won't come looking for it."

Winston smirked. "If I was Swan, I wouldn't want to look at myself any longer than necessary, either." He paused, then turned and marched the painting to where the majority of his works lay tilted in a domino line against the wall. After frowning at Mike Swan for a moment, he slipped him between two other canvases, hiding him in the middle of the stack.

"Your version of him is pretty tolerable."

Guitar-girl bobbed an eyebrow and twanged her instrument, turning her face away.

Winston straightened. "Well, I'm fine without pleasing the masses, as long as my work is liked by…" he looked Ivan up and down, "…the right people."

Actually, Ivan had changed his mind. Coming here today had clearly been the right decision.

"You know what?" the large man behind Ivan boomed. "I've actually remembered Katie and I have that…thing we have to go to, don't we, Katie?"

Winston went a faint red.

Katie strummed another few chords before getting up quite suddenly. "Ah yes, I do remember that appointment being rather important. Winston, I'm sorry, but we have to leave."

Ivan was growing rather alarmed, watching all of this unfold. "I was actually just going to—"

He was silenced with a swift kick from none other than Winston himself. When he looked at the offender, thunderstruck, he was met with an expression that suggested he stop talking. Before he could protest further, Katie and the large man disappeared with a strum and finger guns, respectively.

Winston called a goodbye after them before sighing and turning to Ivan. "They never leave my house."

Ivan frowned, concerned. "Why don't you change your locks?"

Winston snorted. "Uh, no. It's nothing like that. They're my best friends, but I live above a bakery."

"Oh." Ivan was suddenly filled with an ugly, jealous feeling he couldn't yet face. He turned to the paintings again. "They really are," he said, petrified they would fall into silence, "good."

Winston glanced at his work behind him. "They're where they should be, after twenty years of practice. But then it doesn't really count when you're three and doing finger paintings, does it?"

"No," Ivan said, a little surprised they were so close in age. But then, a lot could happen in three years—Ivan had definitely still been hanging on to college friends at twenty-three. He would bet by the time Winston reached twenty-six he'd be right where Ivan was now, isolated except for mandatory dinners for career and family. Or maybe it wasn't like that when you didn't have a real job.

The dreaded silence started to creep in again, and it was just as agonizing as Ivan had known it would be. When he risked a glance at Winston, he found himself being studied.

"What?" He couldn't help it; it came out defensive. Ivan imagined, as a painter, Winston was very observant of detail, and today of all days he wasn't in an ideal state for scrutiny. Or being looked at in general.

"How are you feeling?" Winston asked.

"Better."

Ivan had answered without thinking, but after dark, while relaying the exchange in his head, he would realize Winston had been referring to his bandaged hands, not his life in general.

"Good. You wanna have dinner?"

Ivan balked, uncertain he'd heard correctly. "Are you sure?"

"Hmm." Winston hesitated. "Yeah. Pretty sure," he said, and before Ivan could speak, clarified, "I mean, it won't be like real dinner. I have an agenda."

"Oh?" Ivan somehow doubted this was the only agenda Winston Jinx had hidden in his pocket.

"Yeah." He brushed past Ivan in a whiff of paint and started rummaging through the kitchen. "I still haven't Seen the ocean with color. Katie says it's blue, and that's my favorite so far." Winston held an old looking blanket in his arms. "I know it was the first, but it's yet to be beat. Do you have one?"

"A favorite?" That he and Winston were having such a different experience with this was almost laughable. And Ivan did laugh, though it was a somewhat sterile expression.

"Oh, that's right," Winston said, "I forgot you hated this. Even orange, though?"

Ivan conceded that *fine, orange was his favorite.*

"No no!" Winston protested. "Don't say it just to stroke my ego."

Ivan's face felt hot. "I don't even know the names of most of them." And he didn't want to.

"I can help you!" Winston said, whizzing around the small apartment like a tall orange hummingbird, gathering miscellaneous items. "I'll bring the chart with us. It's been helping me. Also," he brushed past Ivan, "I hope you're not expecting a balanced meal. My mom's given us her leftover shortbread cookies and some other goods that were too ugly to put out, so if you're used to kale chips and rosé, then…"

His eyes flicked up to Ivan's, bright with mischief, and it took Ivan a moment to realize he was being teased. He'd been too ensnared by the sudden aroma of shortbread to retort immediately. God, he was hungry.

"What are you implying?" He was taking this too seriously. He should have played along.

"Nothing." Winston grinned, miraculously undeterred. "Let's go." He picked up a massive basket of shortbread, deformed muffins, and other misfit baked goods that had inexplicably appeared behind them as they'd talked. Ivan hadn't even heard the door open.

"When did tha—" he started.

"The dangers of having a witch for a mother. She's very good at acting silently." Winston took the basket in one hand and grabbed Ivan's with his other, making his stomach swoop. "Is this okay?"

Ivan was overwhelmed. "Yes. But like Wicca or Satanism?" He had been hoping to find out he'd overreacted, and it was none of the above. It seemed like mere seconds before Winston was dragging him out the door, into the street, and away from any heart or discipline he might have had to voice his concerns. If this stranger and his mother decided to gut him for some ritual sacrifice and leave him for the tides, well, it at least would be a new *kind* of misery. And it really was only courtesy that he went on at least one proper date with his apparent "Soulmate." Anything less would have been an insult to Winston.

Fortunately, it turned out to be neither Wicca nor Satanism. However, Winston explained as they passed a photo lab ("I have no clue how places like this stay in business," he interrupted himself, "with everything going digital"), she was still a witch, only she preferred to make her own rules. "Once I'm sure she's not gonna embarrass me, I'll introduce you to her."

"Plenty of people still take traditional photographs," Ivan said, more dazed than irritated. "And actually, I met her on the way up to see you."

"She didn't mention it?"

The way he said it implied that it was normal to announce one's devil worship to their son's suitors. Though she'd pretty much done just that, hadn't she? That necklace was obvious enough. He wondered if it affected her sales.

"No."

Winston groaned. "What'd she say about me, then? Because if she's not talking about her craft, she's talking about me."

That coaxed a proper smile out of Ivan. "That you're a workaholic."

"So much slander to my good name, recently."

"I could say the same," Ivan said nobly. "I do not eat *kale*." At least, not since he'd quit that cleanse diet back in February.

SAVING SEYMOUR

Winston threw his whole head into it when he laughed. Of course, they probably looked ridiculous, running around the city like children, hollering for a cab. And, everything was in too much color, and they were about to go and sit on a cold beach under a sky that threatened rain to eat bakery food that was too ugly for even a witch to sell in her shop, but Ivan, for whatever reason, was still happy he'd come.

9

That day was neither the first nor the last time that Winston dragged someone to the ocean. A lone Victorian lighthouse watched the tall grasses whip at his and Ivan's waists while their ankles ripped through tangles of wildflowers. Winston helped Ivan over the pile of driftwood that marked the sandline after the latter slipped on a piece of loose bark and nearly broke his ankle.

When Winston had been little, he'd begged his father, on the rare occasions he'd been home, to come down to the water with him and look for whales. Jonathan Jinx, having just returned from spending weeks to months on foreign beaches, had been understandably reluctant, but also had given in almost every time, pointing out starfish and anemones when the Rezzies hadn't been around. Gretchen, meanwhile, had taken full advantage of the time away from the shop to collect materials for her craft, glass jars filled with sand, shells, and seawater in a canvas bag, clinking when she leaned in for a kiss from her husband.

As he'd grown older, Winston developed a tendency to go down to the waves with Barney as soon as they got out of detention, grab a pair of kayaks, and forget about the homework that Katie was at home doing. Upon their return, Gretchen Jinx curbed the beginnings of hypothermia with herbal tea and any pastries too ugly to sell.

He'd probably spent more time around Barney, Katie, and the Rezzies growing up than he had his actual parents. Any other day, this might have made Winston considerably less tense in the face of the sublime expanse than Ivan, whom he guessed had spent his after-school time more like Katie than Barney. However, today was not any day, and when Winston and Ivan stopped at the mosaic of pebbles tracing the surf's edge, its blue stole the breath from both of their lungs. It darkened as the water's depth increased, approaching the color of the night sky as it neared the horizon.

Ivan dropped Winston's hand and wrapped an arm around himself, his chest still heaving from the journey. Winston had been distracted by a little green cricket on the side of a building when Ivan had stopped them both in their tracks and announced solemnly, staring off over the water: "I See it." Winston had raised his eyes and broken into a run for the Sound, partially because he had to See the thing he viewed his life in, and partially because it felt nice to have someone run with him, childish as it was.

Briefly, Winston tore his eyes from the sea and looked Ivan up and down, suddenly questioning the practicality of this expedition. He certainly didn't want to be the reason that a $900 jacket was ruined by the brine. Ivan looked like something out of a photoshoot as he kicked his shoes off in twin sprays of sand, the wind toying with his hair. He hadn't slicked it back today. It looked nice.

Winston kept his own shoes on as he led them along the shore. Recognizing the translucent gleam of jellyfish in the sand was instinctive to him at this point, but today there were a few distractions that would get in the way of that. Ivan brushed off his warning, still apparently too traumatized by the addition of blue to his own color palette to begin to consider jellyfish, and Winston wondered if he would be doing more first aid later that day.

They were not alone on the beach, as the dawning summer had encouraged even more people than usual to brave the tail end of rush hour. Still, perhaps because of the rain on the horizon, it was not entirely difficult to find a quiet spot after they'd walked for a few minutes. With a bit of trouble, Ivan followed Winston over a rather large boulder with clusters of starfish at its base, and the people were sparser on the other side.

The blanket hovered stubbornly in the breeze when Winston fanned it out, and Ivan helped him coax it down to the sand, which was still cool from an earlier drizzle. The latter did not, however, sit, and Winston, impatient, kicked off his shoes without further preamble, throwing himself down in a puff of sand.

Ivan soon followed, albeit more gracefully, and Winston set the food between them, dearly wishing he could stop the heat from rising to his face, and even more that Ivan couldn't See it so clearly.

"I should have asked if you had any allergies," Winston said, a little surprised at himself for not remembering. He'd been so flustered when Ivan had shown up that he'd overlooked the few precautions that usually anchored him.

Ivan was frowning at the basket in a way that made it obvious he could See its wicker. "I'm pretty low maintenance."

Winston snorted, and when Ivan looked up sharply, glanced pointedly at his bandaged palms.

"I can change the wrappings when we're done here, if you like."

Ivan rolled his eyes. "Perfect ending to a perfect day."

Winston asked whether cheap wine would make it better, and though Ivan initially wrinkled his nose at the dusty clearance rack bottle that emerged from the basket, the wine did, ultimately, improve things. Although, even after a few swigs (which grew exponentially less strained as they multiplied), Ivan took one look at the poppy seeds dotting the misshapen caps of some of the muffins (at least, that was what Winston assumed he Saw—it was the only blue in the basket, but it was possible Ivan was Seeing another color he hadn't been enlightened to yet) and immediately returned to the bottle's graces. Or rather, he tried to before Winston snatched it away.

"You need to eat something," Winston said. When Ivan protested, he continued, "Before you give yourself a whole different kind of reaction." Ivan was both thinner and shorter than Winston, and Winston was already feeling a little buzzed. In hindsight, he probably should have brought the food out first.

"I was just—"

"Look," Winston said, "Katie told me the more we See, the weirder processed foods are going to look to us. Better to enjoy it now while it's just a few poppyseeds."

"Are you *serious?*"

Winston confirmed this, though the truth was that Katie had been speaking, more specifically, of things that were processed far beyond baking and refrigeration. He was currently

91

trying to eat all his old cereal before he found out what it "really" looked like.

Ivan ruefully took a lemon poppyseed muffin, hardly looking at the rest of the basket's contents. "It's not just poppyseeds," he said. Maybe he was drowsy from the wine, but his voice was suddenly quieter than the seagulls investigating them from above. "I can See almost everything here." He nodded to the basket.

Winston wanted to sympathize, but more than anything, he was just jealous. "You'll have to eat sometime."

Ivan scoffed and shook his head, as though to say *eating is bullshit*, though he did, to Winston's relief, eat. To soften his own intoxication, Winston took a handful of deformed honey-shortbread cookies, still lukewarm from the oven, and munched them nostalgically, watching the Sound.

"I don't get how you can have a favorite," Ivan said, setting the muffin stump aside. "I can hardly look at myself in the mirror anymore." Winston's speechlessness must have registered as confusion, because Ivan clarified, albeit reluctantly: "I can See skin now, too."

"I'm sorry." Truly, Winston was, but the hesitation preceding the words, coupled with their simplicity, left them sounding insincere, even to his own ear. "Maybe I'll change my mind," he added, "when the same thing happens to me."

"Yeah, maybe." Ivan shot him a brief glance before returning to glaring at a crow approaching the abandoned muffin hopefully.

Winston picked up the stump and started peeling away its wrapping. "For what it's worth," he said, emboldened by the wine, "I think you're pretty easy to look at."

When he looked up from unwrapping the muffin (which he'd suddenly realized called for a medical kind of precision), Ivan was glaring at him so intensely, it was almost provocative.

"You're brave," Ivan scoffed, going back into the basket and removing the top from the other muffin, "I'll give you that."

The arch response caught Winston off-guard. "*I'm* brave?" Ivan had been a bit vicious at their first meeting, true, but if anyone was flirting with trouble here, it definitely wasn't Winston, and Ivan knew it. Buzzing with alcohol and Ivan, Winston continued, "That's funny, because I'd assume out of the two of us, I'm the only one that's been to prison."

Ivan nearly spat muffin everywhere, startling the crow into flight. Winston pat Ivan on the back until the coughing fit passed, restraining his smile until he was sure he wasn't actually choking.

"*Prison?*"

"Yeah."

"Stop that."

"Stop what?"

Ivan rolled his eyes, turning to look at the waves. "Bullshit."

"It's true!"

"*Where?*"

Winston told him, and Ivan had to lie down, his dark hair mingling with the sand. The thought of him having another conniption trying to get the grains out didn't help Winston control his facial expression at all.

"It was only a few months," Winston said, "and it was years ago."

Ivan pressed his bandages into his eyes. "And you were going to tell me this when?"

93

Not on a first date. "When it came up, I guess." He honestly hadn't thought Ivan would stick around long enough, Bond or no Bond, for it to do so.

Ivan uncovered his eyes and stared at the sky, muttering something about second thoughts. "Well then, what did you do? Was it a protest?"

Winston took a bite of the muffin stump. The bake was perfect, but he could see why his mother had tossed the batch. Too much lemon.

"I got in trouble a lot in high school. Barney and I used to flip through *The Anarchist's Cookbook* at lunch." Alright, they'd only done it for like a week, but it was fun to watch Ivan freak out.

"The Anarchist's *what now*?" Perfect.

"Oh, we were teenagers," Winston said through a mouth of food. "Didn't you do stupid things as a teenager?"

"I didn't read *The Anarchist's Cookbook*!"

Winston wondered if Ivan had been a private school kid. Probably. Someplace the politicians and news anchors sent their kids, where every student got a free laptop.

"Whatever," Winston said, "that wasn't what they busted us for."

"Then what?"

"Activist stuff," Winston said, hoping Ivan "scab" Notte would be deterred enough by the first word not to push the issue. He dug his fingers through the sand, and when he looked up, Ivan was staring at him with an expression halfway between a sneer and openmouthed awe.

"Winst…why would you bring this up on a first date? I should leave right now. Politics and your prison sentence."

The word went through Winston's body like a ripple, making him intensely aware of the arrangement of all his limbs and crystallizing the image of himself, in his mind's eye, taking Katie's notion of "Platonic Soulmates," stuffing it into a bottle, and hurling it to shatter against the coastal rocks. Not, of course, that it wasn't real. Just not, if the way Ivan was fidgeting was any indication, for him and Winston.

"At least," Winston said, "you know what you're getting into." Although, of course, the very best part of what they were getting into was how it was nudging them out of their respective realities, and it was, therefore, inherently beyond knowing.

The pair exchanged swigs through the rest of the bottle, and had made their way through most of the basket before the clouds started to thicken. The food offset the booze enough that both of them finished the meal (Ivan asserted this was a strained application of the word) no more than pleasantly buzzed off sugar and wine. Winston was appraising a leftover clove snap and trying to calm his heartbeat when Ivan inquired as to which colors precisely he Saw, which instantly destroyed all progress he'd made, to his annoyance and delight.

Winston told him, and Ivan was surprised that the list included only blue and green, which made Winston guess Ivan was definitely having a more jarring experience than him. Rotten luck. To make him feel a little better, Winston informed him that a few colors, black, white, and grey, which everyone Saw, would be remaining the same, but he got the sense Ivan was more insulted at the notion that color had always been in his life than relieved at the prospect of some remaining the same.

"Is that how you'll paint?" Ivan asked. "In…greyscale, I mean." He hesitated over the word Winston had taught him moments before. The only other group on this part of the beach was getting up to leave, an older couple rounding up their toddler and Labrador, walking with the calm acceptance of people used to coordinating with fussy weather.

Winston watched the dog leap up the boulder and receive an affectionate ear ruffle at the top. "I guess I'll have to invest in some colored paints and relearn everything."

"But most of your customers won't even know the difference."

"Yeah," Winston said, feeling a little more sober, "but the ones that do will have art for them for the first time ever."

Ivan frowned at the blanket.

"Maybe I was a little overdramatic," Winston said. "It won't be relearning everything; it's just a lot of new factors to take into account. Katie said the whales are the same, though. The Rezzies."

"Are the 'Rezzies,'" Ivan sneered around the word, but it was weirdly gentle, "your muse, then?"

"That position actually belongs to Mike Swan."

Ivan gave a curt laugh, then said, regarding the paint, "You could take classes to speed up the learning process. I'm sure some of the local colleges have them."

A smirk more sardonic than its predecessors that night pulled at Winston's mouth.

"Yeah, I'm not really a classroom kind of person."

Ivan raised a brow, cloying and soft. The gaze Winston parried it with, in contrast, was taloned.

"I'm kind of an art school dropout."

With melodrama worthy of an opera, Ivan fell backwards into the sand. "*Honestly!* Is there anything else you want to tell me?" he exclaimed. "Are you vegan, too?"

Winston tilted his head indulgently. "Sometimes."

"What, you're vegan when you eat a garden salad?"

Winston snorted at that.

"You dropped out of college?" Ivan asked.

"Yeah, well," Winston forced himself to look flippant, "it's not for everyone, I guess."

"But don't you worry?"

"About what?"

Ivan buried his face in his hands. "I don't know." His voice was muffled, but the defeat in it was quite audible. "Everything." He raised his head to the clouds and asked, miserably, "Why me?"

Though the words had undoubtedly been addressed to himself, thanks to the wine, they were heard by more than the intended party, and Winston, perhaps refreshed by the rain on the breeze, elected to answer.

"Because," he said, "you desperately needed some chocolate and booze, and I was willing to give it to you." When Ivan appeared unconvinced, Winston added, "I mean, you did bring the painting back." In fact, as far as Ivan knew, what Winston had done today could have just been courtesy, though Winston was sure it showed on his face that it wasn't.

The wind tossed the blanket around them, crumbs and sand alike taking flight. The tide had crept up the beach in the time they'd spent together, resubmerging nearly half of the deflated starfish and anemones clustered at the boulder's base.

"And you think," Ivan said, "I did that because of the Bond."

"Not really," Winston said, "but I like you."

Despite the fact that it answered his earlier question, the statement only seemed to confuse Ivan more. Before he could inquire about it, however, the beach rang out with a series of electric chimes, making Winston jump.

It was later than he'd thought. He didn't need to look at the label glaring from his phone, because every night at nine o'clock came the same reminder:

Seymour.

Winston cursed and, ignoring Ivan's questions, started throwing things into the basket, silently begging the rain to hold off just a little bit longer. If it was pouring when he got to Galaxsea, he'd have more cover.

"I have to go," he announced, holding out a hand. "Give me your phone."

Ivan obeyed, and Winston fiercely entered his number into it.

"I don't understand. Do you have another commitment? I thought—"

"That I wasn't the biggest tease in the universe?" Winston placed Ivan's phone back in his hand. "Because *that*—" He leaned in dangerously close, so much so that there couldn't have been half an inch between their lips. Winston was certain that Ivan's would have tasted of sugar and herbs had he not just come up with his most wicked idea all week. Ivan parted his lips ever so slightly. "—was your mistake." And Winston quickly changed course, planting the quickest and chastest of kisses on the tip of Ivan's nose, not bothering to hold back a massive grin as he retreated to witness the aftermath.

Unfortunately, it appeared to have rendered Ivan frustratingly catatonic, so Winston, in his haste, actually pulled the blanket out from *under* Ivan. "I'm free this weekend, so text me!" The overall effect of his exit would have been much more blasé and cool if he hadn't stepped into a tidepool and fallen flat on his back as he retreated. Fucking booze.

Ivan appeared to have recovered from his shellshock. "You okay, Casanova?"

"Shut up!" Winston called, peeling a piece of seaweed from his leg. When he reached the top of the boulder, he turned around to look at Ivan, just one last time. As expected, he was Prince Charming in the flesh, squinting upwards through the fog. Winston set the blanket and basket down, cupping his hands around his mouth. "And get ready!" he said. "Next time, I'll be critiquing *your* life's choices!"

10

Even after Winston dashed off, his presence lingered, and Ivan carried it home like a balloon. Come nightfall, he dreamt to muffled rain that Winston was even closer than he'd been on the beach, his lips tasting of honeyed shortbread and his skin smudged with blue paint.

Ivan fell out of the dream violently, at the awkward hour indulgent to sleep to during the week, but wasteful on the weekends. Try as he might to calm down and fall back asleep, it soon became apparent that wouldn't happen, so Ivan stared at his ceiling, sweaty, guilty, and pissed that Winston had made him waste one of his two opportunities to sleep in for the week.

He lifted a hand and examined it in the morning sun. Sand had gotten into his bandages last night, so he'd ended up unwrapping them when he got home. The sunlight gleamed on the healing flesh of some of the larger scars, which existed somewhere between blush and blood.

Ivan had told himself when he'd shut the door behind him last night that he wouldn't do any more thinking about Winston until his head was clear. He'd definitely been intoxicated last night, after all.

That had been the plan, but now his eyes drifted from his palm to his cell phone and he found himself caught in a rush of shivering questions. What did witchcraft look like? How had Winston known art school wasn't for him? Where had Winston met his Seer friends? Were the people in prison all normal, or had he been the odd one out? Did he like photography? Why did he like the Resident orcas so much? Where did he get off? Really, why was he like that?

Ivan rolled over onto his other side. The answers didn't matter. What he and Winston were flirting with was primitive. It was mating, not "Soulmates." He wasn't about to let Winston turn him into one of those people who believed it was anything more. Maybe he only felt good after last night because he wasn't hungry. Ivan had forgotten how much he enjoyed food.

He slid his hand out from under the blanket again. An unnamed "made up" color, with little black hairs foresting the bony ridges sloping down from his knuckles. Wiggling his fingers, he watched his veins contort and flex under the skin, and surprised himself when he realized he'd been doing it for several minutes without thinking anything about it. What surprised Ivan further was that he felt shame for not feeling shame.

Although…maybe it was possible color wasn't that bad. He didn't know if he'd ever See it the way Winston did, but Ivan supposed he could picture a future for himself where it was at least a mundane aspect of his life. The sand at the beach had been as cool and rocky as always. And he was almost starting to get used to his skin. And the ocean was terrifying, but the way that Winston spoke of its blue made that terror seem almost okay.

Ivan gave a tight exhale, not sinking any deeper into his mattress. Winston fucking Jinx. Son of a witch, ex-convict, protester, whale-lover, and painter. Sometimes vegan. And *that* was his alleged Soulmate. Right.

It has to be.

Ivan thought the words sarcastically, but they lingered heavy. The fact that it was difficult for him to acknowledge the *correct* perspective was further evidence that, as usual, he was getting carried away by his emotions. The real troubling thought: he wasn't certain anymore that it was a bad thing. Winston was emotional, and he was good to be around. Infuriating, but good.

A hot and blurry rendition of a sunny, wretched day snaked its way to the front of his mind, then. A silent crowd dressed in their darkest clothing, standing watch over an elaborate casket. Someone's phone rang, two others were discussing a home renovation in low tones, and the eldest son, the weakest of them, wept.

Ivan shot up in bed, suddenly filled with a fire he'd almost forgotten he had.

This ended today.

Just because things felt good didn't mean they were good *for you*. He didn't want to See. He didn't want to know. This Bond was a damn IV drip of poison, and he could already feel himself slipping into leniency. College fucking dropout and painter for hire. Who *did* that? People who had never learned how to live in the real world, that's who. Mike was right to look down his nose at Winston. Ivan had a better life alone than he would ever have spending time with people that delusional, entitled, and childish.

If he pursued anything with Winston, he would surely be trading in his career. Undoubtedly, he would lose focus if he surrounded himself with burnouts like that, and if he lost focus, he would surely lose his job, and then all of his money, and then he would be a failure, as was proved by the fact that this Bond had formed at all in the first place. Ivan might have been genetically defective, but he still had willpower. Yes, burning the bridge as soon as possible was the best course of action. A quick phone call would be best. Not quite so impersonal as text, but still a polite invitation to stay the fuck away.

Untangling himself from sheets and comforters, Ivan snatched his phone and padded barefoot into the parlor, hating the color of his floors, hating himself, and hating Winston as he stared at his name in his contacts, wishing he could slip into the monochrome screen. Wishing they both could.

On the third ring, Winston picked up. Perhaps if Ivan had gotten the first word, he would have stood a fighting chance. Unfortunately, however, he did not, and before he could even open his mouth, Winston said hi. Not even as a question.

Oh, God, Ivan thought, as the hideous Thesis Against Artist Boy he'd spent the past half hour mentally organizing vaporized. It took him a moment to say hello back, and when he did, it felt like someone was sitting on his chest.

"You're not gonna believe this." Winston's enthusiasm had already matured into that which existed between close friends. He sounded genuinely happy to hear from Ivan. *"I just got a new color. I don't know what it's called, but it's in sunlight."*

Ivan was so overwhelmed by the dual damnation of never seeing a normal sun again and seeing Winston even once again that he nearly hung up the phone, but he dug his nails into his palm and drew himself back to reality.

This won't be easy, the shriveled remains of logic said from a corner of his mind, *but you can do i—*

"I hope I didn't wake you up," Ivan said.

"You did, asshole. But I don't really mind, I don't like sleeping away the day."

"I'm the same way," Ivan lied, despite the fact that it ought to have been good news their sleep schedules weren't compatible.

It ends today.

"I was wondering," Ivan started, his heart throwing itself against his ribcage, rattling his frame.

Do not let this become you.

"Mm hm?"

"I just wanted to talk…"

You're better than this. Better off alone. You can't trust anyone, especially not someone as radical as Winston Ji—

"…over coffee." Ivan took a huge gulp of air, suddenly able to breathe again.

"Are you asking me out to coffee?" Winston sounded decidedly more awake now.

Ivan confirmed this.

"You might have to carry me there." The smile was audible in his voice.

Ivan could have died. It was too early to be calling on a weekend. He probably looked so desperate. "We don't have to."

"Yes, we do. I won't accomplish anything today unless I drink some overpriced coffee with a certain rude client's money."

"At least it's going to a good cause," Ivan said, though he would be damned if he let Winston pay. He was already pulling his shoes on by the time they hung up.

It was fine, he could just break it off in person.

The instant the sun hit his face, Ivan regretted not taking more time to put himself together. While Winston Jinx wasn't exactly in a place to be judging him on his appearance, today was the one day Ivan couldn't hide in the fog. Not a drop of the previous night's rain lingered in the air. He should have put more product in his hair. And chosen a different shirt. But then, if Winston could See its color now, pretty much anything in his closet was going to look like a disaster.

The closer he got to the coffee shop, the more it dawned on Ivan that it was actually worse to look like a mess in front of someone like Winston than someone like Mike. Yes, Winston seemed excited to see him, but Winston was a bankrupt painter and a college drop out. What did it say that he was Ivan's Soulmate? Probably that Ivan couldn't take someone like Mike, someone who told the truth when you looked like shit.

After pushing his way between what looked like some kind of Bible study group and a stand of Instant Keto Coffee that left him gagging on flashbacks to an old New Year's resolution, Ivan took a place in line, which temporarily calmed him down, perhaps because as long as he was waiting between the elastic guardrails he didn't have to make a choice between staying or leaving. As soon as he got to the front, his heart started to pound again, but it was only when he emerged with their drinks to find Winston watching him from across the room that panic truly set in, because *how* could Ivan possibly break things off with *that*?

Their drinks smelled unbelievable, and their sweetness teased Ivan's nose as he navigated to the window seat Winston had selected. In a fit of manic irritation, it had been satisfying to order the most ridiculous drink off the menu, but Ivan regretted it more with every step. Not at the possibility that Winston wouldn't like it, but at the possibility that Ivan would.

"Thanks Isaac." Winston relieved him of one of the drinks, smirking at the black Sharpie scrawled across its hull.

"Of course…" Ivan squinted at his own—"…William." Ivan wanted to personally thank every god Gretchen Jinx worshipped that they were by a window. It gave him somewhere to look that wasn't across the table, even if that somewhere was bright blue.

Ivan counted 14 seconds of frothing milk and clinking plates before he cracked. "It was kind of busy when I got here, so I thought I'd just order for the both of us."

"That was probably a good idea."

Winston really had no mercy. To buy himself time, Ivan took a sip from his drink, which he hadn't intended to touch. When he looked up, Winston was making a face at his cup.

"What?" Ivan asked, the taste of caramel still on his tongue.

Winston smiled wryly. "Your cup's marked the same as mine."

"So?"

"Have I mischaracterized you as the 'no room for cream' type?"

Ivan was so unbelievably relieved that Winston saw him this way that it took him a moment to realize his mistake.

"Oh," said Ivan, suddenly wishing he hadn't had a single sip. He probably looked so stupid. "I thought this was more your speed."

"What, 15 percent actual coffee with five pumps of caramel syrup, and coconut milk?"

"Didn't know if you were feeling vegan today."

Winston snorted. "How generous of you to sink to my level for a day."

Ivan felt hot. Winston sat back and took another sip of his drink, looking very pleased with himself.

"Fine, you've caught me," Ivan conceded. "I'm not a 'no room for cream' person. But I'm trying to be."

Winston lifted his cup. "Well, here's to failure."

Ivan hesitated, then completed the toast. "To failure." Winston was so weird.

They both took hearty swigs, and Winston, after removing a trace amount of melting whipped cream from his lips, said, "Speaking of failure."

In the span of a few seconds, Ivan went through a full cycle of confusion, rage, and resignation, eventually arriving at the memory of the words Winston had called over his shoulder through the fog.

"Oh, right. Go ahead, then."

Winston leaned across the table exactly like Ivan's sadistic fifth-grade teacher had the only time Ivan ever got in trouble, after helping a classmate stick a sleeping pigtailed girl to her desk by means of a Valu Pack of Extra-Sticky Cherry Chewing Gum. Winston started easy. "Tell me, Ivan Notte, did *you* finish college?"

Ivan opened his mouth to answer, but Winston cut him off.

"No, wait, let me guess. You have a Master of Business from…Stanford."

"Stanford doesn't have a business program," Ivan said, before he could stop himself. He felt his face go red before he even saw Winston's expression, which was twisted into an infuriating and mesmerizing bastardization of Mike Swan's caustic, open-mouthed grin. Ivan had the sneaking suspicion he was going to pay in the next few minutes for his vegan comment. "Alright," he spoke in the hopes of letting whatever remark Winston was about to make die unspoken, "you were close enough. It was Cornell and it was a bachelor's. Business was right." Business analytics, but Winston wouldn't care.

Winston's smile faltered, and for a split second, Ivan felt a guilt that he reassured himself was misplaced. If Winston was allowed to be as smug as he'd been last night about dropping out of art school, Ivan was allowed to be proud of graduating from Cornell. However, when he tried to muster some kind of the same swaggering confidence Winston had worn last night, there was only a cold vacancy where any kind of ownership over his education ought to have been.

"Damn, okay," Winston said, giving him a kick under the table, temporarily bringing him back to the present. "That's impressive. But tell me this: why doesn't a man who went to Cornell drive?"

"Maybe it's for environmental purposes."

"I don't think so," Winston said merrily.

Carefully avoiding eye contact, Ivan moved his knee so it rested against Winston's and watched his face go red. "Traffic."

Winston gave him a knowing look, but didn't move. "Nice try. You're biting your lip, like you do when you're nervous."

Ivan was equal parts irritated and touched that Winston had picked up on that in so little time. Though he supposed anyone would notice it if they made him nervous as often as Winston did.

He surrendered. "Fine. I lost my license."

Winston laughed, and Ivan insisted it was true.

"C'mon. Spill."

Most people would have had to surgically extract this story from Ivan, but today he didn't make Winston ask twice. In fact, as he started to retell the events that had shadowed him in shame since they passed, he began to feel like he'd given them too much weight.

"I just got irritated at this BMW…"

Winston was already starting to laugh, and it was a little bit contagious.

"And may or may not," he embellished, "have gotten into an altercation…"

"Mmhm?"

"Anditwasreallystupidandisntworthgettinginto." Ivan took a sip of his drink.

"Oh, no you don't. You got into a fight because of road rage and the cops got involved?"

"More or less."

"*Fuck*, how long is your—"

"*Shhhhhh.*"

Ivan caught the rather malevolent eye of a mother of two who was sitting near them with her hands over her youngest's ears. He glared back at her until she turned back to her coffee with a huff.

Winston, having seen the entire thing, lowered his voice. "Sorry. How long is it suspended for?"

"Only a couple more months. It was her fault, though. Isn't my problem the fossil was too stiff to use her damn turn signal."

Winston snorted. "You got your license suspended because an old lady didn't use her turn signal?"

"The fact that she was old didn't exactly help my case!" If Ivan felt silly after saying this, it was nothing compared to how he felt after taking in Winston's expression. "Please don't say you drive a BMW."

To Ivan's relief, Winston said, "I paint for a living and you think I can afford a car. Funny."

"It's a better fate."

Winston leaned back in his seat, pressing his knee into Ivan's as his feet slid forward. He tapped an inharmonious rhythm with his coffee cup. "Amazing. You know, maybe we are Soulmates."

Ivan's stomach flipped, and he tried to calm himself. As flustered as he was right now, he knew the moment he returned home he would be desperate for the suspended license to go back to being a freak accident. If he let it go, it would become his new normal, and that was unacceptable.

"I don't like to tell people about it," he said, and Winston looked at him quizzically.

"You think I do?"

Ivan bit his lip. Winston didn't seem like the type to hide it, per se. He had a cut between his thumb and forefinger, the deep red Ivan now associated with healing, and Ivan wondered what illicit activity he'd gotten it from.

Before Ivan could prosecute him on this, however, he himself was questioned.

"Do you have a lot of those?" Winston asked. "Angry encounters?"

Ivan recognized the feigned nonchalance he often encountered in the Galaxsea conference room.

"Not getting angry now, am I?" Ivan said, moving his leg away.

Winston opened his mouth, but took a moment more to ponder before speaking. Ivan, already feeling like he'd proved he was the exact kind of jackass the car incident made him out to be, took it as a mercy and gave a real answer.

"I don't know," he confessed. "To be honest, I assumed out of the two of us, you'd be the angry one."

"Me?" Winston laughed. "We Bonded when you shoved me!"

"Shhhh," Ivan hushed him again, but it was too late. At the mention of the Bond, the cardiganed mother got up and moved her flock to an empty table with a half-finished cappuccino still sitting on it.

"Don't worry about her." Winston drew Ivan back into their conversation. "What made you think that?"

"I don't know!" Ivan said, growing tired of those three words. "You went to prison, and you protest, and have those posters…"

The puzzlement that initially clouded Winston's expression melted away into bemusement. "You're right," he said. "Clearly, I'm a danger to society."

"I'm sorry," Ivan said, completely serious. "I was just trying to get through."

Winston watched him for a long, heavy moment, and Ivan felt a prickle of inadequacy inside of his chest. It didn't compare to the overwhelming despondency that filled his skull after a humiliation from Robert Cass, but for some reason, he felt it would be even more disastrous to ignore.

"Look," he said, no longer plotting out his words, "I don't have an excuse, okay? It was rude."

Something changed behind Winston's eyes then. Not the kind of change you Saw, but still obvious enough it couldn't be missed. At the moment, Ivan identified it as a passed test. In the far future, he would come to recognize it as a silent understanding.

"It's okay," Winston said eventually. "It's just...you work with Mike Swan. The man who implied he'd have my eyes...you know."

If Ivan had felt he'd passed a test seconds earlier, he knew he failed this one when he didn't catch Winston's drift. Winston took pity and explained, in hushed tones which required him to lean across the table, what exactly had happened. Ivan was aware of his own stillness, but he still felt like he was manufacturing the horror in his eyes when he leaned back. He couldn't help it. Mike didn't agree with the Seer movement, but he would never commit a hate crime.

"I'm not like him," Ivan said.

Winston sighed, for a moment seeming like he was the older of the two of them. "I know." He took a long sip of coffee, and Ivan watched the cut on his hand curl around the cup. To his surprise, he missed the feeling of Winston's hands around his. He wished he'd enjoyed it more when Winston had just taken his and run with it.

The cardiganed mother was leading her children out into the sunshine, her eyes (a color Ivan would later learn was called "hazel") fixed straight ahead. One of the children, a little girl with the same color eyes, cast a curious glance at him on her way out, and Ivan wondered what stories she'd been told about them.

Suddenly inspired, Ivan stood, holding out a hand to Winston.

"It's too loud in here," he said.

11

To Winston's slight disappointment, Ivan had not led him out of the café in pursuit of the bigoted mother and her kids; the family had already disappeared into the anonymous throngs of foot traffic. However, the possessive squeeze of Ivan's hand made short work of that letdown, compacting it down to size until it broke and fell, like sand, through an invisible gap in their fingers. Winston was still reeling from Ivan's phone call, let alone his proposition they continue past coffee, and it made him clumsy in keeping pace as they walked. Usually, Winston was the one doing the dragging.

It was an unusual day. The sun dazzled in every window, mirror, or puddle that they passed. Of these last, there were few. Summer had arrived to stay, bringing with it many squinting eyes after months of incessant rain. When Winston looked up, the light shone through the leaves of landscaped trees, illuminating them a brighter green. He tried to be less blatant about the staring—though there were no physical signs of the Bond, Seers were stereotyped and often singled out for the childlike rubbernecking that came with the colors—to protect both of them, but it seemed like the longer they went, the more persistent the pockets of color became. If Winston hadn't known better, he'd have thought Ivan was leading them into a thicket of it. But then, Ivan didn't See green yet, so it was possible he wasn't doing so knowingly.

Ivan wound them through the Saturday crowds to a compact little park, a deep green sanctuary paved with bricks and heavily shaded by spruces, alder, and yew. Beyond the path, lush green tangles of grass waved, dry for the first time in months.

"It's peaceful," Winston said as their steps slowed. Water was trickling somewhere, smelling unusually sweet in comparison to the salty tang of that in the Galaxsea tanks, some of which had gone directly up his nose last night. A crow stalked across the path in front of them.

"I know you like the...green, I think it was."

Winston looked at him, surprised. "You didn't have to—"

"Don't," Ivan cut him off, then took a breath. "I mean, it's better if I'm not being handed reasons to run from it."

That hurt to hear. Maybe in a good way. Winston was more enchanted by the fact that Ivan had brought them here voluntarily than he was by the green grotto itself.

Despite the trip's apparent intentionality, when they came to a little koi pond, Ivan's grip on him tightened almost imperceptibly, and Winston turned to him just in time to see astonishment flash across his face.

"What's up?" Winston jabbed him in the ribs, and he stopped before walking past the edge of the pond. All the fish were at the other side of the gurgling fountain in the middle, making even more noise as they gobbled up oats tossed by a gaggle of teenage girls.

"Nothing," Ivan said loudly, as the girls dumped the flour at the bottom of the bag and left. "I just thought you'd like the fish."

The gesture was warm, but confusing. "Why?"

Ivan looked at him. "The whales."

The sudden laugh that escaped Winston was so loud that the crow took flight. He covered his mouth, but when Ivan smiled, he dissolved into chuckles again, and didn't censor himself in saying, "Whales are fucking *mammals,* dipshit."

"I knew that," Ivan said, with an ironic lilt.

"You're lucky you're pretty."

"Speaking of pretty," Ivan said, "I didn't know fish had color. I mean I know koi are bred for their fins, but that one's got red on his nose…" He trailed off. "Can you See any of them?"

The fish pushed lilies out of the way in their dash across the pond; from their speed, it might have been inferred they hadn't eaten for months. Their mouths gaped and their eyes bulged as they begged for food, pushing past each other to get nearer to Ivan and Winston's reflections. Winston wished Seymour was that eager to eat.

Most of the koi were the color of sunlight, but a few had little splats of black or white here and there, and one particularly fat one was an entirely new color all over, warmer and more saturated than the sun. However, Winston had barely opened his mouth to ask if Ivan Saw it when the glint of sunglasses drew his eye to a familiar face further down the path.

"Which is that one?" Winston asked, his heart racing.

"I don't know the *genus*," Ivan said. Winston jerked his arm, sending him dangerously close to falling into the water, and laughed.

"The color," Winston clarified, when Ivan had calmed down about the injustice almost done him. To be fair, Winston probably wouldn't have let go of his hand if he'd accidentally pulled too hard. If nothing else, it would have made the whole thing look less incriminating to Mike Swan, who was now smirking at them from behind his camera. Winston did his best to ignore him. He wouldn't let this be ruined.

Ivan's gaze tempered into something that almost resembled tenderness.

"That's…uh…orange. You must have just gotten it. See?" He let go of Winston's hand and reached up to uncurl a strand of hair. Winston nearly went cross eyed trying to focus on it, but the color was unmistakably the same as that of the fat koi.

"Oh my God," Winston said, paralyzed by more than Ivan's touch. If they continued to see each other regularly, at this rate they'd have fully-developed colored vision in a week. Maybe a week and a half, if Winston's pace eventually slowed to match Ivan's. Considering his previous apprehension towards color, Ivan was making no small sacrifice in continuing to see him. "Thank you."

"Of course." Ivan released his curl, but was delayed in lowering his arm. His eyes, black and pensive in the trees' shadows, remained fixed on Winston's face. Winston might have kissed him, if he hadn't been so worried about Swan seeing them. The combination of the new color, Ivan's magnetism, and Swan's now unknown location were enough to overwhelm him.

"Oh, please don't cry," Ivan said, alarmed. "I didn't mean to upset y—"

"No, no!" Winston insisted with a sniff. "It's just…I'm surprised."

"That makes two of us."

The tone was perfectly genial, but just a touch too much so, an excess that came from compensating for being cold on the inside. There was still an aborted "thank you" lingering on Winston's lips when he turned to see Mike Swan standing just beyond the shade of a spruce, his eyes locked on Ivan.

Something plummeted inside of Winston, and he swore he saw it fall in Ivan as well, shattering on the bricks beneath them. For some reason, he thought of Katie.

"Mike." Ivan's voice was devoid of warmth.

Get him, Winston thought. Ivan had mentioned he worked with this guy; he would know how to deal with him. If worse came to worst, they could always throw him to the koi.

"You know, I hadn't realized when I gave you that painting I was playing matchmaker."

Ivan watched him steadily, and Winston was very, very aware that they were no longer holding hands.

Swan continued speaking to Ivan as though Winston wasn't there. "I hadn't thought you ran with this kind of person."

"What kind of person is that?"

Mike Swan laughed, though the sound actually seemed to drain joy from the surrounding vicinity. "A person who hurt me. Although I guess I shouldn't have expected you to care about that. Maybe I was presumptuous."

"You are," Ivan said, "being presumptuous. You know nothing of our..."

He trailed off, and Mike Swan's next word landed like a dart quivering in a bullseye.

"Relationship?"

His eyes darted between Winston and Ivan, and recognition reared behind them like a cobra's head.

"*Oh*," he lilted, "I see. Or, you do."

"You see nothing." Ivan's voice remained even, which somehow rendered his rancor even more obvious.

"Me?" Mike Swan put a hand to his chest. "Oh, God no."

Ivan sent Winston an accusatory glare that he received with a pang. He wondered how many people were within shouting distance.

"We were just," Ivan said, turning smoothly back to Swan, "setting up some boundaries."

Swan made a face. "Ivan," he said softly, "we all know the signs. I'm sure it's all," he gestured to the foliage around them, "beautiful in its true form. What was that new color they just came out with? Salmon? Named after a fish. Can you name one after me next?"

"This is really unprofessional," Ivan said.

Swan went very quiet before taking a step towards Ivan and into the shade, cocking his fair head to the side. He was close enough that Winston might have taken a step backwards, if it wouldn't have meant falling into the pond.

"You know what's unprofessional?" he asked. "The fact that you're Bonded with someone I told you threatened me into buying artwork I didn't want. You could have been with someone who understands you, who encourages you, but instead you decided to *mate*? I mean, Christ, Ivan, you're above this. Whatever you're going through that's made you think this is the answer, I can help."

"Alright, that's enough."

Mike Swan looked at Winston as though he hadn't even realized he was there.

"Look," Winston seethed, beginning to suspect Swan was more than a coworker, "I don't know shit about the relationship between you two, but Ivan is right. You're being inappropriate, and you don't know anything about us, either. So take your bigotry elsewhere."

It took a moment for Winston to realize his mistake. He waited for Ivan to shoot him another glare, and somehow felt worse when it never came.

"Us," Swan echoed, turning back to Ivan. "So it's true, then. You're Bonded. Or, excuse me, maybe 'Soulmates' is more PC?"

Ivan had gone very pale. "Look, he ran into me. It was out of my control—"

Winston's ears were ringing.

"I didn't mean to imply it was your fault. I just didn't expect you would embrace it. I thought you were better than that."

"I'm not embracing it! There's no need to make me feel worse about it."

"I would never make you feel worse," Swan said. "Actually, I want nothing more than for you to get better."

"Fuck better!" Winston exploded, ready to start throwing punches.

The fact that Mike Swan turned to him as slowly as a parent faced with a child's tantrum did nothing but stoke his fury. *Fucking psychopath.*

"Excuse me?" Swan asked. Ivan still wouldn't look at Winston.

"I said, fuck better. Look, you may think I'm better-off-blind, but anyone can see that you're a manipulative bastard who takes joy in—"

"Okay, just stop, alright?"

It was Ivan who had spoken.

"You've said enough."

Winston gaped at him. The park and the city beyond continued to move, people milling about and enjoying their Saturday. It seemed a mockery that just yards away, a group of children laughed without a care in the world.

"The language," Mike Swan shook his head, and Winston felt his face getting hotter, "speaks for itself. He said it, not me."

Deep shame welled up in Winston, the bitter aftertaste of the slur still in his mouth.

"What do you want?" There was a slight tremor in Ivan's voice.

Swan appeared to choose his words with the utmost care, but the warmth in his eyes was saccharine and contrived. "I just want to make sure you're okay. And I want you to know that if you need to talk about anything, I can listen. I hope I haven't overstepped." He paused, then stepped away. "Either way, I'll see you on Monday."

And with that, he retreated, disappearing into the buzz of the metropolis to go and do whatever douchebags of epic proportions did with their Saturdays. Half of Winston wanted to scream, to demand what the hell had just happened, and the other half felt deeply, irrationally, like he'd done something wrong.

He thought of Katie again, and the former half won out. Winston turned to Ivan, whose eyes were locked on Swan's retreating form, and was tempted to shove *him* into the koi pond.

"Do you want to tell me what the hell that was?"

Somehow, just the look on Ivan's face was enough to make Winston feel stupid, and he hated it.

"That's called self-preservation," Ivan snapped back. "Do you have any idea what this means for my professional life?"

Winston couldn't believe what he was hearing.

"You—? You want to talk to *me* about self-preservation?"

"Yes, actually. You know, some of us actually have to *work* to get what we want in life. I have to convince these people every single day that I deserve to be where I'm at."

Winston scoffed, wishing he'd bought his own coffee. "Do you not remember that was a man who threatened a hate crime because he didn't like the painting he commissioned from me? Do you not remember the fact that he told me I was better-off…you know?"

"Yes, I do, actually, and now all that shit is going to be directed at me!"

"Welcome to the real world!" Winston exclaimed. "Oh, and you can lie to yourself about Seeing all you want, but you can't say it's my fault. You bumped into me. God, you're just pissed because now you're treated the same way the world has treated people like Katie every day since birth."

"Christ," Ivan cursed, "this isn't about your friend or her politics."

The word stilled the air around them. Suddenly, Winston was overcome with an eerie calm.

"No, you're right," he said coldly. "It isn't."

Ivan blinked.

"It's about you," Winston continued, his words sharpening like a blade, "and your ego. And I'm sorry to have played a part in corrupting your relationship with it."

Ivan didn't look even the slightest bit wounded, and Winston got even angrier. How stupid had he been, to think this could have been anything? What did it mean if his Soulmate would throw him to someone like Mike Swan to preserve his pride? What did that say about Winston?

"But it's okay," he said, taking a step away, "because I won't get in your way again."

He should have left it there, but Ivan's continued silence was too much of a provocation to resist, and as he walked away, he halted and turned over his shoulder.

"You know, I guess I was wrong. People like you are all the same."

12

Winston took his time getting home that day.

When he'd first given Katie a key to his apartment, there had still been used textbooks and plastic dorm cubbies lying around the place. Most days, he looked back on that decision fondly; it was nice to come home to the sound of composition. Today, however, he crossed his fingers she would not be there.

The sun began to cast the sky in a grand painting of gold, orange, and what Winston would eventually learn was red. It was with great difficulty that he tore himself away from the spectacle and stepped inside *Takes the Cake*. Anger burnt up everything inside of him like dandelion puffs, their ashes leaving tiny scorches inside his ribcage. His irritation was not quelled by the fact that Katie was on his laptop when he arrived.

They shared a look, and while he could tell from her expression she understood something was wrong, she went back to typing without saying anything. Winston might have been more irritated by this if he hadn't, for one, known that this was the warmest reaction he could have expected from Katie and, in addition, recognized the email signature on the screen. It belonged to the record label representative she'd been waiting to hear from for six months.

Her poker face made it impossible to tell whether the news was good or bad, and Winston didn't want to risk asking about it. He was in enough of a crisis as it was; getting any more bad news right now would push him past his breaking point.

A little too loudly, he set his key down on the kitchen counter, heaving a sigh.

"Something happened," Katie observed, not looking up from her typing.

He resisted the urge to sigh again. Maybe if he breathed enough, he could breathe Ivan right out of his body. Maybe he could get his mom do to some black magic on Swan's portrait. Maybe he could reclaim at least some of his dignity. Enough to get him through the rest of the time he had with color, before the Bond faded.

"Alright, then." She closed the laptop lid without clicking send, which he appreciated, and grabbed what was left of his bottle of cheap wine off the kitchen counter. He glared at it, then her, and she rolled her eyes. "We're not letting it go to waste just because his mouth has been on it."

Winston was perfectly fine with doing just that, but he said nothing, because, as usual, she was right. Although, he could have done without the reminder of Ivan's lips, spitting hatred and stretching into arrogant sneers.

"Why are you always right?" he sat down at the counter, pressing his palms to his eyes. How could he have been so selfish, to focus on "Soulmates" at such a critical time in the Seymour operation?

The bottle sloshed as Katie held it out. "If it'll make you talk plainly," she said, "take a swig."

Winston shook his head. "If I drink, I'll cry." Mostly because of the mammoth task in front of him. But not entirely.

"If I have to ask what's wrong one more time…"

He stood up suddenly, marching over to the stack of paintings against the wall and flipping through them a little more violently than necessary. He pulled out the one he was looking for.

Swan's face pulled him right back into the shitshow he'd experienced just moments before. Though they obviously weren't accurately colored in the painting, the memory of those fucking blue eyes came rushing back to him in company with the echoes of insults and hot shame. Mike Swan took the color of the ocean and bastardized it so that every time Winston felt sea spray on his face, he would be reminded of the fact that his Soulmate had chosen bigotry over him. And the fact that he himself had chosen a bigot's love over the Rezzies.

His fingers dug into the canvas before he cursed softly and tossed it to the side like an empty pizza box. "That fucker Mike Swan showed up to harass us at the park."

Katie raised her eyebrows.

"Yeah." Winston's voice rose. "And he said some things about being Bonded, and Ivan sided with him."

"Do you know if Swan has power over him in the workplace?" she asked.

"No," Winston said miserably, sitting down again and taking a drink of wine. He chose not to mention his suspicion that Swan and Ivan had a romantic history. Whatever Katie would have had to say about that, he doubted he had the heart to listen to it. Despair pressed in on him like thick, cold mud. "Look, I get it now. Bonding doesn't mean Soulmates.

Whatever. The word is bullshit, and it's shitty that the community pushes it on everyone. But I l—"

"Don't say it," she said sharply.

"It's true," he said, a lump growing in his throat. "I thought he felt the same way." He'd been so astonished by Ivan's lack of cruelty that he'd taken it to mean love, or at least the beginning of it. He'd thought he was immune to the magnetism she'd warned him about from the start, but he never trusted anyone as quickly as he had Ivan.

Katie sighed. It was clear from her tone she was regretting bringing out the booze. "You couldn't have loved him. You barely knew him."

Winston, had he not been overwhelmed, embarrassed, and brokenhearted, might have agreed. Unfortunately, he was all three of those things, and the wine was only adding to the problem. He had just had a feeling about Ivan. There was something unnamable, but very potent, that distinguished their meetings, their conversations, their first date, from every other relationship he'd had for years. Could all of that really just be the Bond?

"This is why I say the Soulmate narrative is bullshit." Katie's words were firm, but to Winston, they were as distant as if she'd shouted them from the street outside his window. "The two of you live completely different lives. You have different values, different dreams, different budgets. It's better that you're clashing sooner rather than later."

Winston wept.

"You can't change him."

"I didn't want to!" he said, fully aware of how stupid he sounded. "I thought that maybe..."

"The two of you could get along despite the fact that he was a self-hating bigot with a belief system polar opposite to yours, and proceed to ride off into the rainbow horizon with Seymour in tow?"

It took Winston a moment to recall the meaning of the new word, "rainbow." When he did, he stared at the kitchen counter. The white plastic was fascinating all of a sudden.

"Winst, listen," she said. "Nature thinks you're genetic matches. Don't mistake that for love."

It was terrible to think what he'd tried so hard not to since starting this whole thing, but at the edges of his mind, the possibility started creeping in that maybe, just maybe, this was for the best. How must Katie have felt, seeing him so infatuated with someone that pronounced his hatred for Seeing every other minute? It wasn't only Winston's humanity that he was pushing aside by keeping Ivan's company. He felt a rush of shame for lusting after someone that held Katie in so little respect.

"I'm so sorry," he broke the silence. "I was thinking about myself."

"Not really," she said, tilting her head to look at him in a way that was both hawkish and tender. She reached out and gave his hand a squeeze, and they sat quietly until the sunset had faded to a deep blue and the wine was completely drained.

Even if he had loved him, Winston was still a liability to Ivan's reputation. He had to accept that to the other man, he was a novelty, nothing more. He wasn't oblivious. He knew he was the physical embodiment of what people like Ivan thought was wrong with the country. Something inside of Winston twisted terribly as thought after thought rushed through his mind, rewriting every moment they'd shared together into something jaded and awful. How much of his time with Ivan could have been spent on more important things? When had he turned into such a bootlicker?

Katie broke the silence with a deep sigh.

"I'm sorry," she said, and though he knew it was sincere, he still felt childish hearing it, as though he was thirteen again, crying to her about his first break-up at recess.

Winston sniffed, shooting the empty bottle a nasty look.

"Don't be," he said hoarsely. His sorrow was starting to ebb, and his initial anger was freshly kindled.

"Listen to me," Katie said. She had him anchored in place, but his mind was already miles away. "You are so much more than what you See. This Bond is not who you are."

With a surge of blind rage, Winston wondered how many times Ivan had told himself that.

"No, fuck it." Winston broke free of her grip, opening a drawer and digging out one of his disposable phones. "It's time to stop apologizing."

"What are you—?"

"I'm texting Barney." His fingers flew across the keyboard. "I lost focus, and it's time I moved the plan into its next stages."

Katie stiffened, alarmed, likely recalling their last discussion on this stage of the plan. "We still don't have enough information—"

"That's why," Winston interrupted her, "we're going to get the information, straight from the source."

"Winst, I'm just not there yet with the hacking. I've been so busy with my music…"

Her face fell when she realized he'd spoken literally.

"Absolutely not," she said. "There are ways to get the information other than *marching into headquarters* and taking—hell, do you even know what you need?"

"I know," Winston said, his mind working a mile a minute, "that we need to know what our assets are. We need to know when they're going to be doing construction, when they're going to keep the park open late, if they still have any guards or cameras I don't know about. We need to know if they have a means to transport the whale on site, or if we're going to need to bring something ourselves. If so, then we need to figure out how to get that in. We need incident reports, we need records of payment, we need calendars."

Waves of disapproval seemed to radiate out from her.

"So, in short," she said, "we need everything."

"I won't," Winston halted his rapid texting, "let them keep him there."

"Oh, for God's sake!" Katie exclaimed. "He's one whale! This is your second offense!"

"We're all just one!" Dammit, he hated fighting with her. "When the hell will anyone get it through their head that they use that argument to keep us all suffering?"

"There's still time to petition for a sea pen—"

"Why the hell would they invest in a sea pen for a dying whale?" Winston snapped. Besides, Seymour belonged with the Rezzies, with his family. Putting him in a sea pen, where he might even be able to hear their calls, and yet still be unable to follow them, almost seemed crueler than keeping him in the park. He was embarrassed that he was taking offense on behalf of a whale, but what else was there to do? Not care? "You can't look," he said, "at a whale floating motionless at the top of his pool and say he's not bored. I'm not going to let him die degraded like that when the ocean is barely a mile away. You can't tell me leaving him like that isn't evil."

"Saving him won't change what happened to you."

Winston's blood ran cold.

"I'm not," he said, "going to look the other way while an animal I watched grow up in the wild gets neglected." Katie usually was so understanding about his neglect, what with her own abusive household.

The silence that followed filled the room like a dense fog.

Katie regarded him coolly. "So what am I, then?" she asked. "What do you expect me to do when you're doing time for half your life, and Seymour is long dead, and your mother and father have to watch you waste away behind bars when you could be making art?"

They won't be watching at all, just like last time.

Winston stared her down for a long moment before looking away. "That won't happen."

"As your friend, I can't let you do this."

"As your friend, I'm begging you to let me."

She shook her head. "Sometimes I think you just do this shit so someone will pull you back in."

Winston wiped a tear away and eyed the empty bottle with loathing. After a beat, he said, "I don't expect you to help me any more than you're comfortable with."

She huffed and turned back to her email.

§❧

For the rest of the weekend, they planned. In Winston's mind, there was nothing else to be done. To his dismay, Katie cancelled a few smaller gigs she'd booked, and Barney cleared his work schedule, leaving him with no other choice but to let them help. He ended up needing every bit of it, and didn't even have time to visit Seymour. During that time, Katie mostly talked to Barney.

Perhaps it would have been more prudent to put this thing together when they weren't running off of 5 shots of espresso a piece at four a.m., but any prolongation of Seymour's escape was suddenly unbearable for Winston to entertain. He knew, somewhere deep down, that it was better if they didn't rush into this, but he had stopped caring about caution, no matter how many concerned glances Katie sent his way. Caution wasn't going to save the world; there was too much work to be done. Action, unrestrained and unapologetic, was the only way to bring Seymour home.

It felt like he was running off a high. While Katie and Barney tired or paused to grab some scraps from downstairs, Winston bristled with irritation and continued working. Some dormant part of his brain was aware his eyes were aching from endless scrutinizing of the building's blueprints, of the details of their fake passes, of the bullshit documents they had to bring in late from the D.C. park location (because their flight was delayed several hours, so inconvenient, really), of the reliability of the flash drives they'd be copying the needed files to. However, while that part of his brain usually took some kind of effort to ignore, in those few days, it was like the signals it was sending him weren't even necessary. He worked the same regardless of whether or not he ate, drank, and slept, so he didn't bother with it. Katie and Barney forced him to have a slice of apple here, a piece of bread there, but it all was sand in his mouth. Water no longer quenched his thirst, and sleeping was an unforgivable waste of time. The one time he did catch a few hours, he woke up feeling the same as he had before he'd laid down, only disgruntled and anxious to beat. By the time Sunday rolled around, sunlight definitely looked less yellow, but he tried to ignore that.

Get the information, get out, save Seymour. If someone confronts you, you're a representative from the D.C. location come to manually transfer extremely classified information. You would have waited, but your flight home is departing soon, and you're on thin ice with your supervisor who wants the information, pronto. You know it's unprofessional to be hanging around the building so late, but you thought as long as you had your ID, it would be fine.

Winston repeated the words in his mind like a prayer, though he dearly hoped that no confrontation or explanation would be needed. Most people were satisfied with a quick glance at something that looked even vaguely like ID, but anything more scrutinizing could cause the entire plan to come crashing down.

"Well," Winston said on Monday afternoon, his temples throbbing.

The group stood around his kitchen table, staring at the floorplan of Galaxsea headquarters. Perhaps there still was some detail they had overlooked. Surely they couldn't have finished this in a mere two days. If they'd worked at this rate the entire time, then Seymour would already be in the ocean.

Katie looked up at him. "Well."

"Maybe it's a little too late to ask," Barney said, "but is this, like, terrorism?"

"They won't be afraid." Winston ruthlessly put a lid on whatever much needed barrel of laughs Barney had been about to open. The other side wouldn't be afraid.

"Better for us," Katie said. "The less they fear, the less trouble we'll run into."

"It isn't terrorism," Winston clarified, though his stomach had lurched at the word. "We're doing what's right."

Barney gave him a long look. "We've gone to prison for less, Winst."

He felt a prick of guilt and looked down at the table. It wasn't fair, but a part of him resented that questions were being brought up at all.

"I know." There was a beat in which no one said anything, then Winston raised his head again and continued, "I would never ask either of you," he looked at Katie, "to throw your lives away for me." Like Winston, Barney didn't have far to rise. He cut timber for a living, and was considering opening a camera store once he had enough in savings. But Katie was different. Winston needed to believe that someday she'd be treated like she was important, that all the pain meant something. He needed to believe someday she'd be listened to, even just by people who liked her music, because he never would be. Winston didn't think he would ever be able to live with himself if he kept her from that.

"We won't throw away our lives," Katie said, looking back at him. "We'll save one."

"One very big one," Barney added.

"Then let's do it," Winston said, the words rushing through his veins like a drug. "Let's save Seymour."

13

Some part of Ivan had known it was wrong from the start, but it wasn't until twenty-four hours had passed that he began to understand the true scope of his fuckup. He'd reexamined what had happened by the pond countless times, shifting blame to Winston, then Mike, then society itself, but in the end, no matter how he rearranged the narrative, the memory of the look on Winston's face only allowed him to arrive at one conclusion: the blame was his, and his alone.

Lying facedown in bed, his head swimming with the consequences of last night's booze, it was hard to think of any immediate use for that information. After all, he'd only known Winston a few days. It wasn't like Ivan cared about any of this Bond stuff. What did he care if he'd upset Winston?

It hurt to admit it, but he might have gotten a bit more attached than he'd thought. Far too attached to be appropriate for how long they'd known each other. His parents had dated for half a year before even thinking of one another as non-disposable. Maybe that was extreme, but Vera and Charles Notte had never really been capable of settling for less than a picture-perfect love.

Maybe it was the alcohol, but the longer he thought about going back to a life without Winston's eccentricities, the more he felt like dying. And that terrified him. Christ, he hadn't felt this manic when he and Mike had dated. Or even with any of his previous boyfriends. This stupid Bond was making it difficult to think straight.

Ivan could tell from the streaks of warmth on his skin that it was sunny again today. He wanted to lift his head and close the blinds, but he knew looking at the light would hurt almost as much as thinking about everyone milling outside and enjoying the weather. In the hopes of regaining some kind of emotional control, Ivan began to imagine the kinds of things Winston and his friends might get into now that the rain wasn't in their way, like throwing bricks through Galaxsea's windowpanes, or even personally vandalizing his office, but confoundingly, this only saddened him further.

Ivan realized that he was crying, and that he deserved to be. And, as soon as he acknowledged the tears soaking into his pillow, it became impossible to deny the truth any longer. The truth, of course, that Winston had stopped being disposable some time ago, and Ivan wasn't upset just because he'd fought with Winston. He was upset because he'd hurt Winston. And the guilt that this roused in him was so potent that Ivan was struck by another, even harsher truth: he was, perhaps, not a very good person.

The thought had surfaced before, on some of his particularly nasty days. He'd fail at completing some illicit task for Galaxsea, catch a verbal lashing from Cass, and retaliate so relentlessly that he left the conversation feeling less than human. Usually, any guilt he felt in those instances appeared as a sharp pinprick of panic that, despite its potency, was there and gone quickly. After all, even if Robert Cass had feelings, Ivan wouldn't care about hurting them. However, today it lingered, morphing into a realization of such ruthless clarity it made him feel like he was sinking lower into his mattress.

He'd judged Winston from the very start.

The amount of times he now recalled condescending to Winston was enough to make him physically nauseated (although that could have been his stomach). Even as he'd longed to kiss him, Ivan had mocked Winston in the back of his mind. He'd stuck his nose up at his apartment; he'd thought his painting less an admirable passion than a cute quirk; he'd feared his mother's worship; and he'd silently ridiculed his activism. It was especially hard to laugh at this last aspect after seeing the look on Mike's face when he'd said "Mate."

Ivan had never thought of himself as cruel. He'd been taught by his parents to be polite, and careful, and respectful, but never outright to hate Seers. His father had been old-fashioned, sure, but it was hard to imagine him sneering as Mike had, which was on its own confusing. Mike had always, including yesterday, seemed at worst intolerant of Seers, never hateful, but now Ivan felt an inarticulable apprehension towards him. But why should he, if Mike had always been so tolerant? And moreover, if Ivan had always been surrounded by such even-tempered people, how had he become so spiteful? This wasn't even just about Winston; now that Ivan thought about it, he really had a bone to pick with everyone. What if *he* was despicable, not the world?

This disquieting possibility shadowed Ivan through the rest of the weekend. He took a personal day that Monday, partially because he had a pounding hangover, and partially because his entire worldview was collapsing around him. And although he did his best to eat and shower, he was ultimately too miserable to do a proper job of either, and resigned himself, as most men do when trapped in a cataclysm of these proportions, to calling his mother.

Were it anyone else, Vera Notte would have waited proudly until the third ring as a reminder that her time was precious and not to be wasted on anything but the very best gossip (and, to Ivan and Allison's ire, the most convincing telemarketers), but her children were an exception to this rule, and she answered promptly.

"Ivan! Honey, how are you?" There was chatter in the background; she probably had an opening shift at the flower shop today. Ivan felt bad for interrupting her. He would never understand why she'd chosen this, of all jobs, to take up after Dad died. Sometimes he wanted to punch something when she told him the things customers said to her. In fact, it upset him enough that he'd started going out of his way not to talk to her.

"Hi Mom."

"You sound strained." She clocked it nearly immediately. *"How are things at work? Are you and Allison getting along again?"* It had been years since they'd gotten along, but she always pretended it was less.

"Mom." Ivan choked back a sob, hating himself.

"Honey, what's wrong?" The background noise faded as she stepped into another room.

"I, uh…" Ivan tried to breathe. "I think I'm in love."

Vera Notte was either mercifully oblivious to the complete breakdown her son was having on the other side of the line, or she had class enough to pretend she couldn't hear it. Knowing his mother, it was a 50/50 chance.

"Oh, no!" she laughed. *"Honey, that's wonderful! What's his name? I knew it would be you before Allison; she's always been a bit too cutthroat for her own good."*

"There's more." He couldn't say it. He couldn't. He'd thrown himself in with a certain lot; was he going to alienate himself from them as well? The thought of both sides being against him, of spending the rest of his life alone, was soul crushing. "It's...we're Bonded. I'm a Seer now."

The silence that followed couldn't have lasted more than half a second, but it felt like half a year.

"You...See things, then?"

Ivan took a shaky breath, nailing shut his coffin. "Yeah."

"Is it true that there are more colors, now, or are they really making things up? Because Carly told me that they're being too harsh on these talk shows. She's always going on about what we have in the shop, roses are red..."

It took Ivan a moment to process what she'd said. "Wait, you're not...?"

"Ivan, don't stutter, it's unbecoming."

"You're not disappointed? I mean, Dad always said—"

"Don't worry about what your father said; you know he liked to grumble. Carly is Mate—excuse me, Bonded, and she and her husband are perfectly normal, lovely people, so I don't see it like Dad did, anymore. Nothing wrong with a bit of biology, since we're all so disconnected these days."

"Oh," was all he said, but he wanted to beg her not to coddle him, not to pretend it was fine when it wasn't. As a prompt and a self-sabotage, he said, "He's a painter."

"Would I recognize his name?"

"Definitely not."

The beat of silence that followed went through Ivan like a stake. God, there he went again, criticizing Winston every chance he got. He liked Winston's art, so what, or who, was he criticizing it for?

Against his better instincts, Ivan continued, "He's kind of broke, actually. His mother is a pagan and a witch, and he's an incredible artist, but it's not like you and Dad wanted."

"Oh, don't worry *so much, Ivan!"* she cried. *"I wish you'd do it less. God knows your father should have."* There was a pause. *"You were always like him in so many ways, but that was the one I worried about. Is your Soulmate a worrier?"*

"No." Ivan looked out his windows, where grey clouds were moving in over the Sound. "No, he's not."

"Good. As long as he's good for you, I don't care if his mother worships the devil himself."

"Mom!"

"Oh, you know what I mean. There's a little wiggle room, as long as he's a good man. Working has made me realize that perhaps your father was a bit too absolute in his views. There are so many strange and wonderful people out there."

True, but there were just as many evil people as there were good. Ivan felt a rush of indignation. His dad had been cautious around certain types to protect the family.

"I know you miss him, honey. I do, too."

"Do you?" Ivan snapped. Somehow, it hurt more that she responded to his irritation with tenderness. She hadn't even cried at the funeral, and had probably encouraged the concerned murmurs circulating the wake about Ivan's more emotive mourning.

"Yes," she said patiently, *"and I still think he could learn a thing or two from you, me and your sister. Do tell her to call me, yes? The both of you never call or visit."*

They said their goodbyes, both knowing Ivan would not be talking to Allison, and hung up. Ivan sniffled, and wiped his eyes with a paper towel he then scrunched into a ball.

In a way, he almost felt cheated. Where was the lecture on morality and civilized behavior? The crying? He'd been the only one doing that. If his mother didn't hate him for being like this, was it possible that others might accept him, too? Could that world exist? A world where he could just live his truth and not worry about what other people thought?

Somehow, he had a terrible feeling that every second from this point counted twofold. Every minute that ticked away allowed Winston's image of him to further sour, but how the hell was he going to fix this? If he'd learned anything from his mother's experiences in retail, and his own in love, it was that even the most sociopathic lovers were capable of buying a bouquet of flowers to smooth over a disagreement. Winston would know that. And, as pissed as he inevitably would be, he might be brash enough to point it out.

In the distance, streaks of rain shaded the sky over the sea. The shower would probably hit Seattle in an hour or two, but somehow, it looked less real through his window than on Winston's canvas.

The thought lit up Ivan's hopes like a Christmas tree. Without worrying about how he looked, he threw on some jeans and a sweatshirt before grabbing his keys and fleeing into the darkening city.

&❧

By the time Ivan arrived at *Takes the Cake* with a small palette of colored paints nestled in the front pocket of his sweatshirt, the rain had reached Seattle. Although he had to dodge the tiny waterfalls streaming off the bakery's overhang, and he had no umbrella to keep himself from getting completely soaked, he welcomed the smell of it over his cab's smell of cigarettes and vomit.

The taxi drove away, its beams pausing at a stop sign Ivan had trouble Seeing, maybe because of the dark and rain, before rounding the corner and becoming another light in the city. For a moment, he regretted not asking the driver to wait, as he didn't even know if *Takes the Cake* would be open at this hour, but he need not have, because the doors readily admitted him into the shop's familiar cinnamon glow. Gretchen's bakery had a pleasant aura to it, for a place run by a witch. Ivan wondered if she always worked this late, or if one of her crystal balls or something had told her he'd be stopping by.

Christ, he was hungry. If he hadn't been here on such important business, he might have stopped to buy a hand-pie.

As usual, any precautions he took to ascend the staircase silently proved fruitless, and by the time he stood dripping rainwater outside Winston's door, Ivan was feeling painfully conspicuous. After briefly considering whether to wring out his shirt or continue looking like he'd just jumped in a lake, he determined both options would leave him looking equally pathetic. Taking a deep breath, his heartbeat hammering in his ears, he knocked.

Despite his mother's reassurances, in those few agonizing seconds before the door opened, his mind was a whirlwind of worry. Ivan wasn't confident that he could look at Winston without suffering a complete breakdown of language. However, as it turned out, he need not have worried about this at all, as when the door swung open, he was greeted not by Winston Jinx, but by his friend Katie, who looked more upset to see him than he could ever have expected Winston to.

Ivan tried to be subtle when craning his neck to look around her, but this only deepened her scowl. Despite the obvious fact that no one else was in the apartment, he still summoned the nerve to ask, "Is Winston there?"

Her stare less resembled daggers than it did a military-grade assault weapon.

"No."

Ivan believed her. Winston had a strong enough presence that he doubted they could be in the same building without him knowing it. But if he wasn't here, where was he? It was hard to decide what was worse: Winston, feet away, pretending not to be there, or Winston out somewhere, dancing under flashing lights and moving on with his life.

"You're alone in his apartment?" Ivan asked, trying to summon some kind of bravado.

"Oh," she smiled contemptuously, "well, you see, since I too am peasant, Seeing scum, he doesn't have to worry about me robbing him or stinking the place up."

"Look, I—"

"You know," her voice increased, "you've got a lot of nerve coming here without so much as flowers. Three-hundred-dollar Italian shoes, and you couldn't be bothered to get the guy a damn rose."

Ivan glanced down at his drenched gym shoes, and when he met Katie's eyes again, there was an inferno behind them.

"Goodbye, asshole."

And she slammed the door in his face so violently that Ivan flew back against the opposite wall.

"Katie?" He shook himself, then knocked on the door again. "It is Katie, isn't it? I'm not empty-handed. Do you know when he'll be back?"

"Do you know what time it is?" was the only reply he got, as cool as the water still rolling off his clothes.

Ivan ran his fingers through his hair, which was still damp and curling. "I have to see him, Katie. Do you know when he'll be back?"

There was no response, though Ivan thought he could hear one distinct tap of a laptop key.

He pressed on, heart aching. "Look, I don't know how much he told you, but I've made a terrible mistake, and I think I deserve to be heard out."

A chair scooted loudly, followed by a series of stomps that incrementally increased in volume before the door swung back open.

"You think you *deserve* to be heard?"

Involuntarily, Ivan took a step back, which placed most of Winston's kitchen counter in his range of view. There, a strangely familiar view of an office door glowed on a laptop screen.

"I didn't mean…" he started.

"What?" she demanded. "You didn't mean the part where you humiliated him? You didn't mean the part where you sided with a man that thinks people like me, and Winston, and you, by the way, are on par with animals? A man who threatened to cut his eyes out? You broke his heart, Ivan! He loved you!"

144

Ivan blinked, uncertain he'd heard correctly.

"He loves me?"

Katie laughed. "Of course he does. You're three days into a Bond, for God's sake. Most people are inseparable at that stage. Even you should know that."

It was a bit challenging to breathe.

"Oh, don't act surprised. You knew you had him wrapped around your finger. You knew you had him the moment you looked at him, just like you know when you look at anything it can be yours. Because people like you don't get told no, and they certainly don't get told no by people like me and Winston. So consider this a first for both of us."

"Wait, don't—!"

She slammed the door again. Ivan shivered, then began to hammer with his fist on the aged wood.

"Dammit, can't we just talk?" He continued pounding on the door. "So help me, I'll break this thing down!"

He knew they were both aware this was physically impossible for him to accomplish, but the threat was his only comfort in his increasing state of hopelessness.

And then, Ivan was struck by a sudden recognition.

"Katie?" he called. "Was that my office?"

The thought of it being true was more bizarre than anything he could have imagined would take place that night, and yet, the longer the silence on the other side of the door, the more Ivan began to believe that it had indeed been his office on her screen. What this meant, he had no idea.

Surely, it couldn't be good.

After a pause, there was a set of slower, quieter footsteps, and the door opened again.

"What did you just say?" Katie asked.

Ivan noticed she had turned the laptop away from his view.

"I said," he took a step over the doorframe, though her arm blocked his way, "was that my office on your computer?"

"What do you mean *your* office?"

Slowly, he turned his head to look at her. Obstinate eyes stared back at him.

Suddenly, all the stress of the past week that had previously dissipated realigned itself into a neat little boulder which was promptly, metaphorically, dropped on Ivan's shoulders.

"I mean *my office*," he shrilled, pushing past her and striding into the familiar scent of paint and sea unique to Winston's apartment. Any other day, it would have been welcomed. Today, it had no effect on Ivan as he rushed to the computer.

"Wait, Ivan, don't!" Katie swung the door shut again and raced towards him, but it was too late. Ivan stared in horror at the screen, which displayed a collage of live camera feeds not only from his office, but from the entire Galaxsea corporate headquarters.

14

As Ivan stared at the screen, an old conversation, interrupted by each jolting thump of his heart, replayed in his mind.

"You hate Cass, too?"

"Of course I do. He's an ass."

Once the memory appeared, there was no steering himself away from the conclusion it pointed to. Ivan knew, as surely as if he had seen him, that Winston was currently at Galaxsea headquarters, and he was, most definitely, not doing anything legal.

Ivan also knew he was supposed to feel validated by this discovery, but he didn't. Here it was, the confirmation that Winston and his friends were bad news, the excuse to go back to his normal life, and the only thing he could confidently say he felt was Katie's eyes on his back.

He turned to look at her. "Tell me he's not in there."

"Tell me," she said, "you don't work for those bastards."

Ivan turned back to the screen. There really weren't many people he "worked for," per se, but given Katie's current mood, he wasn't eager to enlighten her.

"Does Winston know?" she asked.

Ivan bit his lip. Winston hadn't hated Galaxsea that much, had he? Christ, there'd been an uproar about the whale, but most people were satisfied with making a poster, shouting for a few hours, and calling it a day. It wasn't like Galaxsea had *all* of the Southern Residents in captivity. What was Winston thinking, doing this on top of his criminal record?

"It never came up."

In his peripheral vision, Katie had gone frightfully still.

"Give me," she said, "the laptop."

Ivan turned to look at her again and found her closer than he'd expected. He retreated with the laptop into the nearest corner of the kitchen countertop, in front of a dusty knife block. "No."

She was bigger than him. Definitely stronger, too. But he was less afraid of the immediate threat she posed than of whatever Winston was doing at Galaxsea.

"Do you want Winston back?"

"Yes."

"Well, so do I!" She made a swipe for the computer, which Ivan dodged, stepping to the opposite corner of the kitchen. "Give it to me!"

"Not until you tell me what he's doing!" Ivan shouted. There was movement on the screen as he hugged it to his chest, but he didn't get to scrutinize it closer before pain exploded in his shin. Cursing, he doubled over, and the computer was yanked from his grip.

"Jesus!" Through the tears in his eyes, Ivan saw Katie dash to the sofa. When his vision cleared, he saw that she was texting furiously, the light from her phone's screen giving her eyes a rabid gleam.

Ivan stormed over to her. "What the hell?"

"Shut up."

"No." Ivan grabbed the computer again. "What's going on?"

"It's none of your business."

"It literally is!" Ivan continued to pull with no regard for the laptop's safety, but as it was clear he was fighting a losing game, he changed tactics. "Tell me what you're doing, or I'm calling the police."

Katie's face paled, but when she looked up from her phone, her glare hadn't softened at all. "You really didn't know a damn thing about him, did you?"

That threw him. "I knew he was an activist," Ivan said, wondering if that was what she was getting at. He'd loosened his grip on the computer without thinking, and Katie promptly transferred it back to her lap, returning to clicking, texting, and, infuriatingly, ignoring him. The least she could do was admit he'd proved her wrong.

"Katie," Ivan said, pointing at the laptop, "this isn't activism."

She smirked, asked what was, and before Ivan could compose a more nuanced definition than "public airing of grievances," closed the case. "That's what I thought."

"But this isn't right!" Ivan said. Winston might have been smuggling a bull elephant into the building, for all he knew, but Ivan was certain that people who advocated for social change the right way didn't do so by the glow of a laptop screen at 11pm.

"Oh yeah? Tell me this: if Barney, Winston and I stand outside your building with signs that say 'Free Seymour,' is your soft corporate heart going to be motivated to do a damn thing besides snap your fingers to close the blinds?"

Though technically incorrect, as Galaxsea's windows automatically tinted when it got sunny (not Cass's most prudent investment), her statement was rooted in an ugly truth: regardless of his feelings for Winston, Ivan still wasn't moved by the protesters, and he was damn sure his coworkers weren't, either.

"Just tell me no one's going to die," Ivan said.

Texts continued flowing. "You've already stabbed Winston in the back once. I'm not telling you what we're doing just so you can hand him over to the police."

"Please," Ivan said, desperation mounting, "I don't know what else to say. I fucked up."

"You work for a theme park that tortures whales."

"I can't help where I work!"

Ivan regretted it as soon as he said it, and Katie scoffed when his face went red.

"Fine," he conceded, hating her. "Maybe I can. But I can also help you get him out of there without getting caught. Please. He already has a record."

She looked at him with raised brows, and Ivan was bracing himself for another verbal lashing when, like Gretchen Jinx's magic, she pulled him down by the sleeve of his hoodie. Bewildered but over the moon, Ivan immediately started scanning the camera feeds for Winston, and ended up finding him next to the hulking form of Barney, the bearded man from the day he'd returned the painting. The two of them, bending stiffly in ill-fitted suits, were crouched in front of Robert Cass's desktop computer doing God knows what with the modem.

"They're gathering information," Katie said, reading Ivan's mind.

Ivan felt a little prick of regret, and then dread. When he told Winston where he worked, would he be obligated to take part in this? "What for?"

"Winston is planning to..." she trailed off, then shook her head. "I'll let him tell you about it. I don't think it's going to happen, but he's determined."

Ivan frowned. That wasn't much for him to go off of. For all he knew, there could still be explosives involved. Broken windows. Destroyed property. A bloody revenge for the stolen Southern Resident.

Suddenly, Katie started, and her curse intermingled with the complaining couch springs. "Look, I'd love to tell you the details, if just to watch you squirm, but there's no time now. Just help me keep them out of *her* way."

She turned the screen towards him, and Ivan's stomach dropped when his eyes landed on what was unmistakably his sister marching rapidly down the hallway.

"She won't be going into his office," Ivan said. "Just tell them to hide behind his desk. She's a fast walker, and they don't have time for anything else." Dammit, why the hell did she always have to be better than everyone else? It wasn't enough to stay until five, no; she had to stay until midnight to put a fucking folder on someone's desk. Maybe classified information that Ivan and the interns and the rest of the worker bees weren't privy to.

If it had been anyone but Allison, they might have stood a chance, but the younger Notte sibling had a photographic memory and an ability to persuade that ruled out the possibility of ambiguity in the courtroom. That is, if they even made it to the courtroom—Ivan imagined if her first instincts rendered

Barney a threat, her years of childhood kickboxing would take over until there was at least one broken bone per man.

Katie typed out the order, and Winston and Barney scrambled behind the desk, which, for most average sized humans, would have been a suitable hiding place. Unfortunately, Barney was built like a boulder, and Winston taller than Ivan recalled, so even on the grainy camera footage, it was obvious they were not completely concealed.

While Allison might have overlooked their exposed shoulders if she was just passing by, unfortunately, she was *not* just passing by. Katie and Ivan swore in unison as she began keying in the code to get inside Cass's office.

"What's the new plan?" Katie asked. "Do they fight her?"

She started to text again, but Ivan grabbed her wrist to stop her, earning him a look that could wither flowers. After dropping her arm hastily, he said, "Don't tell him. There's no time, and he'll do something stupid."

"Then what—?"

Katie's voice grew shriller with panic, but Ivan had stopped processing what she was saying because, like most men faced with a catastrophe of such proportion, he was thinking of his mother, and the clarity she had offered that morning. And that was all it took to organize his mind.

Ivan dialed Allison's number with shaking hands, and Katie's jaw dropped as, right when Allison swung Cass's office door open, she took her iPhone out of her pocket, pausing where tile met carpet.

Allison didn't pick up until the fourth ring. *"Hello?"*

To hopefully erase the distracting expression on Katie's face, Ivan mouthed "sister" at her. She closed her mouth and nodded, but her eyes lit up with a knowing look that he didn't like much better.

On the line, Allison huffed, and Ivan stammered out something about who he was, only to be cut off and told she already knew.

"Right. Shouldn't have assumed you needed an explanation for anything."

Katie smacked him, and the two engaged in a brief struggle wherein Ivan attempted to convey, while uttering a series of ums and wells to keep his sister engaged, that he did not intend to doom his Soulmate to prison just so he could insult his sister one more time.

"Is it important?"

"Yes!" Ivan said, detaching himself from Katie and migrating a few steps to the kitchen.

"Because it's been a really long night and I don't have time to deal with this."

Across the room, Katie inhaled sharply, and Ivan didn't have to speculate as to what that meant his least favorite busybody was doing.

"I'm sorry!" Ivan blurted. "I shouldn't have snapped. It's been a long night for me, too. Just please stop whatever you're doing and talk to me for a second."

There were an agonizing few seconds of silence on the line and stillness from Katie, filled only with the buzz of the bulb inside the scuba lamp's helmet. Finally, mercifully, miraculously, Katie turned around and, unsmiling, gave him a thumbs up. Any temporary relief this might have given him was overshadowed by the dispiriting reality of having his sister on the phone expecting some kind of urgent conversation.

"You're not sick, are you? You weren't in today."

"No, I'm not."

"Nothing stage four."

"No."

"Then why are you calling?"

Ivan bristled at her tone, but for some reason, tonight it also hurt to listen to.

"I talked to Mom, Alli," he said, using the name he'd abandoned when she'd come to Galaxsea.

"And? Why are you calling me that?"

Ivan rolled his eyes, since she couldn't see it. He was ready for this conversation to be over. She would never move. She always had to win, mow down everything in her path, including him. Including Dad. "She said she wishes we wouldn't fight, alright?"

The line was silent.

"Hello?"

"I thought you weren't talking to Mom."

It felt like Katie's eyes were on him, but when he looked at her, she was texting Winston and Barney. "Not for a while. She says you haven't been calling her either."

"I'm overwhelmed!" she exclaimed. *"And I'm sure you're going to interpret that as a personal attack, just like everything else I do, but it's the truth. Cass is—"* she lowered her voice, though the only other people in the office with her were unlikely to take offense at whatever she said next—*"he's a nightmare to have over your shoulder all the time. You know how he changes his mind at the drop of a hat. I know you want to be where I am, but if I could switch places—"*

"Don't say it. You wouldn't."

There was a beat of silence, but Ivan didn't get the same vindicating rush of anger he usually did when he caught her like that. He was relieved when she spoke again.

"You're right, I wouldn't. Because I love you. And I need this. It's all I have to cope."

Her voice cracked on the last word. Ivan retreated further from Katie's line of vision, though truthfully there wasn't anywhere to go. He pressed his back against Winston's refrigerator, feeling its hum and smelling its salmon. What did that mean, to cope? To get over Dad's death, she was going to do the same thing that killed him?

"It's really late for you to be working."

"You think this is voluntary?" she asked, a note of defensiveness in her voice. *"With the way Cass is running the place? I can't stop. Why did you call me?"*

Something in Ivan's stomach twisted at her words. *Can't stop.* He remembered his father, dark circles under his eyes, losing his fatherly pudge and popping veins at his temples, catching emails at dinner.

"Mom said to ask you to call her."

"Is that it?"

"Please, Alli." He arranged his face into something neutral and looked at Katie, who gave him a nod. Barney and Winston were in the clear.

"Okay. Now I have to get back to work."

It took a moment for Ivan to realize she had hung up. Even when he did, he kept the phone at his ear, as if by doing so he could communicate what he hadn't said. That he was sorry. That she needed to go to bed.

The rain was barely there on the rooftop, the footsteps of a mouse who preferred not to be noticed. Ivan hoped Winston and Barney's escape didn't involve any kind of outdoor climbing.

"The family business?" Katie closed and set aside the laptop.

Ivan shook his head, sliding his phone into the pocket of his hoodie. Its weight combined with that of the paints made the shirt hang awkwardly. He moved it to his jeans.

"He'll take you back in a heartbeat, you know."

Ivan, in spite of Katie's tone, felt no less of the euphoric terror the words brought.

"I wouldn't encourage telling him right away," she continued.

"I can't lie to him," Ivan said, even though he suspected he might need to.

"Not forever. Only until you quit."

He stared at her, and her expression darkened.

"You are planning on quitting, right?"

In truth, he hadn't been. At least, not any more than he usually did throughout the course of a typical work day.

"Surely he'll understand."

"I don't think *you* understand." She stood so that they faced one another, eye to eye. "It's not about that documentary. Galaxsea is a very personal grudge to Winston. Asking him to accept that part of you is asking the impossible."

"I got over personal things for him," he pointed out.

"You got over—or, started to get over—bigotry for him. It's different."

He shook his head, confused.

"Look," Katie said, turning her body towards the door, beyond which faint footsteps could be heard, "just don't think he's too stupid to find out the truth. Oh, and if you want him to stick around long enough for that to happen, don't ever call him stupid again."

Ivan recalled what he'd said earlier that night. "I didn't mean it like that," he protested. "I didn't mean stupid, I just meant—"

A key turned in the door, and Ivan abandoned his defense of himself, at least temporarily. In such quick sequence that it felt a bit unreal, the door swung open to reveal Winston, scuffed and damp but alive and safe all the same. His still-colorless eyes found Ivan's almost instantly, shackling him to the floor where he stood. Winston, too, planted his feet, leaving poor Barney stuck just beyond the doorframe.

Though he'd helped him escape, Ivan couldn't deny Winston introduced a manic energy to the room that was a little off-putting, maybe because it made him look a little more like the kind of person who would break into Galaxsea headquarters, maybe because it reminded Ivan of himself. There was no other word for it but *stress*, and it, combined with the suit he wore, left Ivan a little deprived of jeans and laughter.

Barney cleared his throat from outside the door. "Is anyone going to tell me what's happening, or am I just gonna have to set you aside myself?"

He said this last bit to Winston, who abruptly stepped to the side. Barney's eyes, when they landed on Ivan, had a much different look to them than Winston's.

"Motherfucker!"

"Barney, don't."

It was not Winston who stopped him from barreling into Ivan, but Katie, who probably was stronger, anyway.

"What're you doing?" Barney protested, his hands making fists the size of Ivan's skull.

"He saved your asses," Katie said.

"What do you mean?" Winston asked. Though there was nothing but suspicion in his voice, Ivan thought it was nice just to hear him talk. Unfortunately, he couldn't really sink into it like he wanted, as three pairs of eyes were on him, waiting to hear his explanation.

For a horrifying few seconds, he couldn't speak. He'd gone over what he would say a hundred times, recited it to himself in the back of the cab like a maniac, but staring all of them in the face, it was like he hadn't prepared at all.

"She was my sister," he finally choked out. "The woman who opened the door."

Understanding dawned on Winston before Barney. "You called her."

"Yeah."

"Thank you."

Somehow, it was the worst possible response. "I hate you" would have been better. "I hate you" would have been provocative; this was dismissive, detached.

Ivan removed the colored oil paints he'd spent all afternoon chasing from his pocket, but as soon as Winston's eyes landed on them, he felt that they were trivial, tokenizing. When Ivan took a step towards him, Winston shrunk away like an injured animal.

"I got you these."

Winston looked at the paints with a spark of interest, but this was quickly extinguished by the time his eyes found Ivan's again.

"Where'd you find them?" His voice was deadpan. Ivan was very aware of a look Katie and Barney exchanged in his peripheral vision.

"I found a shop up in Wallingford," Ivan said. "They sell art supplies for Seers—"

"I've been there," Winston interrupted him. "It's expensive as hell."

Ivan had opened his mouth to say the paints were pocket change before it occurred to him that they probably weren't for Winston. He held them out. "I came to say sorry."

Wordlessly, Winston walked over to Katie and handed her three flash drives. Ivan was a bit chilled at the prospect of what was on them, but not quite so chilled as he was by Winston's response. "You're disgusted by Seeing. You said it yourself."

"I didn't mean that, I—" Ivan retracted the paints— "I was afraid."

Their reactions were simultaneous, but Ivan heard each one:

"So was Winston!"

"That's no excuse."

"So was I."

All three of them, of course, were right. Ivan's voice was getting smaller and smaller, and when he spoke next, it was properly quiet.

"I'm sorry," he said. "I put you at his mercy."

He would have done anything to be able to say it then. *I love you too, don't you know?* But apologies were no time for endearments. In fact, Ivan was shaken by the amount of endearment he'd faced so far that night, though he would welcome the challenge of just a little more.

"I would give anything to take it back," he continued.

After a beat, Winston glanced at his friends. "Can you give us a minute?" Only after the door had shut behind them did he step forward and gently remove the paints from Ivan's grip. A few tears slipped past Ivan's defenses and rolled down his cheeks.

"You put yourself at his mercy, too." Winston examined the package. "You know that, right?"

He raised his eyes, and Ivan nodded, even though he was too upset to be sure he properly understood.

"Who is he?" Winston asked, his voice now a murmur.

Ivan's pulse skipped, but not in a good way. He looked at the floor, as though the answer would be at their feet. With Katie's warning in mind, he admitted, "We have a history. We're just coworkers now." At this time, Winston opened his mouth to say, or perhaps to ask, something, but Ivan realized this only after he'd blurted, "I understand if you don't forgive me."

Winston shook his head, and it hit Ivan like a bullet that he was close to tears, too. He could only watch as he tried and failed to blink them back, searching for something to say.

"There are some things," when it finally surfaced, Winston's voice was quiet but sharp, "I can't compromise, Ivan."

"Then let me compromise," Ivan said. He took a step towards Winston, who stepped backwards.

"I can't ask you to put my interests before your sister's."

"Her job doesn't matter! I don't have a shred of loyalty to Galaxsea."

Funnily enough, as he said it, he realized that it was partially true. It was difficult to be preoccupied with his sister's job, and with his job, when Winston Jinx was in his life. It was like trying to water houseplants after discovering one possessed a winning lottery ticket. Winston trumped everything.

Winston sighed, tapping the paints in his palm. There were little cuts on it, glistening red, possibly from his escape.

"Thank you for saving us. I don't know how much Katie told you."

Not enough. Ivan relayed to him all the information he had, and Winston exhaled in what must have been relief.

"Good, that's good." He nodded to himself. "Look, I know you say you hate Galaxsea, but it makes me nervous that your sister is so high up in corporate there."

Ivan took another half-step closer to him. *Fuck Galaxsea. Oh, fuck Galaxsea to hell.*

"Don't tell me anything you don't want to," he said. "I just want you to be safe."

Winston cracked a smile, and Ivan went a little weak in the knees. "Now you're sounding like Katie, who, by the way, is definitely at the door listening to all of this."

Ivan didn't find that hard to believe at all.

"Are you saying makeup sex is out of the question?"

"Unfortunately."

And centuries before Ivan could have prepared himself, Winston closed what little gap there was between them, throwing his arms around Ivan, who found it oddly easier to breathe in the crushing embrace.

"Thank you for the paints," Winston murmured into Ivan's neck. "And I'm sorry for what I said. You're not like Swan."

If Ivan was giddy at the contact, he no less than glowed after those words. So delirious was he to have Winston's gangly limbs wrapped around him that he forgot, as quickly as he'd committed it to memory, what Katie had said. "From now on," he said as he pulled away, "only you get to make the stupid decisions. I'm not very good at it."

Winston smirked, but it didn't reach his eyes. "That's okay," he said, "Barney has enough stupid to go around the whole group."

The muffled exclamation that followed from outside the door made Winston laugh, but Ivan still hid behind him when his friends reentered the room.

15

Ivan and Winston took a week or so to ease back into familiarity. Sweet, meaningless text conversations consisting of gentle teasing about mundanities stretched out over the course of each day. Winston got into the habit of sticking his brush behind his ear when he typed out a reply, ending the day with hints of his new paints in his hair. He had to kill the habit just as quickly as it started when Katie, Barney, and, horrifyingly, his mother came up with a number of breathtakingly obscene names for the phenomenon.

However, both Barney and Katie's teasing grew sparser as the days passed. The former, who was less resigned than Katie to the shadows under Winston's eyes and the trembling in his hands, dropped by his apartment the next week.

"Winst, you need a fucking break."

As usual, Winston was both touched and annoyed by his friend's concern. He didn't respond to Barney, instead continuing to paint and conjecture wildly (mostly to himself) about Seymour's rescue, and the terrible reality that there were still dozens of variables permanently outside their control. The stress of holding a ten-thousand-pound life in his hands was not diminished by the fact that he was swooning over someone whose sister's hand governed its suffering. He knew that it wasn't fair, and that it truly might not have come up by coincidence alone, but finding out that Ivan's sister worked for Galaxsea had made Winston feel a little bit misled. He couldn't shake the possibility that Ivan might have hidden it on purpose to avoid scaring him away, which was both flattering and troubling.

"When did you last eat?"

When he couldn't recall, Barney physically lifted him up, carried him down the stairs, and sat him down in the bakery, where he was scolded (by Barney, not his mother) and forced to eat some bread so fresh out of the oven that it burnt his tongue.

"There's no point in asking you to sleep, is there?"

Winston shook his head, chewing miserably. The more he ate, the hungrier he realized he was.

Barney sighed, his chest deflating like a large plaid balloon, and proposed Winston take at least one afternoon off, an idea which he shut down almost immediately. If he took a break, Seymour might not eat as much the next time he saw him. If he didn't catch as many fish, he might start to forget everything he'd learned since Winston had started going to see him, regressing into the passive apathy that a lifetime at Galaxsea had induced in him. If that happened, then the release might fail, and Seymour would starve once he was back in the ocean, and then Winston would be just as complicit in his death as Galaxsea.

Of course, Barney didn't back down. He'd heard J Pod might be moving into the Sound, and they could go out and kayak tomorrow. Yeah, it was going to be a clear day, nothing like the rain he and Winston favored, but at this point he was more concerned than excited about putting his friend's health at further risk.

As tempting as the prospect was, Winston knew seeing the Southern Residents was only going to make him feel guilty for neglecting the Seymour project, so he declined, which apparently called for desperate measures, because Barney, who hated Ivan as much as he hated dress shoes and vegetarian meat substitutes, invited him along for the trip, shoving him into the backseat of his RAM pickup as they drove up to Winston's favorite little bay by Edmonds.

So, for better or for worse, Winston now found himself standing with an apprehensive Ivan and an impatient Barney, each separated from the next person by a small kayak trailed by a long path of disturbed sand that was dark and volcanic, glittering in the sun. The water lapped at the tips of their vessels, giving little icy kisses to their feet.

It was more difficult to appreciate the scene when Ivan was present. Even if it wasn't for his ability to make tattered gym-shoes look classy, the past week seemed to have had the opposite effect on him than Winston. His smiles reached his eyes a little more, and while it was unlikely he'd gained any weight in such a short amount of time, it did look to Winston like he was less severe in his angles.

"Are you sure this is safe?" he asked, his cheeks slightly red—because of course, that new color glowing on his face could be nothing else.

God help me, thought Winston.

"You never been kayaking before?" Barney asked.

"Not on the ocean."

Barney muttered something derisive about private lakes.

"You'll be fine," Winston said, sloshing out into the water with his kayak.

Ivan hurried after him, visibly recoiling at the water temperature. "What if it storms?" he paused ankle deep in wet sand. "There's no one else on this beach. We're kind of in the middle of nowhe—"

Winston paused in the middle of stepping into his kayak, water streaming off his legs. "That's kind of the point."

Well, they weren't truly in the middle of nowhere. Unless they were many more miles north of Seattle, there wouldn't be any true isolation to be found. Even if they took to the sea, they would have to do a substantial amount of weaving between islands and peninsulas before they hit open water.

"You two do this a lot?"

"Not really," Winston admitted. At Ivan's visible horror, he clarified, "We like it when it's rainy. Fewer whale watchers." They'd figured that out when they were in grade school.

Barney, already situated, discreetly glided past them in one fluid motion, making quick work of the waves' best efforts to push him back to shore.

"Anyway," Winston continued, helping Ivan into his kayak, "we know the Resident orca feeding routes pretty well, so hopefully we can see some." The bay was well hidden, and far enough outside the city that he hoped, despite the good weather, they wouldn't run into any tourists.

"We're going to be in the *feeding route*?" Ivan asked. Barney laughed from where he was bobbing in place.

"They eat fish, transplant!"

Ivan glared, but Winston, suddenly antsy, offered him no sympathy.

"I mean," he said, "they do eat salmon."

This information looked to give little comfort to Ivan, but he must have channeled his nerves into fighting the current, because before Winston could blink, he was bobbing halfway between shore and the bay's mouth with Barney, leaving Winston standing stupidly in calf-deep water. He pushed himself off to join them, any pity he may have had for Ivan's inexperience quickly blown away by the bittersweet sea breeze.

If Winston was being honest with himself, he did find Ivan's concern strangely refreshing. Obviously, he knew how to be sea-safe now that he was older, but he could have used a little of that concern earlier in life. Though his mother's hands-off parenting had been a blessing in a lot of ways, it had also been shockingly cold in others. Winston and Barney had racked up more than their share of close calls as children, the most severe being an encounter with a mother grizzly. Winston still thought about the way his own mother had laughed when he'd told her how it charged him and Barney, only changing its trajectory when they hugged one another, causing it to mistake them for one animal, and not two terrified children.

The afternoon was pleasant, if a little hotter than Winston would have liked, especially when they moved beyond the shaded boundaries of the bay and had to battle the current. As expected, Ivan struggled with this more than him and Barney, but Winston was deprived enough of sleep and food that he didn't have to hold himself back that much to stay by his side. Barney, however, did, and he eventually got fed up and ended up leading the way by a hundred feet or so. Winston felt a little bad about it, though not too much, as for the better half of the afternoon, Barney frightened away all traces of wildlife before he and Ivan could see them. Though this wouldn't have bothered

167

him most days, it made their journey down the coast a good deal more grueling. Ivan's frustration started to show when one side of his paddle became so weighed down with kelp that he couldn't lift it out of the water, causing him to spin 180 degrees and utter a string of curse words that made Winston struggle to choke back laughter. Winston was just beginning to worry that the jellyfish he and Ivan found in the bundle of kelp would be the only wildlife they saw that afternoon when he heard a spout of water.

As Ivan turned to him in panic, he called out to Barney, who was at their side in moments, shading his eyes with a blistered palm. For several tense seconds, there was nothing, and Winston's heart sunk to think he'd gotten Ivan's hopes up. However, he soon heard another spout of water, and spotted the great black fin with it. This was followed by several others big and small, all about two-hundred yards away, close to the cliffside, and not a tour-boat in sight. A pod of orcas was coming up behind them, making their way towards the Sound just as Barney had predicted. Fins that would have blended with the waves in his former vision now jutted out from the water like spines on the back of a terrible serpent, monochromatic in the blue-green sea.

Winston reached out and pulled Ivan's kayak until it clanked with his. When Ivan looked at him curiously, he explained, "It makes us look bigger." Barney floated up to Winston's side so they were three across. It was really all that could be done at this point; if they tried to move into open water, they'd be even more in the pod's way. Better to stay in the shallows with the weeds and wait for them to pass.

Ivan currently looked as though he believed having someone block your path was no reason for aggression at all.

"Winst," he said, "we should probably start moving to safet—"

A massive spout of seawater erupted directly next to them, and Ivan nearly fell out of his kayak.

"Cookie!" Barney and Winston recognized the whale on sight.

Almost immediately, two larger, much louder spouts came up just in front of them. Barney labeled them Tsuchi and (tentatively) Mako. Winston had missed J Pod.

"Winst...is this *safe*?"

"Mostly," Winston answered. "Really illegal, though."

"I thought you said we wouldn't be doing anything illegal!" Ivan wailed, leaning over sideways to watch another orca glide past underwater. "Oh, God, it's looking at me."

Winston grinned. "Whales don't always follow the law."

Ivan laughed once, pitched and hysterical. The next time a fin surfaced next to him, he reached out an arm to touch it, and Winston shouted so immediately that Ivan appeared hurt.

"What?" Ivan asked.

Winston removed some of the sharpness from his tone, but was no less serious when he said, "You touch them, you turn into whale soup." He punctuated this with a glance at the frothy water.

Ivan did not try to touch them again, and the three of them watched the pod pass.

&❧

Ironically, as their day of leisure went on, the effects of Winston's sleepless nights grew even more potent. When the party turned around and returned to the beach, Winston did his best to put a dent in the massive spread Ivan had packed them for lunch, but it did little to address the root of his exhaustion besides make him even more sluggish and sleepy. In the interest of staying awake he stopped after two prosciutto sandwiches, an ingredient which Barney was so vicious to Ivan about that Winston had to banish him away to photograph the cliffside. Ivan took little interest in the food himself, and had only eaten a handful of grapes and half a sandwich before he started packing it up. At that point, the sun was still high in the sky, but Winston knew full well as soon as he laid down he would not be easily moved, so he hastily threw together a driftwood fire while Ivan watched, pleased when it roared high in spite of his negligence.

Winston and Ivan laid out to dry in the heat of the sun and fire, muscles aching. They spent the afternoon warming their feet, digging in the sand, watching the eagles circle and commenting occasionally to one another that they really should be putting some sunscreen on, or they really should make sure poor Barney hadn't gotten eaten by a grizzly, but neither of them moved. At sunset, with no rain in sight, the sky exploded into a symphony of red, orange, and gold, the sea deep indigo underneath it.

"You're quiet," Winston commented. He sat up and threw another piece of driftwood onto the fire, watching it flash blue from the salt. It hadn't particularly needed it, but he'd wanted to watch the color change again.

"I'm thinking," Ivan said, sitting up to watch this. "Do you think other things will make it change different colors?"

"Only one way to find out."

This led to a brief episode of pyromania, wherein Ivan took samples of nearly every material in their immediate vicinity and tossed them into the fire, twice nearly extinguishing it completely with sand and, Winston nearly cracked a rib laughing, water.

"Alright, I didn't think!" Ivan protested. The point of his shoe nudged Winston. "Why aren't *you* up?"

"Hmph, I'm not as big a fan of combustion as Barney is."

That shut Ivan up for a good ten seconds. Winston looked up at him from his place in the sand. It wasn't a terribly flattering angle, but he didn't care.

Ultimately, Ivan sighed and repeated, "Combustion."

"Yes," Winston said, while Ivan kicked his shoes off again and resettled next to him, "combustion. One of those 'problem science kids,' you know. Barney is the poster child for why you don't tell kids they can't develop their own film until they're sophomores."

"Because he did it himself."

"Well, to do it himself he had to pay for ingredients, and to know what to substitute when one was too expensive, he needed to understand the chemical process. He got obsessed with reaction summer after freshman year."

"My mom wouldn't let me develop my own film either," Ivan said. "She was worried about the chemicals. But I never thought about going behind her back to do it." He added, as an afterthought, "I wouldn't have known where to start."

Winston was so floored by this new information about Ivan that when he finally responded, it came out stuttering and distracted.

"You like photography, then?"

171

"Kind of."

Winston rolled over to look at him. "You should talk to Barney about it!"

Ivan scoffed.

"I'm serious," Winston continued, falling onto his back again. "He would love someone to talk photography with. I know he can be a little harsh, but I wouldn't be friends with him if he had bad intentions." He trailed off at the end of this, realizing how similar he sounded to his mom. Most people had good intentions. And Barney had really been rude to Ivan from the start; it wasn't unwarranted if they didn't want to spend time together.

"Did he go to prison with you?" Ivan asked.

Winston's heart sank.

"Yeah, he did. Why do you ask?"

Ivan was quiet for a moment, frowning at the sky. Finally, he said:

"The fire, I guess. I know you wouldn't do anything to hurt people. But was there any correlation to that kind of…activism?"

A visceral memory of a knee forced into his back jabbed at Winston through the sand. He shivered, and an eagle snickered.

"It was Katie."

"Her?" The surprise in Ivan's voice irritated Winston a little, though it might have been just retroactive anger from the memory.

"Her parents wanted so badly for her to be a prodigy, and they thought Seeing…" Winston trailed off, dragging his fingers through the sand. That wasn't his story to tell. "Well, it's not important. But she got bullied at school, too. It was bad when I first met her, but in high school, things really picked up. That's when I started to get involved."

"So you turned to…"

"No," Winston resisted the urge to roll his eyes. "Nothing extreme, obviously. I was more aware of politics, though, and I was an impulsive 18-year-old. Barney was, too."

"What did you do?" Ivan asked, his voice softer than the crackling fire.

Winston took a breath.

"A rumor started to go around that Barney and I were going to do something terrible. You know."

Ivan didn't answer, but Winston got the sense he knew.

"And…one day I was at a protest calling for protective legislation for Seers, and I let my temper get the best of me. Katie had gotten cut by a girl in the locker room recently. They were asking her if she could See what her blood looked like. Protesting is usually cathartic, like I'm taking steps towards a solution," he said, "but it wasn't, that time. There were a bunch of counter protesters videotaping us, calling us animals, better-off-blind, snowflakes, and I just felt so *angry.*" His heart was pounding just at the memory. "It isn't just an opinion, or an insult; it's them telling us not just that they don't care if we're hurt or killed or spit on, but that they need us to know it. So I snapped and threw a glass bottle."

Ivan sucked in a breath.

"And," Winston continued, "more or less started a riot."

He was glad they were lying on their backs. He wasn't sure he wanted to see Ivan's face. And he wasn't sure he wanted Ivan to see his. Truth be told, if there was anything he regretted in his life more than anything, it was the moment he threw that bottle.

There had been so many young people there, kids that still had faces of babyfat, who made snappy posters and didn't know you weren't supposed to wear contact lenses. He still thought of them sometimes, how he'd put them in danger, set a rotten example.

"I didn't mean to," Winston said. "Barney kinda lost it, too. So that plus the rumors were enough."

"Why didn't Katie bail you out?" Ivan asked.

"Her parents wouldn't let her leave the house past eight. They wouldn't lend her thousands of dollars for bail."

Ivan's silence said he understood where this was going. Eventually, he said, "You were only 18."

"I was," Winston said, "but that's kind of the point, isn't it? I had no idea what I was doing, and people got hurt. I ruined my life." And possibly those of others.

There was such a long silence that Winston began to wonder if Ivan had fallen asleep. When he finally spoke, his voice was soft, but it still startled him.

"I think it's cool you did it," Ivan said.

"What?"

"Stood up for your friend."

A gust of wind ruffled the evergreens, whistling through the cliffs. Winston's heart skipped a beat when Ivan rolled over to face him again, propping himself up on an elbow. The gesture transformed him into something younger; an Ivy-League undergrad, boyish and smitten. Perhaps if Winston's muscles had not been so sore, if he had not been so damn tired, he would have kissed him then.

"Besides," Ivan said, "I'm with your lot now anyway, for almost touching that whale."

Winston didn't know where to start with that one. "And the pleasure of your company makes a life of crime worth it, huh?"

"Am I wrong?"

"No, you're very pretty, I admit. But only as long as you don't try to touch Blackberry again."

"God, they're like pets to you," Ivan marveled, ignoring the threat. "How can you tell the difference?"

Winston closed his eyes to rest them. "There's little ways to tell. The saddle patches behind their fins, other distinctive characteristics like notches on the dorsals or discoloration or scars. You need a sharp eye. I started learning when I was really little, but if I go too long without seeing them, I start to forget. It was a nightmare after prison."

"Do you have a favorite?"

There were dozens of names he could have given, but he was tired, and so the only name that his tongue would have was, of course...

"Seymour." He paused, then clarified. "The Galaxsea whale."

"I know who Seymour is." The odd silence that followed was broken by an oddly spoken question. "Why?"

Winston knew Ivan meant well, but in all honesty the prospect of having to explain why he loved the whale was more depressing than anything else. Trying to explain why Seymour was important was trying to explain why laughter was. The love of something as separated from humanity as a killer whale cannot be summed up in a logical flow. No human tongue lends itself well to that kind of mystery. It was the reason people prayed, the reason that he painted. The reason he remained in Ivan's magnetic field in spite of everything that had happened.

Trying to quantify the value of things whose entire worth was unearthly made him feel overheated, claustrophobic.

"I guess because he was the first I knew," Winston said. "He was the only calf in L Pod at the time. My dad helped me spot him." Winston regretted this last part as soon as he said it. Not because it was untrue, but because it was so perfectly rational that he knew Ivan would immediately latch onto it as a Freudian explanation for his love of the whales, of Seymour, a displaced attachment to a distant father, nothing more. This would have made the trauma of Seymour being airlifted out of the sea even more potent. And yet, Winston knew it wasn't the reason he cared.

"I only wish that people cared," Winston said after a moment. "They're a family."

"A...pod."

"No, a family." Winston suppressed a yawn. "They scream for their young when they're taken." This felt like another justification, and Ivan seemed to hear it in his voice.

"You don't believe that."

Winston sighed, "I don't know if I have to."

"But you can never know for certain what they think," Ivan persisted.

"That's the point."

Ivan was silent.

"I don't know," Winston said. "Not everything needs to have a logical reason behind it. Some things are just nice."

Out in the water, a fish jumped. From behind the arm he'd thrown over his eyes, he felt Ivan looking at him.

"You look tired," he said, and Winston came the closest to tears he'd been all night.

"I am."

"I can look out for Barney," Ivan said. "I'm not tired, if you want to sleep."

Winston's heart skipped a beat at the suggestion, which had suddenly made him a good deal more awake.

"Do you know what to do if a bear comes?" he tried to summon the appropriate level of drowsiness back into his voice.

"Scream and run around in circles?"

"Attaboy."

The two intertwined their legs by the fire, and Winston fell asleep wondering if the absolute fool with his arms around him had worn cologne to go kayaking.

16

Ivan had assumed that the more time he spent around Winston, the easier it would become to detach himself from the painter. Now, he realized just how profoundly incorrect that conviction had been. Perhaps Ivan could have said he liked Winston in spite of his lack of a real job or his unapologetic enjoyment of sweets and Seeing, that these flaws were rendered null because he was funny, or tall, or dedicated. However, such a rationalization was no longer viable, because the terrible truth of it all was that the things Ivan loved the most about Winston were the precise things he had spent years training himself to hate.

Ivan probably should have been concerned he was being indoctrinated or something, but for the time being, he was mostly content using the Bond to explain it all away. Katie had said its pull would make them inseparable by the third day, and even Mike agreed there was little to be done at this point. All of this suggested Ivan should have felt disassociated, alienated from himself because of the Bond, but the truth was that he actually felt more present than ever. Paradoxically, the irritation he felt at the way Winston tapped his foot when he was thinking or the fact that he never cleaned his fridge actually strengthened Ivan's overall sentiment for him. Actually, the mysterious fishy smell around the fridge was perhaps the only thing in his apartment which Ivan hadn't yet warmed to. He was a little scared to open it, and declined food and drink when he was at Winston's after work, unless it was from the bakery downstairs. This proved to be wise, as nothing could have prepared Ivan for the sweltering evening he finally opened the door and found himself faced with dozens of pairs of unblinking, glassy eyes.

Ivan scrutinized the bag of freshly caught wild salmon laying on its side, behind which a traumatized-looking bottle of apple juice hid. He temporarily forgot the latter, which Winston had asked for. "Didn't you say you were sometimes vegan?"

"Yeah."

Gesturing to the open fridge, Ivan asked, "Do you just have a *salmon habit*, then?"

Winston turned and frowned. "That's just for a project."

Ivan knew it wasn't fair for him to resent Winston for hiding things from him, given his own secret, but at that moment, he couldn't help it. It was one thing if Winston wanted to remain discreet about the Galaxsea break-in; in fact, a part of Ivan appreciated that it was kept outside his sphere of influence. But it was another thing entirely to keep him in the dark on the smaller things, like whatever art project the fish were a part of. The small things were, after all, what sustained Ivan, now that he had them.

"It's a long story," Winston continued, seeming to sense his discontent. "Actually, what time is it?"

Ivan announced it was almost ten, and Winston swore quietly, setting his palette aside as Ivan maneuvered the juice out of the fridge. "Did you still want—?"

"No, don't worry about that," Winston said, dashing across the room to pick up a pair of gloves. Ivan became slightly

179

concerned when subsequently, with the self-assurance of a catwalk model, he strode to a locked drawer in the kitchen and removed a rather frightening knife, a flashlight, and a number of other suggestive instruments that if purchased together would have made any cashier suspicious. "I'm so sorry to leave like this." Winston lifted the massive bag of fish carcasses out of the fridge. "I actually really need to be somewhere."

And where the hell was that? Ivan studied him, a little hurt. Logically, he should have been concerned about that knife more than anything, but at the moment, it seemed more critical that it was Friday night and Winston was going somewhere without him. God, it wasn't like he'd slept over yet. What if this had been happening all week?

"Big evening plans?"

Winston paused, and it was clear from the shake of his head that he'd read Ivan's expression accurately. "I know how it looks."

"No, no." Ivan tried to sound polite, something that would have worked more effectively had they not gotten so damn good at being impolite to one another lately. "Hadn't even crossed my mind."

Winston's face fell, and Ivan realized his mistake.

"Really?"

Ivan looked at the floor, surrendering. "No. Where are you going?" Silence followed, and Ivan started to get irritated. For Christ's sake, Winston was already half out the damn door. "You wanted me to ask."

Winston sighed, bouncing on the balls of his feet a few times. "I'll tell you later, but I really have to go now."

"Okay."

"I promise it's not what you think."

Ivan was thinking of romance and crime, and not in a glamorous way. "Is it dangerous?"

Winston bit his lip, and Ivan's jaw dropped.

"Seriously? Are you going back to Galaxsea?"

Again, Winston didn't answer him. His eyes remained trained on his feet, and Ivan, chilled, closed the distance between them, pulling Winston back into the apartment and the door shut behind him.

"You're going back," Ivan whispered. He saw it on his face.

"In a sense."

"What the hell does that mean?" Ivan asked, panicking. It was too soon to tell him. He couldn't tell him. Not while he still worked there, at least. "Winst, you got lucky last time, and that was with Katie, me, and Barney helping you." Something dawned on him. "They're already there, aren't they?"

"I'm not going to the headquarters. We're done there."

Surely he wasn't talking about the theme park. "Then what—?"

"I can't tell you, okay?" Winston exclaimed. "Not until I think it through more."

"You're seriously gonna make me wait back here while you risk your life?" Ivan asked. "How the hell am I supposed to sleep? What if you don't come back? What am I supposed to do then?"

Winston had a weird look on his face. "You really care that much?"

"Of course I do!" Ivan exclaimed. "I don't know what the hell I would do without you."

181

Something lit up behind Winston's eyes, and he set the bag of fish down on the table. It slumped under its own weight, and Ivan saw himself reflected in one of the carcass's glassy eyes. He shivered.

"Okay," Winston said quietly. "I trust you."

Ivan breathed. "I trust you too."

"The truth is," Winston said, "we—I, I mean… I'm going to free Seymour the orca."

Throughout his life, Ivan would go on to experience many awkward silences, but none would harbor confusion or anticlimax the way the one that followed did. He wasn't certain he understood until his eyes landed on a painting leaning against the wall detailing a black fin jutting from deep blue waters, transporting him back to their day on the sea.

"You can't tell your sister," Winston continued.

"Are you going to stage a protest?" Ivan asked. If so, he sincerely doubted his sister would so much as bat an eyelash at a protest, at this point.

Winston glanced around the room before raising his voice theatrically. "Of Course I'm Going To Protest Peacefully And Lawfully, As Any Good Citizen Would."

So it wasn't going to be something safe, with posters. It would be something like the protest that had torn his adult life apart, something with tear gas. God, what if it ruined his ability to See? Even if, by some miracle, he managed to find a doctor that knew how to treat him, Winston adored color. Ivan couldn't fathom how much he must love the orca to risk no longer Seeing.

Ivan bit his lip, feeling a little choked up. "I'll bail you out if you get arrested."

"I'm not gonna get arrested."

Ivan rounded on him. "You don't know that! God, you've already got a record, and you know how Galaxsea people are. Cass is a sadist. He'll catch one glimpse of you with that megaphone or whatever and—"

"Megaphone?"

Ivan looked up at him, and it looked like Winston was just as confused as him. He sniffed.

"Don't…protesters use…?"

"I'm not actually saving Seymour with a protest."

"So how?" Ivan asked, more confused than ever. It was only when a corner of Winston's mouth twitched into a smirk that Ivan realized the scale of the insanity he was courting.

Surely not.

The laugh that escaped Ivan's throat was so inappropriate that he covered his mouth with a hand. He'd sounded a little like Mike.

"No, no." He shook his head with another chuckle. "Even for you, that's a little much."

"Is it really, though?" Winston's eyes sparkled.

"Yeah, it really is."

"I mean, you do know I've gone to prison."

"And I'd *assumed* you didn't like it there."

"It sounds like you disapprove."

"Oh, no, that's ridiculous." Ivan felt himself rapidly boiling over, his cool dissipating with every syllable. "Why on Earth would I disapprove of you *stealing a whale?*"

Winston did not appear in the slightest startled at the increase in Ivan's volume. In fact, he looked almost relieved.

"Look, I know it sounds crazy."

"*Sounds* crazy? Winst, I can't believe I have to tell you this, but you can't steal a five-ton fish!"

"Mammal."

"Christ!" Ivan cursed, pinching the bridge of his nose. "Tell me it's a joke," he ordered. "Tell me you're fucking with me, and we can go to the beach or something instead."

"I was actually going to see him now," Winston gestured to the massive bag of salmon, "if you wanted to come."

"See whom?" Ivan croaked. "The *whale*? To do what, presumably? How the hell are you planning on doing this?"

"Look, I can explain the plan later," Winston said, picking up the bag, "but I'm getting antsy. Do you want to come or not?"

He had to be insane. Weren't the craziest ones always the most charming? "I mean, what, are you just going to carry him out? Attach a bunch of balloons and float him to the ocean?"

Winston ran a hand through his curls. "There goes that plan out the window."

Ivan narrowed his eyes. "This isn't funny. What about security? Cameras? There's a million places you could get caught, and then you'll be locked up forever!" *What about Mike?* Ivan shuddered to think what would happen if he caught wind of this. Just that day, he'd been showing Ivan pictures of an "embarrassing retard" who'd apparently protested at some talk Mike had gone to see. Who knows what he would think of someone who did something this crazy? And what about Alli? If she so much as suspected something was amiss, all three, maybe four, of them were doomed.

Winston's expression softened. "You don't have to worry about that. I've been visiting Seymour for over a year, now. I know the place—"

"A year?" Ivan felt like he was about to start hyperventilating. For the entirety of the time he'd known Winston, he'd been visiting that five-ton problem. Ever since that documentary, Ivan had been hoping that the big fish would just die already.

"Yes. Now are you coming or not?"

Ivan was frozen, his ears filled with the sound of his heartbeat. The air was too hot in here, too close. What had he gotten himself into? He liked hearing about Winston's activism, but he couldn't actually participate! Especially not when it involved sneaking around on private property. Seymour had hurt people in the past. What if that happened to them?

In hindsight, Ivan should have asked Winston for a change of clothes before they left; he was still wearing his work clothes, and though he'd left his jacket on the couch, he was still overdressed to be traveling through abandoned, graffitied tunnels. Anything of Winston's would have been far too large on him, but it might at least have made him look a bit less like he was asking for someone to rob him of his platinum Mastercard.

Had they not been about to commit a crime, the yellow lights, the indigo sky, the tangles of vines disrupting the forest of concrete might have set the scene for a pair in love. Instead, Winston was carrying a massive bag of fish while debating aloud with himself over whether he would have gotten into more trouble with hypothetical siblings than he had with Barney. He really looked like something supernatural under the flickering street lamps, and there was an easiness to his stroll that Ivan found fascinating.

"Do you know where you're going?" Ivan asked, after they'd walked for about half an hour. The streets were narrower now, and the buildings never rose more than five or six stories. They'd put enough distance between themselves and the Sound that they could no longer hear it, only the rush of the distant highway.

"Of course."

"Have you ever even been to Galaxsea?"

"As a tourist?"

They had reached a tall chain-link fence, which they followed to where the beginnings of a sterile, man-made forest cast it into shadow. Ivan could just barely make out the silhouettes of rollercoasters in the distance.

"Yeah."

"Then only once," Winston said, "after Seymour was first put on display. It was more than enough."

They wove through pieces of rubbish escaped from long-abandoned dumpsters. A feline snarl echoed out of one of them when Ivan walked past, making him jump. When they finally stopped, the discussion halted with their steps. It took a moment for Ivan to realize the bag of fish was being held out to him. Taking it reluctantly, he watched Winston grab hold of the fence and hoist himself off the ground in one fluid motion.

He didn't think he could do that. "Winston, I…"

"Here, hand that up to me." Absurdly, Winston was now supporting himself with only one arm, holding out the other for the bag. Ivan tried not to stare as he, unbelievably, took it from him one handed. The jolt that particular sight sent through him somehow organized his vocal cords, and Winston had barely climbed another inch when Ivan spoke, halting his ascent.

"Please come down."

Winston, his arms shaking, turned to look at Ivan incredulously. To his surprise and chagrin, Winston released the fence with a jingle, landing hard, but on his feet, in a crouch.

"What's up?" he asked when he straightened. There was genuine concern in his voice, and it was gasoline on the fire. Ivan felt all the more like it was suddenly too bright, even underneath a new moon.

"I can say something to Allison," Ivan proposed. "The park isn't that far from the water. Maybe she could arrange for a sea pen…" Winston's impatience was so obvious that he trailed off, feeling more foolish than ever.

Winston gave their surroundings a quick once over to ensure that, except for the probably-rabid cat in the dumpster, they were still alone. "That's not really an option."

"For most people, breaking the law isn't an option," Ivan said, desperation mounting.

"Good thing I'm not most people," Winston said, linking his fingers through the fence again.

Ivan wrapped his arms around himself, and took a step back. "I'm…I'm so sorry. I can't do this."

Some of the irritation left Winston's expression, but it was replaced with something much worse. "'This' meaning…?"

"I can't do this," Ivan repeated, loud enough that it echoed around them worryingly. His voice caught as he backed away. "I'm sorry, I can't."

He turned. Somewhere behind him, he heard Winston ask if he would be able to find his way back, and though he meant to respond, the lump in his throat forced him to retreat in silence.

The fence rattled as Winston hopped it, and then the night was silent except for Ivan's footsteps and rapid breaths. And, though he hadn't known what he so desperately had wanted to get away from when he'd stood below Winston, dangling from the fence like a poison apple, the further he walked, the more it felt like he was moving away not just from jumping the fence, but from Winston himself.

Maybe Ivan could find someone else, someone more like him. A Seer that wasn't so much of…well, a Seer. Mike definitely had a point about the movement being corrupt. Who was Ivan to ask that other people cater to him? Furthermore, who was he to get upset over Seymour's captivity? The Resident Orcas weren't his to protect. He'd be a hypocrite if he got all soft over the thing that made him money. Ivan liked the way he lived. He'd be stupid to risk it for love. The Bond wasn't even real love. He wouldn't have loved Winston if they'd met normally.

Above Ivan, the sky was black and empty, a void taking in his sorrows and letting them drift away to nowhere. He wasn't cut out to be a Seer. He didn't have the heart that Winston did. It was too late for him.

With each step, though, the current pushed him back towards square one, that particular thought, which he would ordinarily have allowed to go unquestioned, reminding him that he didn't have to drift. Maybe one day, if he continued on like this, it would be too late. If he kept walking, he might find himself on his deathbed in a grey world, in a lucrative but sinister job with fake friends and family he didn't see often. He might find himself on his deathbed the same as he'd always been.

Ivan was no longer walking. His ears rung, and suddenly, the world felt very small and simple, reduced to *away* and *towards*.

Of course it was petrifying to think of doing the things that Winston did. It was desolating to think that he might have lived his life asleep for so long. What did he like? Who would he be, if not this? The terrific truth was there in the silence, which was, of course, that he now doubted every one of his justifications against Winston, and he felt naked without them.

He was twenty-six, and he hardly knew himself. Ivan didn't think of himself as a Seer. Or a rule-breaker. Or somebody who believed in much at all. But how had the alternative served him?

There was a brief moment of suspension, and then, before he could so much as think *oh*, he spun around and sprinted back the way he came, back to Winston, back to love, back to life, closing the distance in what must have been a fraction of the time it had taken to walk away. The metal cut into his fingers while his feet scrambled for purchase in the chain links, and Ivan gritted his teeth as he waited for the fence to stop swaying under his weight. His arm muscles were screaming by the time he reached the top, but luckily, he quickly spotted what he hadn't from the ground: a large oak branch extending towards the fence, connected to a trunk sporting several easy footholds.

Carefully, Ivan reached around the barbed wire atop the fence to grab the branch with one arm. After testing its stability, he moved his other hand to it, then lifted a leg over the barbed wire and around it, feeling the bark's roughness through his dress pants. The maneuver was probably easy for Winston, but Ivan was shorter, and therefore had less leg to work with, along with a great deal less strength. In a desperate attempt to avoid the barbed wire catching him between the legs as he rolled over, he transferred his other leg over hastily and, as a result, got caught in the back by the wire instead as he swung upside down on the branch like a pathetic, well-dressed sloth.

Ivan hissed with pain and pulled himself right-side-up. He could already feel blood soaking into the back of his shirt, though he tried not to focus on it while he made his way to the ground. Unfortunately, no amount of focus could fully account for the fact that oxfords weren't ideal for tree climbing, so he slipped on a piece of loose bark when he was still a foot above the grass, which caused him to lose his grip entirely and plummet to the ground.

He landed on his fresh cuts, and bit back what might have been a scream if all the air hadn't been knocked out of him. When he sat up and reached a hand to his back, his fingers came away an even deeper scarlet than they'd been the day he'd cut them outside the hospital. However, maybe it was the adrenaline, but he didn't feel much woozier. After a moment of deliberation, he decided not to bother with his wounds now. When he caught up to Winston, *if* he caught up to Winston, they could bandage him up together.

The night air cool on his cuts, Ivan set off across the expanse of grass and trees that bordered the park. If there was anything that could perfectly represent Galaxsea as a company, it was the park's interior fence, which, while initially appearing to be 12-foot, wooden, and, most importantly, unscalable, turned out not even to be a fence at all. When Ivan swung back his leg to give it a kick, he realized it was actually three planks of wood painted to look like a fence, spaced out so as to leave a small path for walking between them. When Ivan did so, he found himself in the main park, where he was immediately struck by guilt, dread, and the oddly-compatible smells of theme park popcorn and industrial motor oil. None of these sensations, however, were as jarring as the lack of color.

The landscaping on either side of the walkway provided a break from the monochrome, but even after blinking a few times, Ivan still felt suffocated in the grey. A dusty teddy bear slumped against a shop window to his left. Another one poked out from a trashcan, where an unidentifiable animal was rummaging.

Some lights along the cobblestoned, gummy walkway were still illuminated, but while they seemed to have all been intended to be left on, more were burnt out than glowing. Ivan wanted to be fair—after all, he couldn't say the place looked depressing just because he Saw it differently—but the truth was, even after taking the lack of color into consideration, the place was superficially and emotionally repulsive. The edges of the topiaries were overgrown, the kitschy murals of dolphins and sea-turtles swimming through the cosmos were chipping paint, and the trash cans were overflowing. And this, this was what he could lose Winston for. This was what his father had…but he couldn't think about that now. He was already having trouble catching his breath as it was.

Ivan vaguely recalled that Seymour's pen was near the rollercoasters, but there were currently rides on either side of him. On his right was a death trap that went straight to the stars for what had to have been at 200 feet before dropping straight back down. On his left was a little rusty thing that Ivan assumed involved water, as it was titled *Moon-soon*. According to the signs and its shadow against the sky, there was also another ride entitled *Supernova* further behind it. He headed to the left which, initially, seemed to be a good choice, as he soon started seeing signs for the stadium that surrounded Seymour's pool. However, this good feeling was brought to an end when a hand emerged suddenly and clamped over his mouth; another arm snaked around his waist, pulling him behind a hot-dog stand. In wild panic, he thought, *Mike,* but the person let go too fast to be him, and when Ivan turned around, he Saw not cold blue eyes, but a shade of orange he could pick out anywhere.

17

Ivan let out a breath and removed Winston's palm from his face.

"You scared the hell out of me."

"*Shhh*." Any true desperation in Winston's voice was overshadowed by the fact that he was laughing. He tilted his head at the enclosure Ivan had been about to walk by. "Sea lions. They'll make a racket if they see you."

Ivan wondered if Winston had learned that one the hard way. "Don't they need to sleep?" he whispered.

"They live in a perpetual state of stress since their enclosure is overcrowded, and they get a majority of their food from guests instead of normal feeding schedules, so I doubt they do a lot of sleeping."

Okay then. "You gonna save the sea lions next?"

Winston smiled dryly. "Hell yeah."

Ivan's heart skipped when Winston took his hand. They took a smaller side path that passed a ride called the *Planet Spin*, where dozens of little pods whirled around a giant sun on fraying cables. Ivan remembered riding something like that with Alli once, though not at Galaxsea. She'd been violently ill afterwards, and he'd laughed at her for months.

Though there were even fewer streetlamps here than on the main promenade, Ivan was still taken aback that Winston didn't even try to keep them in the shadows. "Aren't you worried about security?" he asked, out of breath for a number of reasons. "Or cameras?"

"This place doesn't have the money for that shit since the documentary dropped," Winston replied. "You've seen it, right?"

Oh, he had all right. Though it was one thing to see photos of Seymour's (allegedly) self-inflicted bruises through a screen, with Mike, Cass, and Allison offering commentary, and another to see the Rezzies in the wild. It was difficult to picture the massive animals he and Winston had kayaked with performing for audiences of children sticky with cotton candy and popcorn.

Suddenly, Ivan halted on the gum-caked concrete. "Wait, what happened to the fish?"

Winston smiled again, this time looking pretty pleased with himself. "They're in the Arctic exhibit." Winston gave his arm a little tug, but Ivan prompted him to clarify with a look. "If I wanted to feed him dead fish, I'd have just stolen from the trainers."

Ivan continued to stare at him, and he continued:

"I trade the dead salmon with some live ones from the Arctic exhibit whenever I come here, so he can learn to catch them. The local salmon exhibit is one of the only ones still open in the Arctic building, since they're so damn cheap compared to polar bears or walruses. They just keep replacing the dead ones thinking they died of something else."

Ivan's jaw was practically on the ground.

"Pretty smart, huh?"

Ivan stammered, "Why the hell wouldn't they think something was up by now?" *How the hell did this get past me?* Good God, maybe he *was* bad at his job.

"Because they're dumbasses."

Ivan couldn't argue with that. He hadn't realized things were this bad. Watching their stocks fall was one thing, but being here to see how much this location alone had been let go was another entirely. Ivan wasn't sure, suddenly, that he wanted to see what awaited him in Seymour's pen. A lack of security was one thing, but animal abuse was another.

After a bit more walking, they arrived in the shadow of the stadium. Ivan caught the gleam of starlight on a few rows of metallic benches before he was pulled into a pitch-dark hallway, up some stairs, and back out into the night.

"Watch your step," Winston said.

Ivan did, but his shoes simply weren't made for gripping the slippery turf the trainers tossed fish from. Upon taking just one step onto it, his feet slid out from under him. He would have fallen flat on his face had it not been for Winston, who fortunately spun around in time to catch him.

Ivan muttered an apology as he detached himself, suddenly grateful for the lack of light which hid his reddening face. To avoid looking at Winston, he bent to untie his dress shoes, bearing the sting of his stretched cuts and willing his pulse to slow. He knew he loved Winston, he accepted that now, but it was dangerous here, and he needed to keep his head together.

"You're bleeding."

His shoes clattered as Ivan kicked them both off. Behind Winston, a flopped over fin, sickly and pathetic, drifted past in the unnaturally clear, grey water of the pool. Ivan couldn't take his eyes off it. Seymour was bigger than he'd pictured, even with the Rezzies in mind.

Winston glanced over his shoulder at Seymour before repeating himself.

"I mean, you're bleeding badly."

"I cut myself on the wire." Ivan stared at the whale. As much as he loved being fawned over by Winston, Seymour quite literally seemed to dwarf the pain he felt.

"Let's go see him," Ivan said.

"You're hurt."

Ivan brushed past him and stepped closer to the water, illuminated only by stars and a few flickering lights. Taking care not to slip, he walked until his toes were at the very edge of the pool. Behind him, he heard Winston remove his shoes and pad across the turf until he stood directly beside him.

Seymour appeared even more impossibly large from this distance. His fins were larger than Barney's torso, and he wasn't using them any visible amount. At any given moment, he took up about a sixth of his tank, which was smaller than Ivan's apartment. It hurt to look at. Ivan didn't know why; it wasn't like he'd chosen for this to happen to Seymour. He hadn't said "Let's put this gigantic apex predator into the equivalent of a bathtub and charge people $70 to come to the park and watch him float around." He hadn't said that.

He hadn't said it, but most mornings, he'd brought an umbrella to work and used it to push the protesters aside. He'd watched the whole damn documentary and hadn't for a minute thought to check what kind of conditions Seymour was living in. He'd been too busy worrying about impressing Allison and Mike, and making something of himself, so he'd been content to dismiss Seymour's pain and the people who bore witness to it as melodrama. But now, Ivan saw that the only melodrama had been performed by himself. Watching Seymour drift around like this felt like watching the mane being shaved off an African lion—it was a degrading, ugly sight.

Winston was looking at Seymour, seemingly deep in thought. Winston, who was spending his grocery money on this suffering animal, watched as the aluminum lights reflected off the water's glassy surface and flowed over his face. A billboard behind the pool was painted with cliffsides spiny with trees. A smaller sign listed facts about the Southern Residents. The first was that they were critically endangered. Ivan didn't read the rest.

"I get it now," Ivan said quietly, feeling rather queer all of a sudden. He turned his eyes back to the whale.

"You don't think I'm…?" Winston's question lapsed into nothingness.

What did he think?

"I think," Ivan said, "I wish I was more like you."

Not like Allison, or Mike. Maybe not even like his father. *What a crazy thing to think. Surely I don't mean that.*

But Ivan did mean it, and it was the most frightening and devastating thing he'd ever experienced. More so even than Seeing color for the first time. He wanted to be like Winston. Or with him. Or both.

As though he'd read Ivan's mind, Winston said, "Stupid," and Ivan's head snapped over to him, startled.

The painter was raising a brow at him. There had been a bit of jest in the word, but it'd been weak. There was something heavier behind it, keeping Winston's usual bubbliness from buoying it up. It took him a moment to realize that he was finishing his earlier question.

Ivan recalled what Katie had said, and shook his head, watching poor Seymour drift around in circles. In light of everything, Winston just might be the least stupid person he knew.

How much happier would he have been if he'd spent more time around people like Winston, Katie, and Barney in college? They didn't look like they belonged in an admittance brochure like his actual acquaintances had, but he might have had someone to be honest with. Maybe he'd have allowed himself to cry.

Something large being dragged behind him jolted Ivan out of his reverie. He turned around to see Winston hauling a massive water-filled plastic bag of writhing, live salmon towards the pool. The thing must have weighed three times what the dead fish had.

"Watch this," Winston said. "He's gotten so good at hunting."

"You trained him."

"Nah." Winston started fiddling with the mouth of the bag. "I just brought the fish. He remembered the rest."

"Shouldn't you get away from the water?"

"No, it's fine." Winston was pulling at the bag with a worrying ferocity now, every tug taking him dangerously close to falling over the edge. "I don't know why. This isn't. Opening."

After watching this for half a minute, Ivan couldn't take it anymore. "Here," he moved in to help, "let me."

And just then, Winston managed to get the thing open. Unfortunately, this also sent him over the edge along with a dozen flopping salmon and Ivan himself, who had grabbed him by the collar of his t-shirt just a moment too late. With a great splash, Ivan fell into the pool with Winston.

Hitting the icy water was agonizing. The cold seemed to force itself like a dagger into every cell in his body at once, and this effect was not improved by the wounds on his back, which set alight as soon as the salt water touched them. He opened his mouth in a wordless scream and barely stopped himself from drawing the frigid water into his lungs.

A few salmon brushed past him as gravity slowly pulled him down, and the coldness of the water began to numb him. Ivan felt a clumsy underwater tap on his eyelid, and he forced them open, which stung like a bitch, to find Winston staring directly at him, looking like a creature of myth, his hair flowing out from his head in snakelike tendrils of orange in the darkening water.

The world was silent as he started to tread.

As difficult as it was to see, Ivan sensed movement around them. The source didn't occur to him until he realized the true mass of what had darkened the water behind Winston and, for the second time, nearly gasped his lungs full of saltwater.

He pointed at the whale frantically, but his movements were slowed, and full panic set in as he began kicking to shore, trying and failing to pull Winston, who had reacted a moment later, up to speed with him.

It was like a nightmare. They had to move faster, a thousand times faster, if they weren't going to be devoured. That massive fish would swallow Winston whole and have Ivan for dessert. Their muscles and lungs screaming in protest, Ivan and Winston swam for their lives, certain that the end of all things was right behind them.

Ivan burst out of the water just before Winston, crawling a few feet away from the edge before reaching out and pulling the painter towards him.

The top of the water was almost comically undisturbed. Seymour was swimming faster now, using his fins, but Ivan didn't care about that. He cared that they weren't being made into chew toys.

Ivan coughed and retched out freezing salt water. It felt like every bit of skin exposed to the air was burning, and the pain radiating out from his cuts was indescribable. He was vaguely aware of Winston near him as he blinked salt out of his eyes, and when his vision finally cleared, he scrambled closer to Winston, grabbing hold of him and keeping his eyes locked on the water. He was pretty sure turf was built for the whales to slide out on during shows. Seymour could very easily hop out, glide towards them like a rubbery freight train and drag them to their graves.

Winston stood after a few moments, and Ivan reluctantly let go of him, still shaking too hard to stand. The painter threw the empty fish bag (which he'd impressively held on to) down with a strength that Ivan didn't think he'd have for at least a week, and enthusiastically exclaimed, "Shit!"

Ivan glanced up at him dubiously, and sure enough, he was beaming out at the water as if something *good* had just happened.

Winston turned to Ivan. "Do you know what this means?" He pushed his soaked hair away from his face in a rush, as though to free up his hands for the excited gestures that were about to follow.

Ivan's ears were ringing, and he wasn't sure if his rapid breaths were making him feel more or less faint. They had almost been eaten by a *whale*. Maybe Winston wasn't stupid, but that didn't rule out crazy.

"He didn't give a fuck that we were in there!" Winston said. "He knows salmon are his hunting food! Only captive orcas attack humans, but with the stopping of the shows and everything...I couldn't have asked for this to be going more perfectly. He might actually stand a chance."

Shaking like a leaf, Ivan slowly got to his feet. Good, he heard himself say. Good, that's good. Winston chattered on about his whale, blue lipped with cold, eyes slightly red, and smelling of salt water.

Time slowed, and clarity returned under a black sky. Winston's chest heaved up and down. Moths were drawn in towards the flickering lights. A spider spun downwards like an acrobat. The massive jaws of a whale swallowed a fish, and Ivan recalled the grey water cradling him downwards. It was freezing in the open air; he needed someone close to him.

Before Ivan knew what he was doing, he had taken Winston's face in his hands and crashed their lips together.

Winston tasted of salt and, deeper still, of honey. Just as he relaxed, however, Ivan shoved him away again, startled.

Though the theme park was a village of greys and blacks, Ivan was suddenly aware of the overwhelming color of everything that snuck through the cracks. The spruces outside the stadium were so saturated in their green that Ivan could see every twitch they made as the air shifted, and Winston's hair was as vibrant as if it was under the midday sun. Between his vision and his racing heart, Ivan felt more than a little bit like he was high.

"I'm…" he panted, suddenly overwhelmed with horror. What had gotten into him? "Winst, I am so sorry." He meant it. But how many times could he say sorry and have it mean something? Winston was still buzzing through his veins, so it was very difficult to convince himself his remorse was authentic, but he needed to get his head on straight, to stop acting crazy—

"I'm not."

And before Ivan could so much as raise his gaze, Winston kissed him back. This kiss was hungrier than the last, but Winston was smiling against his mouth, and Ivan wrapped his arms around him and closed his eyes to escape the chaos.

They broke apart when his shivering reached worrying levels.

"Okay, you're gonna get hypothermia," Winston said.

Ivan laughed, but there was little humor in it. "You sound like me."

"Well, if you'd stop hurting yourself," Winston rolled his eyes, "I wouldn't have to."

Ivan shuddered against him, the pain starting to return. "Come home with me," he said suddenly, feeling impulsive, alive.

Winston's eyes flashed, and he glanced over at Seymour, who was once again circling an empty pool. The salmon had all vanished.

"We're bandaging you first."

18

Despite the force he'd kissed Winston with, Ivan proved to be a gentle lover, considerate, if skittish. Winston's heart had broken a little bit at the way he'd kissed his way down Winston's torso, past his waist, between his legs. He didn't know why he felt that way; he'd dated romantics before and wasn't a stranger to the motions they went through. Maybe that was it. Ivan didn't go through the motions in anything he did. He felt everything earnestly and fully, refused to perform, and it made him prone to mistakes. Winston knew, because he was the same way. But he liked that about Ivan, and what hurt his heart about the sex wasn't the sex itself, but the fact that it had taken him so long to meet a man who expressed real love behind the motions. If he had any proof that the Bond matched true Soulmates, Winston guessed that would be it.

Winston must not have gotten a very good look at Ivan's place last night, because when he woke up, he was so jarred by the minimalism and brightness of Ivan's bedroom that he briefly panicked, thinking he'd been moved to solitary. This panic wasn't soothed by the fact that, unfortunately for Ivan's bedsheets, sex had been prioritized over medical attention the previous night. They looked like something out of a crime scene. Winston felt a little bad for letting Ivan persuade him to put off patching him up. He wasn't in bed with Winston, and the latter hoped this wasn't because his cuts had kept him awake.

The smells of warm vanilla and frying butter made reassuring himself easier. Stretching out onto Ivan's side of the bed, Winston let himself doze for a bit longer, slipping in and out of consciousness to the sounds of Ivan shuffling around. Eventually, he dragged himself to the shower, which was the size of his kitchen, to wash whale and blood and God knows what else off him. When he got out, he found his clothing from the day before was neither stiff with salt, nor wrinkled, nor so much as unfolded, and the bed had been stripped as well.

Typical. Winston ruffled his hair with a towel and put on a pair of Ivan's pajama pants instead, not bothering with a shirt.

Ivan's apartment was so much of a maze that Winston was impressed they'd managed to find their way to his room last night. After taking a wrong turn and somehow ending up in a dusty sitting room, he took the opportunity to snoop around a little, but came up empty-handed, which was frustrating. Winston didn't understand why the man had to be so damn hard to read. If Ivan took a half hour to go through *his* stuff, he could probably piece together a near complete picture of his life, but Ivan's minimalism only really told Winston he had money for more space than he could fill.

The only decorations that didn't look like they'd been purchased from Anthropologie (or wherever the hell people with Ivan's kind of money shopped) were the photographs. Winston squinted past the dust that covered one of them. A woman with light hair and Ivan's nose smiled demurely next to her husband, a tall man with a drawn face and the same dark hair and eyes as the two children in front of him. The woman had her hands on the shoulders of Ivan's sister, Allison. The man, Ivan.

Unfortunately, Ivan was a cute kid, which meant yearbook photo and baby picture blackmail would be nonexistent. Winston came to terms with this as he meandered to the main room and kitchen, which had windows so large that the light they admitted hurt his eyes. Squinting, Winston greeted Ivan, who, bed-headed and t-shirt clad, was flipping pancakes with the attentiveness of one diffusing a bomb. He looked up at Winston, tried and failed to bite back a smile, and promptly returned to flipping. Winston both wanted to kiss him and cry.

"Seriously, laundry?"

"Everything smelled like whale." Ivan glanced at Winston's (Ivan's) pants, and they shared a look before Ivan went back to flipping.

"So." Winston sat down at the counter opposite him and grabbed an impressive pancake, fluffy and thicker than his thumb, from the stack next to the stove. "Do you feel better?"

Pancake flip. "Pardon?"

"Your back." Winston hadn't entirely meant his back.

"I think I'll live."

"Clearly, my skills as a butcher are lapsing." It wasn't like they hadn't been entirely irresponsible. Winston had at least managed to ruin the mood and patch him up before they went to sleep ("You might want to consider a tetanus shot, by the way").

"You know," Ivan said, "you've really let yourself go. There were only two times that I felt like I was going to pass out."

Winston found that difficult to believe, with the dramatics that had occurred last night. "If I didn't know better, I'd say your life of crime was starting to harden you."

Ivan snorted.

"I mean," Winston continued, grabbing another pancake before going to the fridge for more butter, "you've known me for three weeks and already you're trespassing." There were a lot of unopened things inside, but no butter to be seen. It took him a moment to realize it was sitting out next to Ivan, who handed him a knife when he sat down again. "I'm just saying, one minute you're befriending a troubled artist, next thing you know, you're shooting black tar heroin…"

This time, Ivan's laugh was genuine and contagious, the easy "ha ha ha" from the back of the throat that made it irresistible for everyone but Winston, who preferred to watch, to join in. After a moment, Winston continued, "By the way, is that what you put in these to get them so big?"

"No," Ivan answered, still chuckling. "I just have a lot of practice."

"Cooking?" It was hard to picture Ivan Notte doing the same work as Gretchen Jinx, but he was clearly good at it.

"Is that surprising?"

"A little bit."

Ivan looked at him, and for a flash, Winston saw the boy in the picture frame.

"Your father?"

Ivan seemed to understand what he meant. He turned the stove off and transferred the last few pancakes to the stack. "Yeah."

"You don't bring him up a lot," Winston said, wishing he was less clumsy with comfort. Anger, he understood. Not grief. He felt helpless waiting for Ivan to blink back the tears that had started to flood his eyes.

"He's not alive."

Winston didn't know what to say. Why the hell would he bring this up? He was so thoughtless. The opposite of Ivan.

"He worried," Ivan said. "Too much."

Don't let it be suicide.

Ivan covered his mouth with a hand and scrunched his eyes shut, but a few tears still rolled down his cheeks. It was a stroke, he said. Allison found him.

Winston stood and rounded the countertop, but when he reached out to Ivan, he was horrified to find himself shrugged off.

"Please don't," Ivan said.

Winston tried again, and was shrugged off again, albeit more weakly. "I brought it up."

"I should be over it," Ivan said. "It's been three years. Alli didn't even cry at the funeral."

Winston flushed with anger on his behalf. "Your dad died. You're allowed to be upset."

Ivan muttered something about shame.

"I mean," Winston, in complete freefall, risked a joke, "we've already slept together, so it's not like you're ruining the mood."

Ivan's laugh was sweet and sad. He gave Winston a quick kiss.

"It's not fair for me to put all this on you," he said. "I need to stop embar—"

"Stop."

The word came out a little bit more authoritarian than Winston intended, but it had the desired effect. Ivan looked at him, plainly anguished. There was a ghost of something expectant in his face, as well, perhaps waiting for a refutation for whatever schema he'd built up in his head that didn't allow him to cry. But Winston, throughout his life, had found that the best way to break down walls was to pretend that they weren't there in the first place. You couldn't debate pain.

"Just stop," he said again.

This time, he held out his arms and waited for Ivan to come into them. He did, wrapping his arms around Winston's waist as he rested his head on his shoulder, re-saturating it with the salt water he'd only washed out that morning.

"Alli's always been stronger," Ivan said.

"Fuck strong," Winston declared, meaning it in full. "Not caring doesn't make you stronger. Maybe your sister acts that way *because* she found him." Of course, it was likely also due to the ruthless capitalist impulse shared by all Galaxsea employees, but he didn't voice this opinion. "Look, I'll be honest. Being poor fucking sucks. But if you want me to stand here and say that the prime state of man is to be rich and detached, you're talking to the wrong person."

Ivan's words of protest were muffled against Winston's chest. Winston cut him off.

"It pisses me off that you're beating yourself up over having a heart." Perhaps Winston could have stopped there, but he felt compelled to tell Ivan this. No one else would. "Society tells us that we'll be eaten alive if we don't harden ourselves. It calls Bonded people dirty for the fact that it couldn't beat out the strand of genetics that lets us See, it tells people to put aside the things they're willing to fight for in favor of a safe, practical option they feel nothing about, and it forces people to believe the lie that it's better to care about nothing, and to never have anything taken away, than to actually experience life with a soul. And then you end up with generation after generation of these heartless, boring-ass people, who deep down are none of those things, but have been taught to fear earnestness so much that they spend their lives shaming everyone who was brave enough to keep their heart warm."

Ivan pulled away a little. "What are you saying?"

Winston sighed, grabbed a pancake, and stuffed it into Ivan's gaping mouth. He sputtered, biting off what was inside and tearing off the rest.

"I *said* you're warm. Also, if it were my funeral, I'd be pretty offended if people didn't cry."

Ivan smiled weakly, chewing his pancake. He removed his arms from around Winston and wrapped them around himself. A strand of hair fell into his face, and he pushed it back.

"God knows I'm going to cry when you free that damn fish."

ᘐ

Brunch was quiet and sweet, but Winston didn't particularly mind the gaps in conversation. Ivan talked about his father and learning to cook, and Winston about not knowing how to. His father, though alive, had never been around to teach him such things. Between the both of them, Ivan and Winston finished the entire stack of pancakes, using jam and butter in place of syrup. Afterwards, Ivan hooked an arm around Winston's waist and pulled him into the living room, where they had sex in the sun, and Winston did his best to at least temporarily dismiss the pain that lived on Ivan's shoulders, and Ivan did the same for him.

Sometime after the sun finally succumbed to the fog, they lay half-dressed on Ivan's sofa as he played with Winston's hair. Winston was pulled out of the rhythm of the touch when Ivan said, "Thank you for saying what you did."

He was rapidly coming back down to earth. They were on a couch. His cheek was on Ivan's chest. "About your dad?"

Ivan tensed. "Yeah. I only worry he would be disappointed with me."

Winston bristled. "Are Alli and Mom bigots?"

Ivan's fingers froze in his hair. "No," he said, "and my father wasn't either."

"Then you have nothing to worry about." Winston turned around and kissed him. He suspected they held more prejudice than Ivan was letting on, but they'd had a good day, and he wasn't about to argue. "If he wanted you happy, that's all you need to know."

Ivan began to stroke his hair again. After a moment, he asked, "Don't you ever feel guilty?"

The scope of the question was broad, but this didn't deter Winston from giving an equally extreme answer.

"No," Winston said, "never." He left out the fact that nothing he did would ever disappoint his parents, because they were too uninvolved to feel that way.

19

A week more of good sleeping, shared breakfasts, and kisses on the nose and Ivan and Winston agreed that they would call this dating. Ivan, however, had only done so on the condition that he would pay for Seymour's salmon going forward. So it was that the only person in Ivan's life aware he had a boyfriend was whoever at the bank noticed the routine withdrawals of cash he made before heading to the farmers' market.

Work became a dreamy in-between time after sleep and before Winston, and Ivan frequently caught himself gazing out his office window, looking beyond the skyscrapers, losing himself in the grey-blue sky and the Sound that supported it. Being with Winston felt like living in one of his paintings. The new, colored ones were just as ephemeral as the monochromatic ones had been, but they had less the disturbing air of a barely-remembered dream than they did the sanctified bliss of sitting perfectly awake, listening to cricketsong. Winston made his life something worth staying awake for, and so the time passed quickly.

Sometimes Winston would spend the night at Ivan's, but more often they found themselves sleeping above *Takes the Cake*—it felt a good deal more like home, anyway, and day by day, Ivan was subtly stocking Winston's pantries and fridge (he'd be damned if Winston ate *cereal* for dinner on his watch). Whether the evening ahead consisted of failed attempts at roux or Ivan distracting Winston from his painting, he never went to sleep feeling the way he had before knowing him.

Yet, although Ivan was happier than he could ever remember being, their discussion of his father had left him brittle. In Winston's grey eyes he caught a glimpse of life before the Bond, and sometimes nostalgia for that life crept out of them. In Winston's arms at night, Ivan suffered recurring moments of panic where he wondered whether perhaps this had all been a huge mistake. What if he was deluding himself by thinking he could ever truly fit into a world of flowers and shortbread and paintings? Ivan dreaded the anger that had permeated every aspect of his life before Winston, but what if that was who he was? What if he *needed* to be miserable to be complete? God knew success had never made him happy, but at least it had given him some sense of identity.

It wasn't that Ivan couldn't face his reflection; it was more that he was no longer capable of identifying with it. The life he was tiptoeing towards was that of a stranger, and a lonely one at that. At least if he was at Galaxsea, he had his mother, his sister, and the memory of his father. His stiff work acquaintanceships couldn't compare to the intimate bonds Winston had with Barney and Katie, but they were still something. Whenever he watched the three interact he felt self-conscious and envious, like them but not like them, socialized for the wrong crowd. It was alarming to realize how isolated grief and money had made him, the juvenile problems it had allowed to proliferate.

It didn't help that he was willingly deceiving Winston about where he worked, and therefore couldn't even get any kind of reassurance from the paramour himself. He faced the paralyzing choice between betraying Winston and betraying Galaxsea completely alone, and after everything Winston had said about the whales, it might have been an easy one to make. The company was shit, he knew that now, but Ivan felt queasy at the thought of being a part of taking it down, which, despite it all, still felt like an act of self-destruction.

Even though they spent nearly every night together now, Ivan never accompanied Winston on visits to Seymour. He would stay awake while Winston was gone, trying not to get nervous if he took a little longer to return than usual.

Tonight, I'll talk to him, Ivan told himself every night, before becoming distracted by the painter's lips. This was only in part due to a lack of self-control: Katie's warning haunted him. What if the conversation he was dreading became their last? He knew it was shameful, but he would rather live a lie with Winston than not have him at all.

If once that plan had seemed sustainable, though, it was no longer. It was hard to enjoy Winston's incredible failures in his attempts to cook, the newest painting he was working on, and whatever unbelievably cryptic internet video he sent next as an attempt at "humor," while Ivan was in the shadow of guilt. He reached a point where he could no longer face the Sound or stomach his job. Everywhere he looked, he saw the whales, and everything he was, was wrong. And, as successful as Ivan was with suppression, there were some factors that were already moving outside of his control. So it was that one day at work, while he was texting Winston about how to make an email sound less passive aggressive, an impetus to disaster came knocking at his office door.

213

"Do you have a minute?"

Ivan raised his eyes, and the smile instantly melted off of his face. Mike took that as his invitation and stepped inside, while Ivan attempted to put his phone away nonchalantly, though he suddenly felt incredibly jittery.

Mike took his time situating himself, slowly dragging an armchair across the room and sitting down opposite Ivan. He hunched over with his head bowed, a posture Ivan found perplexing until it dawned on him that Mike, *Mike*, of all people, was upset. Or, at least, it appeared that way.

"Have you heard the news?" Mike asked.

Unable to take his eyes off the man across from him, Ivan put his computer to sleep. "No."

Mike lifted his head. "I was certain you of all people would know."

Fuck. Ivan's palms were already sweating. Did Mike know about Winston's visits to Seymour? Had some critical civil right been revoked from Seers overnight? Was he fired?

"I guess I've been distracted." He needed to calm down. There would always be conversations with men like Mike.

Mike glanced at where Ivan's phone rested in his pocket. "Were you texting him before I came?"

Ivan was horrified at how easily he had guessed.

It was apparent from Mike's expression that he'd read Ivan's. "Listen. I was being ignorant before. I really wish you the best of happiness. In whatever path you choose in life."

Ivan bristled. He didn't like the pause between those two statements. *I wish you happiness, even, I suppose, if that path is one I consider depraved.* "Thanks."

"I'm sorry if I'm overstepping, I just thought with everything that's happened, I would rather you heard this from me. Cass is demoting Allison."

Absurdly, Ivan nearly laughed. Robert Cass was not known for his critical thinking skills, but demoting Alli would set a new precedent for his disastrous choices.

"Who told you this?"

"She did."

Ivan frowned.

"Don't take this the wrong way, Mike, but why would she tell you?" Alli had never applied for a job she hadn't gotten. She couldn't have taken this lightly, so why hadn't she told Ivan? Had she simply not gotten the chance? Did she still not trust him? God, he'd thought they'd been doing better. Ivan just hoped she was smart enough to let Galaxsea go, even though it would mean the departure of his only remaining ally in the building. Alli could get a matched or better position anywhere else.

"Well, she really had no choice," Mike explained, and Ivan shook his head. Surely, he was missing something.

"No choice?"

"I'm her replacement."

A little jolt went though Ivan not at the words, but at the way they seemed to change the air in the room. He might have been less concerned if it was only the position change itself—Mike had always had power above his paygrade, and this only legitimized it, which meant little to Galaxsea—but he was worried at the genuine warmth the announcement brought out in Mike's face. A warmth that came not from calm, but from satisfaction.

Ivan had a sudden childish longing for Winston. "Congratulations."

"Thanks," Mike Swan said, straightening up a bit. "I just wanted to talk the thing over with you, because your family has taken quite a few hits the past few years…"

While that kind of comment would have ordinarily tempted Ivan to launch himself across his desk, in that moment, it only left him strangely embarrassed.

"I know I shouldn't still miss him." He cast his eyes down to the desk, which he knew Mike knew was suspiciously clear of papers. What would Dad think, if he could see Ivan now? Was it obvious to Mike that Ivan had become the very slacker they'd all thought he was from the start? If Cass was demoting Alli, who had actually worked to get to where she was, what was in store for Ivan, the one who'd gotten his position as a pity handout?

"Well, it helps to have company." Mike's voice was soft as velvet.

Ivan already regretted mentioning his father. He decided to force Mike to get to the point. "Winston," he said. Not *company*.

"Yes. Your…I don't know what the politically-correct word is. Your Mate."

The shame that engulfed Ivan then was potent and dire. All the illusions were dissipating, the mirages clearing to reveal a terrible reality.

"What are you trying to say?" His phone felt like a rock in his pocket.

"Ivan," Mike bit the inside of his cheek, crossing his arms and leaning back to regard his ex-boyfriend, "you've changed a lot since you've met this man. A lot of people…you know, we all cope with grief in different ways. People think taking up yoga, or religion, or art will make them forget that someone they love is dead, but before they know it, they've lost themselves, too."

Ivan was unable to shake the apocalyptic feeling that he was slipping back into an old skin that no longer fit him.

"You're overstepping."

"Why?" Mike cocked his head to the side. "Because I've told you something you don't like?"

"No, I just don't want your input on my private life anymore."

Something moved behind Mike's eyes, but he himself went dangerously still.

"You should."

He took out his cell and slid it across the desk to Ivan, who reluctantly picked it up. What he saw made his stomach drop.

A picture of Winston, at a protest to free Seymour, his face contorted in fury.

"Scroll down."

Ivan was grateful for his long sleeves, because every hair on his arms was now standing up on end.

Picture after picture of Winston at protests. Protests for Seymour, protests for Seers, protests for unrelated but politically-aligned things, and, at the very end, photographs of him at the riot, eighteen and enraged, followed by copies of a hollow-eyed mugshot.

"You have no right to do this." Shakily, he put the phone down, and Mike slid it back towards himself, looking down at the mugshot solemnly.

"Why are you so interested in dating a man who isn't only publicly outspoken against Galaxsea, but who has gone to *prison* for violent crime disguised as 'activism' before?"

"That's not…" Ivan stammered. "It was a long time ago."

Mike pursed his lips, as though considering this. "True, but he hasn't exactly abandoned the activism. I'd say we're overdue for a violent outburst."

"He isn't violent."

Mike smiled. No teeth. "Did he tell you that?"

Ivan looked at him helplessly, unable to respond. Mike had a point. "Did this… finding," he said, "have anything to do with Allison's demotion?"

Mike's eyes glittered. "Now you're getting it."

Suddenly, Ivan stood, shoving his chair back rather violently. Not only had this man threatened a hate crime against his Soulmate, but he had convinced Cass to demote his sister!

"Who the hell do you think you are?"

"Why are you shouting? We're just having a conversation."

"I'm not shouting!" Ivan shouted, then cringed. *Now* he was. "You have no right to do that to her because of my personal life." He pointed a finger at Mike's broad chest. "You don't have the right to know about my personal life at all anymore."

"You keep talking about what rights I have and don't have," Mike said. "Did he teach you that?"

"No, he didn't!" Ivan asserted, unsure if he was more afraid or furious. "Who the hell goes around photographing protesters anyway?"

"The same person who wants to protect themselves and their friends from dangerous people. And he *is* dangerous, Ivan." Mike sighed. "I consider you a trusted friend, and I'm saying this to you because I'm concerned."

"You're no friend of mine," Ivan said icily. "Pray tell, what have I done so far to raise your *concern*?"

"Treat being Bonded like it's normal." There was a hint of an edge in Mike's voice now. "You never used to think it was. Don't be offended, but the truth is that it's not. Only two percent of the world Bonds at all, and even fewer people actually act on the impulse. Especially if their Mate is that mentally ill."

"I hate to break it to you," Ivan said, astounded, "but I wanted to go out with Winston."

"Because you thought if you were a part of something, it would make you forget about the loss."

Ivan, utterly speechless, could only gape at him. That wasn't true. It couldn't be. But all things considered, the fact remained that Winston was going to steal a whale. Winston had been to prison. Winston wasn't exactly moderate. What if Mike was right? What if he *had* been indoctrinated?

"Ivan," Mike said, "sit. It's fine, sit."

Slowly, miserably, he complied.

"You're very protective of him," Mike observed.

"I love him."

"After three weeks?"

"It doesn't take three weeks to notice you're happier."

"You don't look happier to me." Mike's eyes flicked up and down Ivan's body. "In fact, you look angrier. Three weeks to fall in love, and you still want to tell me that you're stable enough to even know what you want at this point?"

Ivan scoffed. "And you know what I want better than I do? Why don't you just mind your own business?"

Mike let that hang in the air between them for a moment before slowly, smoothly, standing. He leaned forward on the desk so he was just a little too close to Ivan.

"Because I'm your superior now, and I'll be damned if I watch this company go under because you let that freak get close to us."

Ivan had to concentrate on not shivering when Mike's breath, cool and minty, ghosted across his face. It brought back years of his life that were both incredibly unhappy and incredibly familiar.

"I'm assuming," Mike straightened up, "he doesn't know you work here?"

It took Ivan a moment to summon his voice. "No."

Mike sighed. "Good. He might not try as hard to convert you if he thinks you're already with him. I'm not trying to hurt your feelings," he added after a moment, "I'm just giving you the truth."

"And what is the truth?"

Mike inhaled.

"Look, you were hired too young to be in the position you're currently in. Everyone knows it now, and they knew it then. Of course you struggled. It isn't surprising you were drawn to Winston. He validated your frustration. Life is simple when you have an identity to blame all your inadequacies on."

Ivan couldn't even look at him anymore. He needed to speak with Winston, or his mother, or, God, maybe even pull Alli aside. They would straighten this out. They would remind him that Mike was a dick. What he said wasn't true.

"Look, don't look like that," Mike said. "The truth is, I *miss* you, Ivan, really, I do. I just want you to be safe. Know who's got your back."

"And that's you, is it?"

A smile, tight but oddly convincing. "I mean, you and Allison aren't fighting at the moment, but who knows what'll change now. Everyone knows she's competitive. There were other reasons she was demoted, by the way."

Other reasons. That seemed reasonable. Maybe this was all reasonable.

"And Winston can't have my back," Ivan followed Mike's earlier assertion to its logical conclusion, "because he's dangerous."

Mike looked at him sadly. "Poverty isn't fun. You've seen how he lives. It isn't exactly a reach to say he sees your money as a way to get out of the shitty life he's set himself up for by going to art school."

"He's my Soul—"

"Oh, for God's sake. Do you honestly think he'd forgive you if he knew where you worked?"

No.

"If you want to ever be worth anything," Mike said, "you need to start thinking for yourself. You always had this problem."

"Why are you doing this?" Ivan asked.

Mike rounded the desk, closing the distance between them in a single, graceful move. Ivan caught a whiff of good cologne.

"Because I know," he said, "what you're capable of. I miss you, and I want the best for you. You're obviously struggling. I want to help."

Ivan suspected he knew what he was getting at.

"I thought you hated me."

Mike huffed. "That sounds like a word they must have taught you. Ivan, I was put on this earth to help people, and you know what I've learned?"

"What?"

"Hate isn't real. It's something invented by the losers of this world to make you feel bad about doing better than them."

He took Ivan's hand, then, probably in the same way he'd taken it a hundred times before, when he'd held Ivan after the funeral and its anniversary, and all the nights the grief was thickest, but now, instead of being comforting, his skin was too soft, far too soft, and as he ran his thumb over Ivan's knuckles, the words he spoke next were, too.

"Call me a softy," he said, releasing Ivan's hand, "I miss you like hell." He took a step back towards the door. "But I have to be honest. If you continue to associate with that Seer, I'll have you fired."

20

Winston was struggling.

Summer was meandering on, and the leaves were growing greener. With the Bond's completion, the world assumed a new vibrancy he wouldn't have been able to picture in his wildest dreams weeks earlier, and yet, with this outward clarity came an internal, less welcome one as well. He was struggling, and he didn't know how to stop.

Frankly, Winston didn't know how he'd continued this long without realizing how bad things had gotten. He kept telling himself if he only held on until Seymour was free, he could rest afterwards, but now even the promise of relief was not enough to soothe him. With Katie recording songs on a tight schedule and tighter budget, and Barney and Ivan both working, Winston faced the unresolved details of Seymour's rescue alone, and certainly not at full capacity. Sleeping, even with Ivan, became a problem, and he lay awake many nights staring into the bluish glow of the moonlight on the ceiling. His paintings suffered from his shaky hand, and each morning in the mirror he was greeted by darker blue circles under his eyes. And yet, the thought of giving up, of being the one responsible for Seymour wasting away at Galaxsea, filled Winston with so much self-disgust he started craving cigarettes, which he hated the taste and smell of and only smoked when he was feeling particularly self-destructive.

Most of the time, he tempered these moods before Ivan came by after work, but nothing could be avoided forever. After a third failed attempt to layer streaks of blue over the bonfire flame he was painting, Winston lit a Camel on impulse, and was so lost in the first drag that he completely missed the familiar sound of Ivan stomping up the stairs.

"I didn't know you smoked."

Winston jumped and turned. "I don't." He took one last drag, held it, and blew a cloud of smoke before snuffing the cigarette out in an old candle lid. After looking at the smoldering remains for a moment, he said, "Sorry, I should have asked if you wanted any."

"Not my thing," Ivan said, cocking his head to the side. After a moment, he started tapping his foot, his eyes drifting over Winston's shoulder to the paintings leaning against the wall where, weeks before, Winston had hidden Mike Swan's portrait.

Winston swallowed. His throat was hoarse from going the day without talking, and he knew his eyes were red and irritated from strain, paint fumes, and now smoke.

"Are you okay?" Ivan asked.

Winston didn't know why he suddenly felt like he was about to cry. He turned partly away. "I'm embarrassed you're seeing me like this." Greasy hair, poor work, bad mood, bad choices.

Ivan set his work bag down at the kitchen table. Actually, now that Winston thought of it, he didn't exactly look like himself, either. The way he was hugging himself made Winston a little uneasy. Maybe the smoking had made him nervous. He had told Winston once he hadn't even tried weed.

"What about you?" Winston asked.

Ivan looked surprised. "I'm fine. I'm just thinking."

"If it's Mike—" Winston was pretty much certain this bigotry issue wouldn't stay out of the workplace forever.

"It's not."

"Because if you need me to start stopping by every once in a while, I could bring you lunch."

Ivan smirked. "You can't cook for shit. And besides," he said, guiding Winston to the sofa, "the last thing you need is another commitment. Take your shirt off."

The twitch of fear prompted by the former, more cryptic sentence, turned into one of excitement. When Winston emerged from his shirt, Ivan was rummaging in his paints.

"Not like that," Ivan, as usual, seemed to read his mind. "Don't get too excited."

"I didn't say anything." Winston was initially too tired to laugh, but when Ivan pulled the same palette of colored paints he'd bought Winston out from the miasma, it was harder not to.

"What are you—?"

"Don't worry about it." With a series of vague pushes and gestures, Ivan guided him so that he was sitting sideways on the sofa, with the warm light of the scuba lamp hitting his back.

"Doubt I'm giving you a very flattering angle to work with."

"Don't worry."

"Well, I don't mean to be a tough client, but if you paint me unflatteringly, I might have to ask for a refUND!" Winston jumped at the cool touch of paint and whirled around. "What the fuck are you doing?"

"Decompressing."

Winston stared. Ivan stared back. Winston fell a little deeper in love.

"Do you want me to stop?"

Unfortunately, the gentle movement of the brush was weirdly relaxing. Winston turned around again, relaxing a little but still occasionally shivering when the brush strayed onto skin that was otherwise bare.

"This is pretty granola, even for you," Winston said.

"*I'm* granola?"

"Look at yourself."

The brush temporarily lifted off the small of his back, and then Ivan said, "Fair. Figured this was sexier than taking candid photographs of each other in used bookshops."

"Would be sexier if I had weed."

"I'd leave you if you did." It sounded like he was only half kidding.

"If I turn around three hours from now and there's something obscene on my back, I'm leaving you."

Ivan muttered something about a ruined plan, and Winston smiled to himself. Ivan was charming all of the time, but he was irresistible when he was being silly. As the two of them settled into the rhythm of painting, Winston tried to track his movements and form a picture in his mind, but he was either less aware of the location of Ivan's hands than he thought he was (unlikely) or Ivan was just more prone to painting in the abstract (likely). It was kind of an interesting exercise, Winston supposed, being the canvas instead of the painter for once. Instead of watching the work progress from a series of disconnected blurs into something concrete, each of Ivan's precise touches blurred together into something Winston couldn't quite visualize.

"What would happen if I had an allergic reaction?" Winston wondered aloud at one point. "This stuff isn't really regulated for contact with human skin." He vaguely recalled seeing some kind of toxicity label on the package when he'd first opened it. Hopefully that didn't prove relevant.

Ivan continued tap, tap, tapping tiny specks of paint everywhere, but Winston swore he could feel him smiling.

"That'd be awkward to explain," Ivan said. "You, walking into the hospital, breaking out in hives with a hyper-realistic phallus on your back."

"What a way to go."

"I didn't realize you were dying in this scenario," Ivan said. "If that's what we're going for, I can try to lay it on a little thicker."

Winston laughed. At least if he did, he'd finally get a fucking rest. Not that this wasn't rest, of course, but nothing would really feel like it until Seymour was free.

After a moment, Ivan inquired, "You really don't have a lot of pictures, do you? You would never do the polaroids-in-bookshops thing."

For whatever reason, the question made Winston more aware of just how large a degree of separation there was between his and Ivan's lives. Barney took pictures as a hobby, yes, but he got the sense that Ivan was talking about group photos with classmates before prom, carefully scrapbooked memories of picnics and family moments and childhood pets. Things that he hadn't had the privilege to take part in.

"How do you know they're not all digital?"

"They're not."

Winston turned around to look at him, surely distorting whatever was on his back. Ivan pulled the brush away.

"Why don't you have any?" Ivan asked.

Given what had taken place when Ivan had come home, Winston was not particularly eager to emphasize their differences in upbringing. Today, he wanted to pull him in, even if it asked him to turn a blind eye. So he turned to the other, secondary reason that he avoided cameras.

"They make me anxious."

Ivan looked confused. He stared deep into Winston's eyes, the helpless stare of a loved child trying to comprehend a neglected one's plight. For a moment, he looked like he was about to say something, but eventually closed his mouth with a finality that made Winston turn back around.

"Could you explain for me?" Ivan asked.

Winston bit his lip, and felt Ivan's at the base of his neck. He wasn't sure he wanted to get into this now, but he was so starved for tenderness that he found the words spilling out anyway, humiliating as they were.

"When I'm painting," he said, "or when I'm by the sea, or at a protest, or with Seymour, I feel like I matter." Like he couldn't be ignored. Like the silence of his childhood couldn't swallow him. "Photographs remind me that I'm..."

"Please don't say it."

"I'm insignificant." Winston wasn't certain if it was worse to raise his voice's volume or keep it lower. Either way, the ever so slight tremor in it was audible. "The art, the activism, Seymour...it's not just because I care about those things. I need someone to *see* me, even if it's a judge in a courtroom, because clearly neither of my parents fucking wanted me."

A picture was a reminder of humanity. Father always at sea, mother letting her son run with bears and orcas, and all that hadn't made him into anything greater. He was still a person, and he was broken.

Winston felt a rush of shame after the outburst. He should have painted all of that, rather than dumping it on Ivan's already heavy shoulders. Ivan was the one who had to work with Mike Swan every day. Winston bowed his head, and a few tears fell on a pink scar on his hand.

Ivan put a hand on his shoulder, turning him around so they faced each other once more. His eyes were pitch dark in the dim room, deep and safe.

"I see you," he said, taking Winston's hands and smearing blue over his knuckles. "You changed everything for me."

There was a buzzing electricity in the room, or perhaps that was only the questionable wiring of the lamp. Ivan was looking through him, and then he wasn't, and Winston wondered if he was thinking what he thought he was thinking.

"I used to love photography," Ivan said.

"Why did you stop?"

"I didn't want to look stupid."

Winston could not place the reason why, but this made him feel a little sick.

"I still like to keep photographs of the people I love, though. So," he met Winston's eyes, "I hope you'll let me."

Winston stared, trying and failing to even consider a way of responding to that. When the people who had brought you into the world treated you like you were a whatever thing, it was hard to conceptualize being told you were loved by someone. Every time, it surprised him.

"You love me."

Ivan nodded, and Winston, awfully, flared up.

"Are you serious?"

Ivan let out a big breath, then asked, "Do you want me to prove it?"

Winston's face had barely gotten hot when Ivan shoved him down onto his back, which was still covered in wet paint. Both of them realized this latter detail a moment too late, and froze.

"I'll buy you a new sofa before Barney and Katie see."

"For both our sakes, please." Winston supposed it was only fair, though, after what they'd done to Ivan's sheets. Ivan kissed him and laced his fingers through Winston's curls, and Winston was just pulling Ivan down by the beltloops when he pulled back.

"I should tell you," Ivan said, slightly out of breath.

Winston paused, his mind going back to Swan, to unnamed workplaces, to eyeless corpses, faces permanently twisted with despair.

"My history with Mike. It wasn't just something casual. He's my ex."

Winston exhaled. He'd thought as much. While it wasn't ideal in terms of timing—maybe the paint fumes had gone to Ivan's head—or in general, he supposed it meant something good that Ivan was willing to share with him. He resumed kissing Ivan's neck with a hum, breathing paint, and sweat, and him. "Doubt he loved you like I do."

"Between you and me, he's an awful kisser. But seriously—"

Winston pulled Ivan's hips down, and Ivan groaned, then pulled back.

"*Seriously*, pause."

Winston paused.

"He's really scaring me lately. He and his friends are keeping tabs on you. I know you wanna stick it to Galaxsea, but please stay away from there if you can."

Winston frowned. "What does Galaxsea have to do with Swan?"

Ivan looked at him and, after a moment, said, "I guess a lot of protesters are photographed there. If Mike gets wind that you're there one day, he can call the cops."

Winston shivered against Ivan. He had been planning to stage a small protest outside of Galaxsea, just one more to remind the public of where the lost Southern Resident was imprisoned, but maybe if it was that bad, he'd see if Katie could run it.

"Fucking freak," Winston muttered. Who kept tabs on activists that closely in their free time? Had Mike Swan been like this when he'd been with Ivan?

Ivan interrupted his thoughts with a kiss. "Really," he said, "I don't know what I would do if those people took you away from me."

Winston looked at his Soulmate, haloed with a golden glow. "Neither do I."

☙

Though there was heat at the pit of Winston's stomach and the impossible distraction of Ivan's hands, he was still aware of a melancholy present in Ivan's kisses that night. However, any worries that might have been born from it were quickly destroyed, along with the painting on Winston's back, which no one, save for Ivan, would ever know the contents of. For the moment, the only art was living, writhing, and covered in blue, and it kept secrets like the dead.

21

In another world, Mike's threat wouldn't have meant anything. But now, it took the rift Ivan's secret had opened between him and Winston and widened it. Four letters meant nothing if they were founded on lies, and Ivan could no longer deny he had lied to both Winston and himself about what he was. Though the better part of him knew the terrible things Mike said about Winston weren't true, every doubt that he had planted lingered, festering. Ivan wanted whales and painting and carbs to feel normal, but the longer he waited to not feel like a moron for indulging in them, the more he felt that giving Mike what he wanted might not only be survivable, but wise. Ivan had thought it would be a relief to stop being cold, but the truth was, a significant part of him missed it. He missed having armor. He missed feeling like people couldn't fuck with him.

Ivan could only guess at the anguish that would follow the split; breaking a Bond had never been a part of what Winston explained to him. And yet, the possible destruction still pulled him nearer like gravity. He found himself meeting Mike's eyes around the office with greater frequency, and though he did his best to look too busy for conversation, they often ended up talking anyway, and never when other people were around. Ivan might have done a better job of telling him to fuck off if it wouldn't have been *so* easy for Mike to frame the whole thing as his doing; a desperate attempt at an inappropriate office romance to gain a better foothold in the company and draw attention away from his Bond. Mike would never have pulled that kind of thing before, but he also hadn't backed Ivan into corners before, nor had he used his shoulders to block doorways. Maybe Ivan was overreacting, but he couldn't shake the suspicion that Mike would actually ruin him if he didn't do what he said. Nor could he shake the suspicion that he deserved it. Besides, as much as he wanted to be, Ivan knew he wasn't ready to leave Galaxsea. He knew Galaxsea, and he knew Mike. He wasn't Winston.

On the day Ivan ruined his life, he remembered his umbrella, and lucky thing he did. For a week, they'd had unusual heat and drought, and the few people that had showed up had just sat in the shade by the building's front, signs propped up against knobby knees. Today was the first cool day since then, and Ivan was still two blocks away from the mob when he started to hear chants. After he strained his ears for a moment, his steps slowed, all the hair on his arms standing up at the unmistakable cry: "Seymour's not yours!"

Winston.

There were almost as many people in front of Galaxsea as there'd been on the day after the documentary dropped. Dreadlocks and t-shirts and sneers, and a few people with orange hair that made his stomach plummet, but so far, none of them were Winston.

It couldn't happen like this. Not today. Ivan debated turning back, but he was already running late, and Mike had tried to call him. As he approached, pulling his unopened umbrella out, people paid him little mind. Even when he was in the thick of the mob, pressed on all sides by bodies and noise, he wasn't acknowledged. In fact, he made eye contact with no one until he burst through the front of the crowd and nearly impaled a woman with the point of his umbrella. Ivan would have traded any amount of physical harassment or foul language, however, for those few seconds of eye contact, because the woman he Saw, and who Saw him, was holding a guitar in one hand and a megaphone in the other.

Katie didn't say anything, and Ivan went inside.

When he stepped out of the elevator, he heard police sirens, thus instead of heading to his office, he turned down the hallway that held the café that was never open, walking as quickly as he dared to a window. From where he stood, there were a few cop cars, but it didn't look like their officers were doing much. As he scanned the crowd for Winston, he got the idea a few times, in a few different ways, to text his boyfriend and make sure he was okay, but he scrapped it every time. He had to trust in Katie. She wouldn't let Winston ruin himself, would she? But then, she'd helped him break into Galaxsea.

"How many of them do you think have jobs?"

Ivan jumped and pocketed his phone, turning to face Mike, who stood with his hands in his pockets.

"He's down there, isn't he?" Mike said. "Your Mate."

Ivan could only pray he wasn't.

"Did you know this would happen?" Mike asked. "Because a warning would have been nice."

"No. And don't call him that."

"Oh, what?" Mike asked. "Mate?"

A woman walked past them, the clops of her heels growing fainter and fainter as she disappeared down the hallway. Ivan would not take the bait. Mike was the enemy here. Not Winston. Not Katie.

"Oh," Mike said, with sudden recognition. "I'm sorry, I always forget there's a special word now. I meant Soulmate."

"It's not a special word," Ivan said, his skin crawling. *Special.*

"Okay," Mike said. "Personally, I think it's easier to call it like it is."

Fear rose up in Ivan like icy water. "You don't know what you're talking about." He hated the way his voice shook. Was he that fragile? That he could only face himself when his image was crafted from soft words?

"And you do?" Mike's laugh was so genuine, his smile so bright, as he said it, that Ivan was transported back to when they'd first started dating. Maybe all along, it had been Ivan with the bad intentions. Maybe Ivan was the manipulator. After all, Mike had been there for him when Dad died. Mike watched out for him at work. Mike would protect him from Winston, from Allison, from himself. "Please don't be like this. I'm sorry if what I said upset you. What worries me is that you won't listen to simple logic."

Ivan was more confused than ever. *What logic? Am I that far gone?*

"I have work to get done." He tried to walk away, but Mike put an arm around him.

"Hey," Mike said, "I know he's told you I'm evil. I know what that crowd thinks of me. But," he removed his arm from Ivan's shoulders and looked at him, "I know you know me. And the reality is I'm no worse than anyone else."

That sounded plausible. Ivan's acquiescence must have shown on his person, because Mike relaxed a little bit, returning to his usual composure.

"Have you considered my offer yet?"

Ivan wanted to leave. "I have."

"And?"

Ivan's heart beat uncomfortably fast in his chest, but he wasn't afraid of Mike, surely. In the beginning, he'd been afraid of Winston. Winston had been the crazy one. Christ, something was very, very wrong, but Ivan didn't know whether that *something* was Winston or Mike. All his head was filled with was the noise outside and eyeless corpses and crushing, inevitable failure.

"I don't know," Ivan said. "Is it possible we could just give them what they want?"

"Give them what they want?"

Ivan nodded.

Mike smiled, no teeth. "I don't think that's something we want to do."

"But if we redirect some of the money Cass wastes towards a sea pen—" Ivan knew he was talking nonsense, but he didn't know what else to do. He couldn't let Mike win this discussion.

"That's not the issue," Mike cut him off. "I want to show you something."

"Are we going outside?" Ivan asked, alarmed, when Mike grabbed his hand, but he might as well have not spoken at all. People were staring at them as they strode downstairs, across the lobby, and out the doors, and all the while Ivan tried not to be repulsed by the smoothness of Mike's palm, which was curled around his with a firmness not dissimilar to a boa constrictor.

"Wait…wait a minute," Ivan said, squinting at the sun. "Mike, this is trouble."

A few people at the back of the group turned around to watch them with accusing eyes, but none laid a hand on them, and Katie was nowhere to be seen. The mob only watched, and Ivan wished he could wring his hands, or cross his arms, anything, but Mike held him fast.

It wasn't only disdain in the protesters' faces. There was some level of fear. Disgust. Despair that spoke, undeniably, of Winston. When he looked at them, Ivan was suddenly faced with responsibility.

I'm part of what he hates.

He'd thought that he was exempt, but as he'd kissed Winston by night, bought him flowers, cooked for him, and proclaimed himself in love, he'd signed papers by day.

He tried to tell me that the whale needed to be freed, and I let him visit the thing alone. I didn't delete Mike's pictures of him. I didn't do anything. I didn't want *to do anything.*

It was clear now to Ivan what he was. Mike was wrong about Winston; Winston was good. He was earnestly, impossibly good, and he most certainly was not Ivan's Soulmate.

Ivan had shown, in his lack of faith in Winston, in his indecision, in his failure to integrate with his friends, that he, in addition to everything else, was a failure in love. He knew Galaxsea was corrupt, but now he also knew he belonged there, and that was a hundred times worse than simply believing the company was good. Self-aware or not, Ivan could never escape what he had been raised to be, and he hadn't been raised to be like Winston.

"They hate me," Ivan said.

Mike yanked his hand free of his and cocked his head to the side.

"Why wouldn't they? You're a successful adult."

"Fuck off!" someone yelled. There were a few middle fingers that made Ivan experience a rush of anger towards Winston for taking away his ability to ignore all this. For dragging his pain out into the light. Still, Ivan scanned the crowd for him, though for the second time that day, he found Katie first.

She was standing towards the center of the mob, but tall as she was, she was easily able to hold Ivan's stare when their gazes met. Looking back, Ivan would realize her eyes carried a warning, but in the moment, all he saw in them was disgust.

When she turned back around, she spoke through the megaphone with such fervor that Ivan took a step back. It was like her voice was made for it.

"I grew up by the Sound," Katie said, "so I've known the Rezzies since I was a little girl. I've known them since the day Seymour was born into L Pod, and so has my best friend."

Mike, at this point, elbowed Ivan in the side.

"—I haven't always understood his love for them, but I do now."

Mike elbowed Ivan again, and this time, Ivan looked at him. They shared a grimace.

"There are some people the system chronically fails," she raised her voice, "there are some people who aren't born into money, or a body that works right, or parents that love them. And sometimes, when you live in a system rigged against you, in a never-ending uphill battle where everywhere you turn you're reminded of what you should have but don't, sometimes it's all you can do to escape to one of the few places that system doesn't exist.

"Those of us that have lived here our whole lives have been lucky to have access to natural spaces, whether it be the Sound, or Mount Rainier, or any of the other national parks surrounding the city. These spaces give us space to reflect, to move, and to enjoy existing without any expectations placed on us."

Mike was gripping Ivan's hand again, very hard.

"Nature allows everyone to experience unconditional love, and places like Galaxsea are trying to take that away from us!" The crowd hooted and shouted in agreement, and Katie increased her volume even more. "They took Seymour, a piece of joy shared by everyone, and they put him behind a paywall. And for what? He was taken as a baby, and now he's an adult with a lifetime of torture to show for it." More shouting. "I don't give a damn whether that whale gets released or put in a sea pen, but I sure as hell don't think being private property is working!" Shouting. "How many trainers does he have to hurt for Galaxsea to realize some things aren't meant to be owned?" Shouting. "Seymour belongs in the ocean, and it's time for us to show Galaxsea that we won't rest until he's back in it!"

The twang of her beloved guitar was entirely absent from the brief, hollow space between the end of her appeal and the wave of voices it summoned.

"Seymour's not yours! Seymour's not yours! Seymour's not yours!"

Ivan inched backwards a little farther, but not far enough that Mike would notice. The other man wore a wild expression between amusement and fury, and Ivan was afraid to drop his hand.

"Fucking bitch!"

Ivan turned to Mike, startled. A protester told him to fuck off. Katie appeared oblivious to the insult.

"Hey sweetie! Sorry to say it, I know you're better-off-blind already, but your voice isn't working so great for you either!"

"Do you work there?" a nameless protester demanded. Mike didn't look at him.

"I'm sorry Daddy didn't love you," Mike called to Katie again, "but violence isn't the answer."

The sun was in his eyes, but Ivan could have sworn he saw her shoulders stiffen at that one. Fortunately, Mike seemed not to notice, and abandoned Katie for the protesters in their immediate vicinity.

"Come on," he hollered, moving his grip to Ivan's elbow, "why don't you babies run back home to Momma?"

"Mike, let's go back inside," Ivan said. Some of the protesters nearest them had pulled out their phones to film.

He may as well not have spoken at all. Mike continued playing with them, and the sun was hot, and the protesters did, in fact, create a similar racket to a crowd of crying infants. Ivan, covering his face with his free hand, tried twisting out of Mike's grip.

Suddenly, a protester backed into him by accident, her dirty shoe scuffing his ankle through his pants. Without thinking, Ivan gave the girl, a waifish thing with black hair down to her waist, a shove that sent her stumbling.

She fell, hard. For a half-second after, he was still Seeing red. And then, all at once, his anger vaporized to be replaced with horror.

Yes, he was a monster, and he was helpless to change it.

"What the *fuck* is your problem?" One shout.

Mike sneered well-intentioned filth over his shoulder, his hands digging into both of Ivan's arms.

"Don't you have somewhere better to be?" Two shouts.

Persistent eye contact. Mike's eyes as blue as the sky above. Pitying and protective.

"Fucking psychopaths!" Three shouts.

Somewhere, Mike asked if he was okay. Ivan tried to get away. Mike held him tighter. He felt safe, right? The protesters' words came in an onslaught and did not waver once they had started. They surrounded Ivan in a whirl. Mike was right, no, Mike was right, and this was wrong. He didn't belong here, but if he didn't belong here, then he didn't belong anywhere. He loved Winston, he hated Winston.

Mike grabbed him by the collar and kissed him.

Had Ivan been asked his own name during the moments leading up to it, he wouldn't have had a clue how to answer. He was no one. Winston had made sure of that.

It had been a beautiful idea, to learn something new, to See a more beautiful world than he always had, one in which people were good, whales swam free, and kisses tasted of honey. But that world didn't exist. Not for Ivan.

When, gasping, he tore himself away from Mike ("Does it *look* like we don't have hearts, people?") his eyes were drawn to a telltale patch of orange in his peripheral vision. Orange with an armful of extra picket signs.

Grey met black, and suddenly, everything good that had happened to him because of Winston was nothing but a cruel mockery. When Winston's eyes met Ivan's, they were the eyes of a stranger, eyes that had looked to the front of the crowd just in time to witness Mike's lips on Ivan's, and had subsequently traveled downwards until they reached the badge hanging around Ivan's neck.

"Stop it."

Ivan didn't say it to anyone in particular. In fact, he said it as he clawed at Mike's suit for balance, his head swimming while Winston handed the signs off to Katie, turned, and disappeared into the metropolis.

"Sorry," Ivan heard Mike say, "I know I'm a handful."

Katie was shouting into the megaphone. Something about cruelty, the faces of animal cruelty.

"Let go of me," Ivan gasped. "Let go."

Mike leaned in confidingly. "You know, you're the one that's holding on to me."

Ivan could still taste mint in his mouth, and his bottom lip tingled where the other man's teeth had raked across it. He dragged his eyes to meet Mike's gaze, and felt himself wilt.

This was all there was, then.

"Dinner?" Though Mike's inflection implied otherwise, it wasn't a question.

"Dinner?"

"Yes," Mike said, with a nod to the protesters, "with me. No judgement or politics."

He made it sound so simple. Maybe that was what life was. It was stupid and simple. Maybe love wasn't about what you wanted, but what you could endure.

"Okay," Ivan said.

"Good," Mike said. "Now let's leave the losers to their screaming match."

And he led Ivan into the air conditioning and out of the sun.

22

Mike Swan wasn't funny, but Ivan wanted him to be. Working at Galaxsea had trained Ivan well in fooling other people with a polite huff, but not in fooling himself. If he could only laugh at it all, look on Winston and the Southern Residents and Seeing with Mike's educated scorn, he would be able to detach himself for good.

Mike's failure to make Ivan laugh, truly laugh, was not for lack of trying on either man's part. Ivan smiled over distressingly-red (how long would he be tortured, before the colors started to fade?) wine when Mike commented, with a smile, that their server looked a lot like Ivan's sister. He rolled his eyes and smirked when Mike muttered, as he ushered Ivan past an overweight Seymour protester in a Street Signs Save Lives t-shirt, that "he'd say she was better-off-blind, but the diabetes would take care of that soon enough." He even laughed, loudly, from the stomach, with Mike when an intern no older than 18 gave an unprompted, tearful manifesto to the half-full conference room about how he couldn't take Cass's degradation anymore, that he quit. It wasn't only Ivan's pity for the kid that kept his mirth hollow; Ivan was so fixated on the way the intern's shame reddened what little of his face wasn't already discolored with acne that he couldn't pay much attention to the meltdown. Ivan was sure his own face was the same color, and he came down with such a migraine after this event that he took a cab home early.

Ivan's inability to find his boyfriend (for Mike had apparently taken his agreement to get dinner as an agreement to get back together) funny kept him dangerously sober to the rest of the subtleties of living on his arm. Mike wasn't physically or verbally abusive, but the way he dished out frequent, silent punishments was all too familiar to Ivan. If Ivan wore a shirt Mike didn't like to an event, Mike would "forget" to save him a seat, so there would be an awkward shuffle when Ivan arrived. If Ivan fell sick at an inconvenient time, as he did on the evening of the intern incident, Mike would strategically place his unlocked phone on the kitchen counter the next morning, so Ivan would see the opinion piece on colored street lights he'd been reading. Even on the very first night they went to dinner, there were subtle notes of expectation in the meal they shared, and though the rest of the slights were irritating, it was times like those which alerted Ivan to the possibility that something in the relationship was gravely wrong.

Halfway through their second week together, Ivan, picturing Winston shaking his head in disapproval, stayed late at work because Mike had an evening meeting with Cass. Mike said nothing when he finally got out, but he graciously opened a large umbrella for the both of them when they crossed the street to the garage where he'd parked. Ivan watched the wet pavement pass them by in glistening streaks, his heart leaping when he Saw a red stop sign standing sentry on the curb. Mike paused for it and drove on without comment, oblivious to the miniscule print at the bottom, the only indication to him that it was any different from a normal sign.

Ivan assumed his silence was because he was processing, but when they reached Mike's apartment and he got out of the car without a word, Ivan realized he had made the mistake of conflating his habits with Winston's. Silence, for Mike, always said something.

When they reached Mike's apartment, an open, modern space that looked more like an art museum than a home, Ivan asked him if he was alright, and Mike, after some prompting, sighed and delivered a sermon to Ivan that left his head spinning. Ivan, he said, was lucky to have him, but he never showed he was grateful. Mike spent money on Ivan, bought him expensive dinners, defended him at work…what did Ivan do for him?

"You know," he said, to a flabbergasted Ivan, "I don't have to date someone that's better-off-blind, right? I feel like I'm being taken advantage of lately."

Ivan couldn't say he blamed Mike for being upset with him. His self-esteem, at the moment, was lower than it had been for years, and it was not difficult to see himself as the mooching, entitled brat Mike did. Ivan would be ashamed to date himself. He hadn't been doing enough to repay Mike for helping him, and he tried, that night and others, to make it up to him during sex, even though he didn't really believe in Mike's kind of fucking. Teeth and cruel words combined with his sterile, minimalist apartment left Ivan feeling like he was a part of some niche porn taking place in an IKEA showroom.

On the most recent of these occasions, Ivan couldn't sleep, unable to stop pondering why he felt even more helpless and lost than he'd ever felt around Winston. Mike turned in his sleep, and Ivan held his breath until he knew for sure he wasn't awake, then picked up his cell from the glass bedside table, guiltily scrolling through old conversations with Winston. He lingered on a particularly animated argument about condiments that had earned him a dirty look from Cass during a staff meeting; his stomach had hurt that day from reining in laughter. Tonight, rereading the texts made him feel like he'd been punched.

Ivan tried to get comfortable, to will himself to appreciate Mike, but his wrists hurt from being grabbed, and his lips were swollen from being bitten, and really, he wanted nothing more than to get away from the man next to him. The more he tried, the more he found his mind swimming with images of his blue eyes glittering with mirth as he'd taunted the protesters, mirth that Ivan now considered, with a chill that reached his bones, had looked genuine because it *was.* In the beginning, Ivan had believed he was doing the right thing when he'd looked down his nose at Winston…Mike probably believed the same. And if he really thought he was doing right treating Winston so poorly, how hard would it be for him to extend the same treatment to Ivan? It was degrading to consider the possibility that Mike had already done so, and had for some time, but was it more degrading than letting it continue?

Ivan sat up in bed, careful not to disturb Mike. He had to leave, and that terrified him.

As he padded in socked feet across Mike's hardwood floors, he did his best to keep his breaths silent. The air conditioning was on such a high setting that he half-expected them to fog. Massive and menacing paintings stared back at Ivan from every wall; it was difficult to picture anything done by Winston hanging among their ranks, serving a prison sentence in this showroom of a home.

When he slipped through the revolving doors of Mike Swan's building for the last time, the night air cooled his bruised skin, and the full moon watched his escape with ambivalence. This might have been calming, but something about the whole scene felt fundamentally wrong. It was only after a couple of blocks that Ivan realized what was throwing him off was the sky itself.

He froze in his tracks, squinting upwards in an attempt to convince himself that no, the deep indigo that had once belonged to midnight was not gone, but it was fruitless. The night sky was black once more, and that piece of Winston, and of himself, had already slipped away from him. At last, the world's colors had begun to fade.

And suddenly, Ivan knew why they'd been screaming. Now, the true depth of the despair experienced by thousands upon thousands of separated Seers took on a whole new meaning. Ivan started walking again in an attempt to calm himself down, but he soon no longer bothered to choke back the sobs crawling up his throat.

What had he done? He didn't want to be with Galaxsea, but the people against it wouldn't have him. He didn't want to be with Mike, but Mike had said it himself that no one else would have him. He didn't want to See color, but he couldn't imagine living in a world where he didn't. He wanted to be himself, but the world didn't, and besides, Ivan didn't know who he was anymore, anyway. Maybe he wasn't anyone.

Ivan wandered through the darkness until he emerged into the light of a flickering, dingy streetlamp, illuminating a few dumpsters surrounded by miscellaneous rubbish, a black cat regarding him with an even, still-yellow gaze, and a familiar barbed wire fence. The metal cut into his fingers, and the rust would definitely stain them, but he paid it no mind. His tears still drying on his cheeks, Ivan focused all his energy on climbing, feeling watched but not endangered. When he swung his leg over onto the tree, he managed to only nick it on a single barb, cursing as a trickle of blood ran down his calf.

Ivan jumped the last foot or so to the ground, but when he straightened up, the cat was no longer to be found, and he shuddered, wondering if he'd been under someone else's observation. He couldn't remember telling his legs to move, only that he came back to himself standing over a concrete pool, with a single, massive, dark spot swimming in circles underneath the flickering surface. Seymour had lost his lethargic drift. The waters rippled above him when he took a turn too quickly, splashing and spilling over the edge of the pool.

Ivan descended a set of stairs to the underwater viewing window facing the empty bleachers. Seymour darkened all three panes of glass each time he glided past, flashing Ivan with a glimpse of his reflection that was just as quickly replaced with barren, grey water.

Maybe it was time Ivan abandoned his glorious future and embraced absurdity. Winston led an absurd life, but he was perhaps the most well-rounded adult Ivan knew. He was the one with friends, with passions, with courage. The way he lived wasn't logical, but maybe people weren't meant to live by logic. Ivan had gone against logic when he'd given love with Winston a chance. Maybe he would have to do the same to love himself, too. Ivan was, he realized with a tearful pang, a person, and no matter how perfect he was, Mike would probably never see him as one.

Suddenly, his arms were covered in goosebumps. When Seymour's form next darkened the glass, Ivan jolted to see another reflection besides his own.

When he whirled around, he was faced with a wall of plaid. Barney looked more terrifying than ever with his face shadowed by the flickering lights around the pool.

"You've got a lot of nerve coming here, you fucking snake."

Ivan took a step backwards, and he bumped up against the wall of glass, unable to put any more distance between himself and the boulder of a man approaching him. His pulse beat like a jackhammer.

"Barney, I—"

"Did you tell anyone?"

"No, I—"

"Do you have any *fucking* idea what you did to him?"

"I made a mistake—" Ivan started, and he knew it didn't even begin to cover what he'd done.

"Oh, you got that right."

Before Ivan could even consider how to respond, his face exploded in pain, and his head slammed against the glass behind him, hard. His hands immediately went to his nose, which was the source of a waterfall of thick blood dripping from his chin onto his shirt.

His knees gave out underneath him, and he slid to the ground. Above him, Barney took a step back, seething and cracking his knuckles.

"You deserved that, and more." Ivan's eyes were scrunched shut, but he knew Barney was still close enough to kick him. He curled up in anticipation. "You'll get the 'more' part if you ever come near my friend again."

Ivan listened to his heavy footsteps receding and spat out a mouthful of blood. His entire face was throbbing—his nose was probably broken.

The full moon shined down as he slid the rest of the way down to the gummy stadium floor. Every now and again, he swallowed a mouthful of blood, forcing himself not to gag. Seymour continued to swim in circles, rhythmically eclipsing him in shadow.

After laying there for God knows how long, a cool breeze, carrying with it a promise of later rain, caressed his face, easing the pain of his nose for just a few seconds. It solidified a painful and sweet clarity that had been dawning on him since he'd fallen, whispering what he had to do.

"I can't believe you broke your nose."

Still upset that he'd awoken alone that morning, Mike had appeared insulted when Ivan arrived unprompted in his office at the end of the day. After delivering a myriad of apologies with as much groveling as he could muster, Ivan managed to convince him to take a private walk on the beach, a walk which he guessed Mike assumed would serve as a backdrop for more apologizing on Ivan's part. Still in their work clothes, they stumbled down from the parking lot into the sand, and Mike's leg snagged so suddenly in the tangled grass carpeting the dunes that he nearly faceplanted. He'd ripped it free with a violence that Ivan couldn't help but feel was directed at him, a suspicion that was compounded when Mike didn't so much as hold out a hand to help him over the bleached logs piled at the edge of the sand. As jittery as Ivan felt, a bit of his confidence returned when he bore witness to Mike's cell phone, unbeknownst to him, slipping from his back pocket and plummeting through the logs to the cool sand beneath.

Ivan followed him in silence, feigning ignorance of his lack of both cell phone and enthusiasm. If Ivan offered to abandon the whole excursion, Mike would definitely take him up on it, so did his best to ignore the uncomfortable silence by focusing on the sand and the Sound as they widened the distance between themselves and the parking lot. The tangles of washed-up kelp, clustered with popping sand-fleas, were the same greenish-yellow Ivan remembered, which was reassuring. Far down the beach, Ivan could see the same boulder he and Winston had climbed over for their picnic, half of its base submerged by the high tide, which lapped at the clustered barnacles and withered anemones still beyond its reach.

"Does it hurt?" Mike asked, when Ivan didn't respond to his first observation. He didn't sound very concerned.

Ivan nodded and winced; Barney hadn't held back at all in his swing. Ivan had walked into work not only with the obscene marks Mike had left on his neck and shoulders, but also with his face swollen, his nose bandaged, two black eyes, and a splotch of zero color in the form of a giant bruise. He looked less like he'd been punched, and more like he'd been kicked by a horse, but he could have handled looking gruesome if it hadn't come with the reminder that he was Seeing less by the day.

"Do I get to know who did it, or will you make me guess?"

"It doesn't matter."

"If I ask you a question, will you answer honestly?"

253

"Yes."

"Did that artist break your nose?"

"No."

Mike stopped in his tracks, his fist tightening dangerously around his sunglasses. "We have to call the police."

"No!" Ivan said a little too loudly, before lowering his voice to deliver a Mike-ready excuse. "No. If you call the police, it makes them martyrs."

"So you have been listening to me."

They began to walk again. Ivan was a bit shocked at how quickly his heart was beating, now that he was faced with having to outright disagree with Mike. *He'll kill me,* Ivan thought. *He'll realize he hasn't fixed me, and he'll kill me. Whether or not he gets people to gouge my eyes out, he'll ruin me. And then he'll come for Winston.* But the Sound looked less blue today, and time was running out. Winston had stood up to Mike Swan, and Ivan could too.

So, he took a breath, and, insignificant as he felt, spoke the truth.

"You're a piece of work, you know that?"

Mike froze midstride once more, and a ghost of offense crossed his face before he remembered himself and started to laugh. Though Ivan felt like the whole world was looking at them, there was no one on this section of beach. He wasn't sure if he preferred to have witnesses for whatever was about to transpire.

Though Ivan's voice trembled, he didn't have to force the words out for long. In spite of the bemusement on Mike's face, they soon were readily flowing off his tongue, his heart running back to the fence, unconcerned about what barbs he would encounter on the way.

"Seriously," Ivan said, "every time you open your mouth, it's like you're trying to teach me something. You're judgmental as hell. I don't wanna be with you anymore."

By the time Ivan was finished, his heart was beating so loudly that it was difficult to hear the waves. Somewhere in the distance, a dog and child splashed together in the surf.

Mike's gaze grew flinty.

"Okay," he said, "I guess I'll add 'accusations of prejudice' to the list of things you have to apologize to me for."

Ivan resisted the urge to point out that he'd said "judgmental," not "prejudice." It said enough that Mike had anticipated that accusation.

"Well, you can stop keeping track, because I've had enough."

"Bigotry is a serious accusation. Even you should know that. God, you've got the exact same victim complex as the idiots that vandalize our building every morning."

"Just because you have a savior complex," said Ivan, "doesn't mean I have a victim one. You *hate* Seers. Every other thing out of your mouth is about how we're making up colors for attention or how we don't have enough self-control for a real relationship. You can't say you never said that stuff."

Mike raised his brows. "Well, those things are true."

"Why the hell are you with me then?"

"Well," Mike tilted his head, "you're not *like*—"

Ivan wasn't even sure if he believed what he was about to say himself, but he cut Mike off anyway. "I'm exactly like them. I'm a Seer, and I like it." Almost feverish with adrenaline, he continued, "In fact, it's probably one of the best things that's ever happened to me."

Mike huffed. "And what? You'd rather be with the baby terrorist? The man who lives above Mommy's bakery?"

Ivan could have hit him, but he didn't think it wise to start throwing punches in his current physical state. "Yeah, actually, I would."

"Be careful what you say."

Ivan crossed his arms to make his shaking hands less obvious. "I am."

Finally, Mike's expression soured. "Why the hell are you defending him?" he asked sharply. "Are you afraid if you leave him, you'll be a bigot? These people call anyone that disagrees with their opinions…"

Actually, that was precisely what Ivan was afraid of. However, he was even more afraid of living a life without color, or Winston, or love. But those were fears beyond someone like Mike.

"…this is how you repay me? You know, not everyone is as tolerant of this Seeing shit as I am. Most people I know think you're all better-off-blind. And you'd better not think of coming to beg my forgiveness when you come to your senses, because it's already too late for that. To think that I'd wasted my time on trying to save someone as ungrateful as…"

Ivan felt a strange rush of pity for the bastard. This was quickly overcome, however, by the memory of every shitty thing he'd done since they'd first shaken hands at Galaxsea three years ago, Ivan's palms sweaty post-interview, Mike holding on a little too long.

"…he'll drag you down with him. In a year, you'll be on the picket lines too, whining about your minimum-wage retail job not paying for your avocado toast and your rights and your Mate and the sixty-seventh new color you've invented this wee—"

Ivan looked at Mike's hands, one of which clutched his precious, designer sunglasses, the other, his shoes. He wondered if it had been a jab at him, not to leave one free for hand-holding. Regardless, the insult, present or not, had little to do with the rather Winston-like idea taking shape in Ivan's mind.

Wordlessly, he pried the shoes from Mike's clutch and chucked them into the Sound.

Mike watched their arc in silence, only balking when they splashed down, as if he was surprised by the result of something falling into water. Never had a sneer disappeared faster. After the surf swallowed the shoes, Mike turned to Ivan and asked an expletive question. When he received no response beyond a horrified stare, he continued, with mounting vitriol, "My shoes!"

"Screw your shoes."

"Is there something," Mike asked, shaking with rage, "you'd like to say to me?"

And oh, Ivan had set out that morning with a fantasy of how this conversation would go. He would set Mike straight, make him feel the shame he'd cultivated in Ivan, leave him speechless and march off victorious. He'd make him pay. He'd make him learn.

But Ivan knew now that he was not like Mike, and that people like Mike, who did not choose to learn, never would.

"There's nothing left to say," he said, starting to back away. "I'll see you at work."

Mike glowered. "I hope you're quitting, or else things are about to get ugly."

"I guess my Soulmate will just have to support the both of us." Ivan shouted over the breeze, turning around.

"Do you mean your Mate?" Mike hollered after him. "What about—Ivan? What about my shoes? Those cost—"

Ivan never got to hear what precisely Mike's shoes cost, because he was far enough away at that point that every word he spoke was stolen away by the breeze. Though his face, pride, and reputation ached, the air of the harsh and untamed sea filled his lungs, cultivating clarity from hurt. It also helped, however, to picture Mike Swan attempting to climb over all that driftwood barefoot.

Once he reached the pile, he turned around to see Mike sloshing into the blue well above where his pants were rolled to. As quickly as he could, Ivan grabbed a few fistfuls of sand and let them fall through his fingers above where the phone had fallen. Maybe it would be found eventually, but with a bit of luck, it would rain before then.

Ivan covered his smirk, but he didn't try to stop, either. He didn't think he deserved to feel stupid for smiling to himself. After all, there was a far bigger fool than him on the beach today, his sunglasses clenched in one fist as he pawed at the water with the other, ass lofted in the air, oblivious to the hum of life around him.

23

The dough was sticky under Winston's palms, and when he stretched his fingers, it webbed between them amphibiously. He threw more flour into the mix and tried to ignore its uncanny grey as he kneaded.

He almost felt he wasn't appropriately sad. This may have been, in part, because his self-pity was mitigated by a worry, in spite of everything, for Ivan's safety. Mike Swan gave Winston a bad feeling, and if he knew Ivan was a Seer, there was no telling how he would treat him. No one deserved to be treated like Mike Swan treated Seers, even a lying asshole like Ivan. Concerned as he was, the memory of the unmistakable badge around Ivan's neck, and the humiliation that had consumed him when his eyes had landed on it for the first time, kept Winston from checking his phone.

The facts were these: Winston should never have taken Ivan back. He should have trusted Katie after they'd run into Mike Swan at the park, because everything Ivan had said to him since that day had been a lie, and Winston had been stupid enough to believe all of it. Ivan, it seemed, was not an exception to any stereotype. He was just like any other soulless capitalist, and Winston was sickened at the thought of everything he'd confided in him. How moronic Ivan must have thought him, as he'd rambled on about the Rezzies and color and art.

Across the room, Katie and Barney were reorganizing the spice cabinet, and the clanging of aluminum tins, married with the occasional spat of rain, served as the *Takes the Cake* kitchen's only protection from total silence. Winston wished one of the oven timers would go off or something.

He was crying into the dough. His mom would have scolded him if she'd seen, would have said that the finished loaf would bring sorrow into the arms of whoever carried it home. Fucking bastard. Fucking soulless bastard. With the back of a hand, he wiped his tears and set the dough aside. At the sink, he scraped the remains of the mixture off his palms, watching clumps of wasted flour disappear down a stainless-steel drain that matched their color.

"Winston?"

He bristled, embarrassed Katie and Barney had to see him like this. Really, the last thing that any of them needed was to hear more about his love life. Katie had started getting phone calls from important people lately, interested in booking her for more pay than usual. This could be the real deal, an important step. They should be supporting her, not idling in the aftermath of another one of his bad decisions, though a dark part of Winston secretly hoped the music wouldn't work out bigtime. Money, it seemed, was taking everyone from him: Seymour, his father, Katie, and Ivan, all pulled away from him so they could make a profit for themselves or someone else while he, the delinquent, was left behind.

"You can be upset," Katie said, pulling him out of his head, "but not now."

Winston dried his hands. "I know."

"Not for me. For——"

"Yeah," he said a little too loudly, "I know." For Seymour.

Winston didn't know if Ivan had told Swan or Galaxsea about the plan to save Seymour, but he didn't care. He'd never told Ivan the exact details, and he'd realized within moments after the protest that calling off the rescue wasn't an option. It would be this week. He and Barney (participating was too much of a risk for Katie now) only had to decide on a day. Seymour was clearly as ready to leave as he'd ever be; it was just a matter of what day posed the least threat. To hold off on the operation was to risk the whale's health declining further, which could render him unsuitable for release.

"You'll find someone else," Katie said.

Winston shook his head. "No one ever Bonds twice."

Technically, it was possible, and would have been even probable among ancient people, but today most people no longer had the ability to Bond at all. The odds of Bonding not just once, but twice, weren't great.

"He was an ass." Barney brushed spices off his hands, traces of the red Winston had come to associate with paprika still clinging to his palms. "You saw the kind of people he hangs out with."

Winston tried to swallow the lump in his throat. Was Ivan in love with Mike Swan? Did he look at him like he had looked at Winston? It was nearly impossible to believe.

"Your person is out there, Winst," Barney added, "but he's not gonna be some corporate slave too chicken to quit working for a company that abuses animals."

Though it was hard to think of Ivan that way, Winston did not voice this. He only said, "You're right," a little louder than he meant it.

"As he always is," said his mother, who swung into the back room in a rush of floral print and rain. "You two didn't have to do all that." She touched Katie's shoulder as she passed, setting bags of fresh spices down underneath the newly-organized cabinet. Winston knew his eye roll didn't pass as entirely benevolent, but he didn't care.

"Don't you start," his mother saw, and pointed a knobby finger. "They don't *have* to help me, because they don't steal half of my merchandise."

If Winston had been feeling generous, he might have appreciated she was trying to preserve normality, but he wasn't. "That's because you give them so much they don't have to," he muttered, and rather than argue, she marched across the room and forced a fat, red apple into his hand.

"Eat this," she ordered, just as the telltale patter of rain on the windows surged.

"Is it raining hard?" Barney asked her.

"Yes, it's a little unusual for this time of year." She silently mouthed *eat* at her son before turning back to her purchases. "But I knew it was on the way. That's why I rushed in."

Winston took a bite of apple. It was a little grainy. "Do I even get to know what spell you're casting on me?"

An impish smile. "Something to help. Just don't eat the whole thing."

Even if he had wanted to, he wouldn't have been able. His appetite the past few days had been shot. But still, he obeyed, if only because it took less mental effort to keep taking mindless bites than to stop. As Winston chewed and listened to the rain, Barney chatted with his mom about whether purchasing large amounts of gunpowder or metaphysical supplies was more likely to get one put on a government list.

Another bite of apple, another solid counterpoint about the stigmas of paganism. Somewhere, an oven smelling of peanut butter dinged. Bread that wasn't infused with tears rose. The bells at the shop's front door tinkled. And endlessly, giant drops of rain splat against the windows. It was enough of a cacophony that no one initially noticed when the door to the sales floor swung open again. To Winston, though, the inaudible occurrence was coupled by the room's previously dull colors lighting up in such a vibrancy that he grabbed the countertop for support.

Unsure even why he was doing it, Winston turned around, perhaps to face some invisible change in pressure, Bond-driven instinct, or the unplaceable sensation that someone was watching you. He nearly dropped the apple when he did.

Standing in a small puddle was a half-drowned Ivan: pale as death, nose thoroughly broken. His hair was plastered to his forehead in black tendrils, and his chest was heaving like he'd been running.

Did you run for me? Winston wondered, his heart beating. *Who did you push to get here?*

There was a buzzing electricity in the room. Katie, Barney, and his mother had ceased their debate. Winston stared at Ivan's bruises, and imagined the ways he would bruise Mike Swan the next time he saw him.

"The door was open," Ivan said, "so I just…"

"Made a big fucking mistake," Barney punctuated his threat with a startling crack of the knuckles. Winston looked from the apple in his fist to his mother, only to find she had disappeared.

"Please," Ivan begged, the words barely a whisper. "Please, just let me talk."

"Always gotta have the last word," Barney muttered.

Winston wasn't sure what he was feeling, but he knew there was a lot of it. "Then talk." Katie stepped forward and put a hand on his arm.

Ivan took a moment to gather his thoughts, but all he eventually came up with was "I love you."

Winston felt very hot, and not in a good way. To his satisfaction, Barney immediately snorted. "That's rich."

Ivan glared at Barney, then softened his expression again for Winston, which only made the latter angrier. "I only hid my job from you because I thought it would hurt you to know."

Such a blind fury overtook Winston that he was spitting fire before he could even think.

"Well, you were right," he said waspishly, a bit surprised at how much strength there was behind his voice, "that it hurt. How the fuck," he shrugged Katie off and stepped forward, "could you have listened to me explain how evil Galaxsea is and still work for the thing that my entire life is dedicated to fighting? How could you?"

Winston was seething by the last word. Now that he had Ivan in front of him, he realized that the reason he hadn't felt sad earlier had been because he wasn't. He was angry, and now he had to clench his hands into fists to keep them from shaking.

In his life, how many fucking times had he fallen through the cracks? How many fucking times had he been invisible to every person that claimed to give a damn about him? And Ivan was going to pretend like he loved Winston *in spite of working for Galaxsea*? Not a chance in hell.

Ivan's eyes were huge. "I thought..." He shook his head. "I didn't think."

"You kissed a man who threatened to kill me."

"He threatened me, too!" Ivan exclaimed. "I didn't know what I wanted! I thought if I did everything I was supposed to do, I'd be happy."

"So which was it?" Barney interjected before Winston could process the first half of what he'd said. "Threat, or you not knowing?"

At the same time, Katie said, "You hurt him twice with the same person."

Helpless, Ivan turned to Winston, who was still burning with anger. "I'm not lying, Winst. It was both."

Winston blinked back tears. "Don't call me that right now. Why didn't you tell me he threatened you? Or tell anyone?"

Ivan fell silent.

"Did he do that to your face?"

"No."

Winston's eyes traveled downwards, and the indigo escaping Ivan's coat sleeves ran through him like jagged glass.

"Did he do that to your wrists?"

Ivan opened his mouth, but nothing came out, and he began to cry instead. Oh, Mike Swan had better hope he didn't cross paths with Winston anytime soon.

"He told me," Ivan said, "I was doing the right thing."

"And you believed him? Ivan, he's a bigot!"

"He made it sound like you were the bigot!" Ivan said. "I didn't know what to think, and even when I thought I knew he sucked, I couldn't tell anyone how he treated me. It would have gotten press, and then you'd have found out."

Winston was utterly disgusted. "And we wouldn't have wanted that, would we?"

"Please," Ivan begged, "I didn't want to hurt you."

Winston inhaled. "I'm sorry about what happened to you with Swan," he said, "and I think you need to press charges. He's a monster. But you still lied to me."

Something broke in Ivan's face, but it was nothing compared to what Winston felt on the inside. He would not cry. He wouldn't. Not for Ivan. Ivan "cognitive dissonance" Notte.

"You lied because you weren't sure if I was worth leaving Galaxsea for."

"I—"

"I was just an experiment for you, wasn't I?" Winston demanded, his temper running away with him.

"Winston, no."

"Wasn't I?" he repeated, crying despite his convictions.

"No, you aren't."

"You choose that evil fucking company every time," Winston said, in freefall. "You choose pride every time."

"Not anymore I don't."

Winston started to turn away. "Forgive me if I don't believe you."

"I lied because I wanted to be with you," Ivan said.

"Maybe I don't want to be with you!" Winston hollered, his chest actually physically aching. "Maybe I don't want to be with a liar, or a bigot, or a coward! My Soulmate is none of those things!"

Though the room was blurry with tears, Winston saw enough to know that at some point during his outburst Katie and Barney had stepped out.

"You can't make me angry," Ivan said, infuriatingly tender.

"You have no fucking clue what it's like!" Winston's words were tumbling out before he could filter them. "You can afford to live in a vacuum, and it shows in how you treat other people! Did you know that where you work has consequences? Did you know that there are other Seers who can't buy their way out of discrimination?"

"Did you miss the part where I told you I was sexually harassed?" Ivan asked coolly.

"Which you told me two seconds ago, instead of when it actually happened, so I wouldn't find out you abuse animals for a living."

"I don't do it myself!" Ivan said. "I didn't even know it was happening!"

A part of Winston was ashamed at the satisfaction he felt when Ivan's voice finally raised back. A larger part wasn't.

"You turned a blind eye to Seymour's suffering," Winston said. "You had the power to change things."

"No, I didn't!"

"Funny," Winston sneered, "because you keep saying that to excuse your shitty behavior, while people like me, Katie, and Barney have to bend over backwards to fix your messes."

Something changed in Ivan's face.

"Do you want me to leave you?" he asked.

"I'd thought you already had!" He hated that Ivan had been hurt. He hated Galaxsea. He hated Swan. He hated Ivan.

They fell into a ringing silence. Winston tried to steady his breathing, but his pulse was thrumming in his ears. Ivan didn't meet his eyes.

"You were gone for two weeks," Winston pointed out. "You said you thought you were better off."

Ivan shook his head. "I…"

"Don't care about the Rezzies. Say it. Make it easier."

"I do care." Ivan took Winston's hand, and his skin was cool and smooth on his, still a bit damp from rain, or sweat, or both. Winston wished he could have enjoyed it.

"You can't care about the Rezzies and work at Galaxsea."

Ivan shook his battered head, his entire form screaming desperation. "I thought it was..."

"For the best?"

"Temporary! I thought it was the smartest—"

Winston jerked his hand out of Ivan's grip. "I can't even look at you anymore." He turned away, his heart breaking all over again. "I wish you didn't know a damn thing about me."

"Winst—"

Winston whirled on him, overcome. "I said I don't want you to know me! I don't want to be your second choice after your job! I don't want you to be embarrassed over spending time with me because I'm poor! I don't give a fuck that you've failed your mission to be the perfect Young Republican, and it isn't my job to help you unlearn all the bigoted baggage you're carrying so you can stop hating yourself! I can't," he said, "keep letting you hurt me for your own personal progress narrative! Because I know I'll let you until I have nothing left!" He shuddered, his hand sticky with the juice he'd squeezed out of the apple.

"But," Ivan's voice cracked, and he started to cry again, "I want to help you save him."

"Please." Winston wasn't falling for crocodile tears anymore. He was done being the fool.

"No, please. Winst, I can't go back there and watch that animal die."

"So leave."

"It isn't that easy! I haven't looked for a job in forever and I'm scared of failing and not having anything—"

"Oh, *you're* scared of failing?" Winston might have laughed, had their current discourse not been so grave. "What, are you scared you'll accidentally buy a third yacht?"

"Fuck you!" said Ivan, with a discomposure that surprised Winston. "Fuck you for not thinking I'm good enough! All I want is to be a person you respect, but I'll never be good enough…"

There was more after this, but it was lost in the sobbing. Perhaps some of it might have been audible, if Winston hadn't been struck dumb by the sight of Ivan doubled over crying, his elbows in the flour Winston had dusted the countertop with an hour ago.

"Lying definitely won't make me respect you," Winston said cautiously.

"It's not just that," Ivan sniffed, straightening up. "You're brave, and confident, and creative, and," he gestured vaguely, "I don't know, steadfast." Winston couldn't help but smirk at this, thinking *Cornell*. "You're like the most incredible person I've ever met; I don't just want you, I want to be like you, too, but I

269

keep chickening out every time I try to change and I know it's totally within your rights not to want me, and I'll be fine if you don't, but I can't leave here with you thinking of me as this entitled, shallow brat with yachts."

Winston was speechless. Eventually, though he was itching to do a number of other things, he steadied himself and asked, "Did you tell them about Seymour?"

Ivan's face, somehow, fell even further. The poor man looked like he belonged in an expressionist painting. "Of course not," he said, hurt. "Did you not hear any of what I just said? I even went to see him."

"What?" At this, Winston's surprise was elevated. *I've been there every night. How closely did we pass? What would have happened if we'd met?*

Ivan didn't restate, only looked at Winston, who ran the former's declarations through his head. He had expected the love, that was a given, but to be respected by someone, moreover someone like Ivan…that surprised him.

He was right about the fuckups, and Winston didn't take running into the arms of Mike Swan lightly, but Winston also didn't take lightly Ivan's ability to acknowledge and own his fuckups. Winston wished he had it within himself to do the same. Maybe someday Ivan would teach him.

They looked at each other for a few seconds, and then Winston, feeling a little drunk, said, "I really love you."

Ivan covered his mouth with a hand, starting to cry again, and looking away as he did so, unpresumptuous, unassuming. Winston came to him and hugged him without concern for the bruises he did or didn't know about. As Ivan's arms wrapped around his waist, Winston buried his nose in his hair, inhaling rain, and forgiveness, and him. Bruised as Winston's ability to trust was, he knew he could trust Ivan to correct his mistakes, and that made Ivan feel safer than the man who never made any in the first place.

I'll always forgive him, the realization hit Winston with a pang. *Ivan, the dead man's son. The better man.*

They held each other, swaying in their little pocket of bread, rosemary, and flour, sheltered from the downpour. Their breathing was even, their fears assuaged, at least before Winston made the mistake of opening his eyes to see Katie, Barney, and his mother all watching them through the window between the back room and the shop front. Katie was pinching the bridge of her nose, while Barney held a hand over his mouth. His mother was rather violently gesturing to the apple he still held.

With a severe glare towards their audience, Winston kissed Ivan on the forehead. "Do me a favor?"

Ivan, blushing, pulled away slightly. "Of course."

"Eat this." Embarrassed, Winston shoved the half-eaten fruit at him.

Eyes widening, Ivan mouthed, "Witchcraft?" before turning around and jumping at the faces in the window. When he swiveled to Winston again, he was nearly as red as the half-eaten fruit.

"Christ."

"Doubtful." Winston wondered what deity they *would* be pissing off if they didn't complete the spell.

"Well," Ivan gave a sympathetic eye roll, "you said it, not me." He took a bite, one arm still wrapped around Winston, and brandished the fruit for Winston's mother, who grinned and clapped as an unenthusiastic Barney and Katie glowered. The sight made Winston want to resolve to start looking for new apartments, which came with the bitter realization that he might not get that far, if the Seymour rescue went awry.

"I think," Winston said, "we're going to need to do some planning, if you want to come."

"We?" Ivan glanced nervously at Katie and Barney. "Now? Don't they need time to decompress?"

"Yeah, they do, but we don't have time. Especially now that I've poisoned you." He glanced at the fruit in Ivan's hand.

Ivan took another bite. "Your ability to say that like you mean it is making me nervous."

"I do mean it."

"Winston."

"Well," Winston took Ivan's free hand, dragging him out the door and past Katie and Barney's jaws, which had dropped to the floor, "My mother says never to trust a man you can't make a little nervous."

24

Ivan could have wept upon the first scent of paint. The sight of the messy tarp, the mismatched furniture, and the ever-watchful scuba lamp was even more a relief than he'd anticipated. Winston's home, like the painter himself, welcomed him back with open arms, which was more than could be said of the latter's friends.

Barney and Katie steamrolled past Ivan as though he wasn't even there, pulling Winston down the hall and out of sight. One resounding slam of a bedroom door later, Ivan was left alone to pretend that he couldn't hear the hushed argument taking place beyond the thin walls. Shivering, Ivan threw the apple core in the trash and wrapped his arms around himself, his soaked clothes like a second skin where the rain had made it past his coat. By the window, the lamp's yellow glow stood guard against a green twilight, and Ivan realized that although there were still droplets of rain on the glass, he could no longer hear its rhythm in the room's silence.

Just as he realized the other implication of this silence, the door opened again, and Katie approached him, trailed by Winston and Barney. Ivan took an involuntary step back.

Winston brushed off his little table, and a few rogue M&M's and pennies clattered to the floor, followed by the flutter of an abandoned playing card. The three of them sat down at once, and it took an expectant moment for Ivan to realize they were waiting for him.

"You work for Galaxsea," Katie said as soon as he joined them.

"I've hated every day of it." As soon as Ivan gave himself permission to say it aloud, he realized how true it was. "And I'm leaving as soon as it's safe."

"You've told no one anything?"

"Nothing. And," he turned to Winston, "I also took some precautionary measures around Mike." He told them about the phone with the pictures, now buried in the sand.

Barney pointed out, "All the photos are probably on his computer, too."

Unfortunately, he was right. Ivan took a moment to think, then said, "I could wipe it. I can't do much about his personal computer, but I still work at Galaxsea, so I at least can get to his work desktop."

"Wipe the whole drive, not just that folder," said Winston.

Ivan nodded. He supposed if he wanted to be even safer about it, he could enlist Alli's help. If he told her even half of what Mike had done to him, she would have no qualms with hurting Galaxsea, especially given how the company had treated her this year.

They fell into a silence, so Ivan turned to Winston again. "Are you sure Seymour's ready to hunt for himself? What about ocean currents?" The Pacific Ocean was no joke, and Ivan wasn't convinced any amount of swimming circles in a stagnant pool would prepare the whale for it.

"He's as ready to hunt as he'll ever be, but there are some things I can't teach him," Winston said. "The currents are one. We also can't know if he'll be able to find his way back to L pod. Or what kinds of diseases he's at risk for. Hell, it'll be a lot colder out there, so even something like hypothermia or pneumonia…"

All of this made release sound like a poorly mediated idea indeed.

"But," Winston continued, "he'll remember what to do."

Ivan supposed they would just have to hope he would. The actual plan, which Winston went on to outline, was less dependent on blind faith than the rest of Seymour's future. Each of them would arrive separately at Seymour's pool. Barney would drive there in his RAM pickup, using a passcode from their break-in to get in through the employee entrance. He would leave the RAM for Winston and Ivan, and spend the night playing lookout from the *Void*, Galaxsea's newest death trap of a ride. In a worst-case scenario where they needed a quick escape, he would be responsible for detonating a series of discreet explosives that would collapse the ride in such a way that, if all went well, would look like the result of a lack of maintenance. Winston would drive the larger truck that would carry Seymour to the ocean.

"Wait, you're going to *drive?*" Ivan asked.

Winston looked at the table. "Yeah."

"Do you have a license?"

"No," he conceded, raising his voice upon seeing the expression on Ivan's face, "but listen, there's no other option. I've driven illegally before, and I'm pretty good at it."

"Maybe with cars!" Ivan shrilled. "Not trucks, much less whatever industrial thing is designed to transport an adult bull orca."

"Look, Barney needs to take the RAM back. This is my production, so I'm driving. I need the wheel between my own two hands."

Ivan turned to Barney. "And you're okay with this?"

Barney raised his eyebrows in a way that made Ivan's nose throb.

"Where are you planning on releasing him?" Ivan asked.

Winston ignored the look Katie and Barney exchanged beside him. "About twenty miles outside of the city, north of Lynnwood, but before Whidbey."

"You're releasing him *in the Sound*?" Ivan couldn't believe how reckless they were being. If Seymour couldn't find his way out into the open ocean in time, they couldn't rule out the possibility of Robert Cass, in all his hotheadedness, attempting to recapture the whale. It wasn't as if there was any shortage of whale watching boats to spot him, either.

Winston's sigh was impatient. "Better to release him into the Sound and hope he finds his way out than to try to make it to open sea and have him die en route. His organs weren't meant to be pressed down under his body-weight like that; to have him out of water for any amount of time is risky. Plus, the Sound is calmer than the ocean. It'll be a kind of practice ground for him."

Ivan had to bring it up. "Winst, he's killed people in the past—"

"Only because he was captive," Winston insisted. At Ivan's silence, he pressed, "He didn't eat *us* when we fell in. The only reason he attacked people in the past was because of stress."

"But Cass doesn't know that," Ivan said. He could just picture him and Mike catching and killing Seymour while he was still in the Sound, playing it off like they were heroes for saving the city from a man-eating whale. "If he stays there too long, people might come after him out of fear."

"Well then," Barney looked rather pointedly at Ivan, "I guess our very own Galaxsea employee will have to stop them."

Ivan couldn't think of a retort or a way he could possibly intervene in something like that. "So we're at the pool with the supplies," he changed the subject, "how are we going to get him to the ocean?"

From there, they would move the chain so one end stuck out either end of the trailer. One end would be attached to the RAM, the other to a large piece of aluminum that Winston had made sure was large enough for Seymour. They would coax Seymour into a net and then onto the sheet of metal, which would be placed on a homemade conveyor of steel pipes. By slowly moving the RAM forward, they would pull Seymour into the trailer. After covering the whale with ice and lotion, they would disconnect the RAM and the all clear would be given to Barney, who would drive it home. They'd reconnect the trailer to the truck, and drive like hell.

"And," Winston finished, looking at him, "of course we need all the hands we can get. It'll be nice having an extra person." Ivan was both pleased they seemed to want him there and relieved they weren't hinging the entire operation on him. A part of him still thought the whole mission was mad, of course, but the thoroughness of Winston's answers made the whole thing seem almost…doable.

Ivan's eyes wandered to a tattered copy of *The Anarchist's Cookbook* lying atop a stack of books nearby. "Are you really going to blow things up?"

Barney said, "Look, it's clear you're not comfortable—"

"I just want to know." Ivan couldn't deny he thought Barney's skepticism was fair. But then, he supposed his own had some merit as well.

"If it's an emergency," Barney answered after a hard silence. "But again, nothing fiery. An explosion and a stolen whale on the same night looks a certain way. But if the ride collapses, and it looks like someone was slacking during inspections…"

"It's more dubious," Ivan finished his thought. "Everyone that's visited in the past God-knows-how-long will be horrified." It would look like Galaxsea not only didn't care about its animals, but also its customers. "Have you thought about doing it even without an emergency?"

"What, you're actually *for* this?"

"Winston."

The painter turned to him and raised his brows, and in spite of everything that had happened between them, Ivan felt jittery. Like they were across a table again, and he'd been bought coffee. Ivan had thought him soft when they'd first met, but he realized now that perhaps he was the soft one. Winston reverse-tamed whales and rode the sea during storms. He risked his life for the things he believed in.

And Ivan…well, he didn't know if he would ever be strong. But he could try.

"I want to save this whale with you."

"Until it goes wrong," Katie's voice was just as edged as Winston's gaze. "Tell us, what are you gonna do when the cops show up? When the rest of us get caught or the whale dies?"

"Then," Ivan said, "I'm paying for all of our lawyers."

This promise—and it *was* a promise—shut her and Barney up thoroughly.

Winston smiled and stood, clapping his hands once. "We'll have to time it perfectly. I've looked at the forecast, and the highest chance of serious rain this week is tomorrow night. If it follows us, it'll cover our tracks a little bit."

"We'll have to hurry, then," Katie said. Winston's head snapped over to her in surprise.

"We? Katie, your…"

"I don't know if I'll have to move once production of the EP starts," she said. "This might be my last chance to do something."

"You mean…?"

"I mean you need as many people as you can get, if you're going to move a whale. I'm going in with you."

Ivan, filled with a profound ache, watched Winston wrap his arms around her.

&

When he tried to follow Katie and Barney out the door, Ivan was surprised to hear Winston call him back. He found him picking his nails, sitting cross-legged on his quilted bed.

"I know we were heated earlier," Winston raised his head. "Did Swan really not break your nose?"

Ivan crossed his arms, too aware of his body. Winston's room never smelled like paint; it smelled like dust and cinnamon incense. "It wasn't him."

"Who, then?"

It wasn't like he could lie, was it? He'd learned that lesson enough times for it to stick. Luckily for him, Winston did the hard part and named the name.

"Was it Barney?"

Ivan lowered his eyes to the carpet. When he finally had the courage to look up again, Winston had his face in his hands.

"Fuck, he made a comment earlier. I didn't want to believe him."

"It's fine—"

"No, it's not!" Winston exclaimed. "Swan manipulated you. You didn't deserve that. Or," he gestured to Ivan's face, "that."

There was a lump in Ivan's throat. Winston sighed.

"I should've been there for you."

"You were," Ivan said, his voice cracking. "I just didn't realize it was this bad." Crying hurt his nose. "I didn't realize I was this bad."

He felt raw and exposed, standing in the doorway, but it was as much startling as relieving when Winston told him to "come here." Nonetheless, Ivan managed to grasp a thread of confidence and sit down on the edge of the bed, doing his best to ignore how dejecting it was to feel like an intruder in what had once been such a familiar place.

"I'll get therapy," he said, and Winston gave a soft, attractive laugh as he wrapped an arm around his shoulders.

"Okay."

"It's all so natural for you. I'm so afraid I don't belong—" Though he was doing his best to maintain a grip on himself, being in such close proximity after a week apart was more than a little intoxicating, and suddenly all his fears were spilling out. He leaned his head on Winston's shoulder, and listened to his response.

"I don't mean to alarm you, but there are more than three Seers in the world. You know that, right?"

Ivan blubbered something so incoherent, about how they were only 2% of the population, that he was surprised Winston understood it.

"Yeah, but we're in the city now. There's a lot more of us in the countryside where it's more colorful. And Seattle's surrounded by national parks, so even for a city, it's not too bad." Winston gave Ivan a squeeze. "I'll tell Barney and them to back off your case. And I know I'm fantastic company, but I think you'll feel much better once you know more people that See."

Ivan sniffed, and bit back a groan of pain. "You shouldn't have to babysit me."

Winston sighed. "Ivan?"

Ivan looked at him.

"You belong. Even if you suck at hopping fences."

"Maybe I'm more of a poster-making guy."

Winston grinned and kissed his forehead. "Or you can just wait for us to get home safe." After a moment, he added, "I hope you know I'll take you back even if you don't help with Seymour. Swan is really dangerous, especially for you."

Ivan appreciated the sentiment, but the truth was that he wasn't doing it for Winston. He wanted to save the whale because it was a good thing to do, and he'd realized that doing good things, for the people and the world around him, was the only thing that really made him feel better. He felt more himself planning to save Seymour than he ever had sitting in the conference room and debating what Galaxsea would do with him. But, being human, this sort of feeling was incredibly hard for him to vocalize, so he only looked at Winston and said, "I really, really want to," praying that his eyes would communicate the rest. "Not just because I want to be your Soulmate."

"I don't think I like that word anymore."

"Why?" Ivan asked, startled.

"It's like I said before. Too much pressure. For both of us."

Ivan blinked. "Is there something you prefer?"

"Boyfriend," Winston said, "works just fine."

25

The next day, as Ivan was walking out of Galaxsea, Alli stopped him halfway through the lobby.

"I did it."

The fountain in the center of the floor trickled, its calm a stark contrast to Ivan's rapid pulse. It wasn't safe for them to discuss this here. There were still potential eavesdroppers behind Bluetooth earpieces, and besides, Ivan didn't want to be in the building when Mike discovered his ravaged computer.

"Thanks." He attempted to end the conversation there, but her fingers tightened around his arm. As he turned to face her again, she dropped it, and they stood looking at each other.

She appeared to struggle for words for a moment, and Ivan waited. His patience was tried by his alarm, however, when her eyes brimmed with tears. She blinked through them furiously, and, looking around, said, "I think this is a bad company."

I'm glad you think so, given that you just wiped the new VP's hard drive, Ivan thought. He might have said it aloud, if not for the expression on his sister's face. For the first time, the full grief of their dad's death was written plainly across it. Together, they were an island of grief for their colleagues to navigate around.

"Yeah," he said, looking down at his shoes. He was restless, being in the same building as Mike.

"You should press charges," she said, the strategist again. "We both should."

Ivan sighed, raising his head to look at her. More than anything, he wanted to get away from Mike and never, ever come back, but today, he was reminded that Alli was his little sister, and if Galaxsea had put him in over his head, it had likely done that and more to her. Ivan wanted to protect her, and if pressing charges would give her justice, then he was happy to support her in it.

Today, however, was not the day for that. "I have to go." He started to back away. "Be careful."

"Oh, of course." She didn't move to follow, and when he turned around, he got a few steps before she called after him, "Ivan!"

He looked over his shoulder.

"I support you," she said, "before…" She trailed off, silently glancing at the suits schooling around them.

It was all he could manage to nod curtly and hope she saw solidarity in his form. He called Winston when he cleared today's gaggle of protesters, none of whom, thankfully, recognized him from a few weeks ago.

"Hey, it's me." Ivan glanced up at a fiery sky as he walked, his ears still ringing with Alli's farewell. "I'm heading out now. I didn't want to slip off too early."

"No, that's smart," Winston said. *"Does it look like rain where you are?"*

There were no clouds to be seen in any direction, and the air was dry. Ivan hesitated to answer, not wanting to exacerbate the anxiety in Winston's voice. Instead, he listened to chatter from pedestrians, bells in doors of coffee shops, someone leaning on their horn. Today, it all seemed like something from another planet.

"Well," Winston read his silence, *"we'll just have to go on with it anyway."*

"We could wait for rain," Ivan suggested, though the idea was slightly maddening. "It's not too late to turn back."

"No, we really couldn't," Winston said. Then he added, *"It isn't too late for you to."*

"Stop." Now was not the time for second guessing.

"Alright. Try to eat something before you come. It's gonna be a long night."

By the time Ivan got home, the calming effects of this conversation had dissipated. Everything, right down to changing clothes, was a challenge. Ivan kept blinking and realizing he'd been staring at the pantry, or into the open fridge, or at the stovetop he'd just lit without the faintest clue of what he intended to cook on it, for several minutes.

Though it was safer for him and Winston not to be seen together tonight, waiting the hours away alone was agonizing. The sky shifted from red to onyx. An hour before they were supposed to meet, Ivan left to pick up a few final supplies the group had asked him to bring. Just as the elevator doors opened in front of him, however, he turned around, went back to his apartment, and shoved two pieces of bread between his teeth before departing once more.

By the time Ivan arrived at Seymour's pool, the air had turned cool and muggy, and his shirt was clinging to his skin. Initially, it seemed that no one was there, and Ivan was just beginning to panic when Katie stepped out of the shadows, giving him a mild spook.

"What took you so long?" she hissed, while his pulse slowed back to as normal as was achievable in their current situation. Katie jerked her head to where Winston was dragging a massive, finely-meshed net behind him like it was high fashion. "He didn't want to start without you. Is that all you brought?"

Ivan glanced down at the value size container of premium lotion in his left hand, and the massive, melting bag of ice in his right. If he'd driven, he could have brought more, but he was out of practice and, even if he had elected to do it illegally, he didn't believe tonight was the wisest of nights to test how much he remembered. Katie appeared dissatisfied with this excuse, but she ultimately settled for an eye roll before going to help Winston, who looked more nervous than Ivan had ever seen him.

Backing up the trailer to the pool was painful. Either trucks had no option not to beep like an atom bomb was about to be tested when they were in reverse, or Winston couldn't find whatever button shut it off. Though Ivan was certain all the noise they were making was loud enough to be heard from Robert Cass's penthouse suite, Winston and Katie both insisted on inching forward and backward until they had the trailer perfectly lined up. In the meantime, Seymour swam, merry and oblivious.

Once it was lined up, Winston and Katie disconnected the trailer from the truck, and drove the latter aside. Ivan, meanwhile, pulled the massive chain through the trailer and attached it to the RAM pickup. The ramp attached to the trailer was already a conveyor of sorts, though the pipes in it were far narrower than the free-rolling steel pipes Winston laid down inside the trailer. Whenever the chain shifted slightly, those closest to the edge rolled precariously.

Finally, Winston, Ivan, and Katie dragged the massive sheet of aluminum Seymour would sit on to the ramp. Afterwards, panting, they all took a moment to survey their work. Ivan didn't have to look at the other two to know they were thinking the same thing he was.

Winston reached into his back pocket with one hand, wiping sweat off his brow with the other. His screen briefly illuminated his face. "It's past midnight."

Ivan wasn't certain if it was prudent to ask whether Winston had really thought through the physics of getting a five-ton animal into the trailer, which suddenly seemed very, very far off the ground. At the moment, even airlifting Seymour out via helicopter looked friendlier.

Ivan turned towards the gentle sound of moving water. Next to him, Winston had a tiny, silver whistle perched between his teeth.

"I thought you were training him to not be trained?" Ivan asked, while Seymour drifted slowly towards them. *That's a massive animal.*

"Except for this," Winston admitted, alarm rushing into his voice. "Alright, grab the net, grab the net—!"

Katie ran to the other side of the pool, while Ivan dropped to his knees and reached into the freezing water up to his shoulder, which actually felt quite good in the humidity. After grasping wildly for a few seconds, his hand finally closed around the net, which was so tightly knit it felt almost like fabric. After slipping once and losing his balance, Ivan successfully dragged it out past Seymour's tail. It was only when he got there that he realized, with a plummeting stomach, what precisely they were going to do.

Across the pool, Winston soothed Seymour (and perhaps himself), rubbing his massive head all over. "Shh, it's gonna be fine." Standing, he raised his voice and called, "Everyone bring me your edges."

Muscles straining, Ivan and Katie heaved their portions of the net out of the water. They were halfway to Winston when Seymour moved. The former swore and blew on his silver whistle, but it was too late. With surprising dexterity, Seymour did a complete 180, turned himself around, and escaped the net completely, gliding to the other end of the pool.

And they did it all again.

And the damned fish did it. Again.

"Don't you know we're trying to help you?" Ivan hollered after the whale's retreating form, no longer caring if the racket they were making forced Barney into demolition mode.

Winston ran a hand through his curls, bowing his head. "Who wants to look at the clock?"

There were several beats of silence before Katie reported, "2:06."

"Christ," Winston swore. Ivan looked miserably up at the benign grey clouds feathered across the stars. Rain or not, they needed to hurry; it wouldn't be long before park employees started showing up for the morning shift.

On the next attempt, Winston successfully hooked the net around Seymour, forming a massive burrito of whale and fear that thrashed so violently it launched Ivan into the frigid water. When he managed to crawl back to shore, the net was hooked up to the chain.

"You okay?" Winston asked.

Whether it was shiver or shudder that wracked his body, Ivan didn't know. "Fine."

Winston nodded at Katie. "Hardest part, then we're out of here fast."

Katie jogged around the trailer to the RAM, the car door shut, and Winston positioned himself in eyeshot of her.

"Slow, okay?"

Ivan didn't hear the response, he just met Winston by Seymour, who was motionless but giving off the vibe that he wanted to eat everyone in the general vicinity.

"Hold onto him," Winston said. "If he panics, we're done."

Ivan nodded, reaching in through the net and rubbing the whale's head with slight hysteria. "Alright?" he murmured. "It's gonna be fine. I know you won't up and die on us."

The chain pulled taut, and the net grew tighter around Seymour, lifting his tail up slightly behind him. Slowly, but still far too fast, he was dragged to the edge of the pool.

"Guide his head up, guide his head up!" Winston ordered, and he and Ivan put their hands under the whale's chin as he was dragged out of the water.

The chain, though it had taken two arms for Ivan to carry, now looked flimsy as a dog leash. Frigid water streamed off the net, soaking both him and Winston as they simultaneously tried to keep flippers from being broken, Seymour from panicking, themselves from getting crushed, and the whale's body from falling off the ramp. Ivan said a string of words that would have made his grandmother faint, pushing at the whale as though he was strong enough to have any effect on what was about to happen.

"Katie, sto—"

"We need the momentum or he's never gonna move!" Ivan snarled, shutting Winston up. He nearly jumped out of his skin when Seymour actually *squealed*.

"Shhhh," Winston hushed desperately, patting the whale's nose, "it's all gonna be—"

Seymour thrashed, and Ivan's heart damn near stopped. His shoes squeaked on the poolside turf as he leaned his entire weight into the whale. Winston guided a massive flipper onto the metal sheet, and Ivan, as soon as Seymour seemed a bit calmer, ran around to guide his chin up again and make sure the sides of the sheet weren't digging into his skin.

All at once, the whale was on the sheet, slowly moving up the ramp as Katie gassed the RAM.

"Keep going," Winston said, his hands still on Seymour. "Come on, just get up into the…"

With a creak, Seymour rolled inside the trailer. Several pipes rolled off its other end and clattered to the ground. Winston hollered for Katie to stop before sprinting with Ivan to the trailer's other side.

Katie had long since taken her foot off the gas, but Seymour continued to roll along the conveyor, whistling and clicking all the way. Winston grabbed the doors and slammed them shut in the whale's face, while Ivan, realizing what was about to happen, spun back the way he'd come, to catch the rebound. On the way, he slipped on the wet ground and fell flat on his back. Without giving himself time to feel the bruise that was undoubtedly starting to form, he grabbed the ramp to the pool and, with all his strength, threw it upwards so Seymour wouldn't slide back into the water.

The whale hit the back door, and Ivan lost his grip. Beside him, the ramp hit the poolside turf, which normally muffled everything that hit it, so loudly it still hurt his ears. Clenching his teeth, Ivan braced himself for a moral-crushing splash, but after several seconds passed with nothing but the ringing in his ears, he opened his eyes to see Seymour had stopped, his tail slightly overhanging the edge of the trailer.

In a blur of orange and stress, Winston rushed to his side, phone in hand. "We've got company. Barney says we have time, but I'd rather leave now."

"What about his tail?" Even on the conveyor, pushing the whale by hand would be impossible, and using the RAM ran the risk of sending him tumbling out the other end.

There could be no emotion to describe the look on Winston's face other than shame. "He's gonna have to get bruised."

Ivan helped Katie clean up while Winston disconnected the chain from the net and pulled it into the back of the RAM, link by link. When this last was finished, Winston reached into the back of the pickup and pulled out a massive bag of water, lifting it for Ivan and Katie to see. "Ice."

Katie wordlessly closed the trailer doors closest to them, while Ivan approached and put his hand on it silently. "It's still cold." And that was what mattered, he hoped. At the very least, the bag proved to be a useful vessel for retrieving extra water from Seymour's pool for Winston to pour over the whale before Ivan followed with the lotion. On one such trip, Winston's heavy footfalls suddenly stopped, and Ivan looked up from covering Seymour's collapsed dorsal fin (which was far heavier than it looked) to see, through the mouth of the trailer, Katie wrapping him in a hug.

"Don't cry," she said. "Crying is for later. Bring that whale home. And you," her voice now bounced off the walls around Ivan, surrounding him, "keep him safe."

Ivan paused, and nodded at her. "I will."

She turned back to Winston. "I love you so much, do you understand?"

He gave a tearful sniff. "Yeah."

"Good," she clapped him on the shoulder, "then make me proud."

And with that, she dashed out of view. Not a minute later, Ivan heard the RAM driving away. As soon as Ivan and Winston left, she'd pick up Barney from the edge of the park, and for the two of them, it would be the end of the night's adventure.

Seymour squealed again, and Ivan tried his best to comfort him as he'd seen Winston do. Suddenly, though, his hands ran along something that didn't feel as rubbery as the rest of Seymour's skin, at the base of his left flipper.

"Can whales get rashes?" he asked as Winston's footsteps clambered closer.

"Yeah," Winston answered, now joining Ivan in spreading lotion, "it's stress."

Ivan was overcome with a rush of pity for Seymour.

Winston's phone pinged again, and he pulled it out, smearing lotion all over the screen as he perused Barney's update. "Alright, five more minutes of this, then we go." Seymour whirred, and Ivan pet his nose. "When this is over," Winston went back to lotioning the whale's other flipper, unpeeling the net from around it in the process, "we're getting steaks."

Ivan blacked out for half a second at the thought. "God, and nice wine." There were worse things he could do than show up to work tomorrow—or, rather, today—a bit tipsy.

"And potatoes," Winston stood up, wiping his hands off on his jeans, "drowned in butter."

Ivan would personally have loved to be drowned in butter himself after this whole thing was over. "With bacon."

"And chocolate cake." Winston grabbed his hand, giving Seymour one last pat with his other, and led Ivan out of the trailer. Winston jumped first, then held a hand up to Ivan to help him down.

They closed the doors on Seymour's tail, forcing it inside. The scene appeared mostly sterile, as Katie had gathered the fallen pipes along with the rest of their straggling supplies, before she'd left. However, one pipe had rolled into Seymour's pool and long since sunk all fifty feet to the bottom. It gleamed frustratingly up at them, but Winston ordered Ivan to leave it before they finally connected the trailer to the truck itself, and Winston climbed into the driver's seat.

Ivan only realized once he'd taken his own seat that he was trembling, his hands barely able to keep steady around the container of lotion in his lap. The empty, greasy bag from the ice was crackling in Winston's similarly affected hands.

"Should one of us be back there with him?" Ivan asked uncertainly.

Winston shook his head. "You could get crushed," he said. "Plus, I need you up here to keep me from...losing my grip." He stared straight ahead, and his phone pinged again. This was it. Ivan took his pruney hand and squeezed it with his own.

"Lucky whale, to have a human like you."

With the first, miraculous crack of thunder in the distance, Winston put the keys in the ignition, and they fled the scene. When the gates opened, Ivan couldn't help but burst out into hysterics that only heightened as they flew down the highway, into the green, towards the storm. Though his eyes were blurry from the mirthful tears in them, Ivan caught Winston casting occasional glances at him, but these ultimately did less to quell the laughter than the horrible ache of his healing face.

Once he calmed, Ivan, feeling a little guilty, watched for cops, while Winston white-knuckled it to their destination. Rare lightning flashed around them, and the front end of rush hour made its way into the city. But they weren't going that way. Mile after mile their hope grew, and the lanes disappeared, until they reached a little side-road nearly completely overgrown by wilderness.

"Huh," Winston said, as they screeched to a stop. "It was bigger on foot."

"No shit!" Ivan said. There was no way they were going to make it down that with a five-ton whale aboard. "We're gonna crack through the pave—Winst, what are you doing?" They were turning. Ivan wasn't certain if he heard another crack of thunder or the crack of a small tree.

"Winston, you can't just—"

"Tell me again what I can't do!" Winston roared, and Ivan decided this was one of those rare occasions in which it was safer not to worry. That didn't stop him, however, from cursing harder than he'd ever cursed before in his *head* while they were crashing through the undergrowth. Trees snapped, pavement cracked, Ivan was certain he got whiplash several separate times, and shrubs were ripped out by the root. If it hadn't been dry for the last few days, they'd probably have gotten stuck in the mud.

Pavement changed to gravel, and they broke through the trees with nothing but water in front of them. Ivan and Winston swore simultaneously, the latter slamming on the brakes as Seymour squealed pitifully behind them.

They ground to a bumpy halt. It was noticeably lighter out now, but behind them, the sky was darkening, the cracks of thunder getting louder. Even Ivan, who'd grown up where thunderstorms were common, felt a prick of apprehension at the wind picking up, an apprehension he hadn't felt for years.

Juvenile trees, their leaves still bright green, had sprouted through the gravel, which was dotted all over with shrubs and completely covered in a carpet of grasses. It was more like driving through an open woodland than driving down a path, but as thick as the trunks of the baby trees were, there was no mistaking the deep blue expanse beyond them. Ivan prayed that Seymour had enough sense to weave his way through the peninsulas and islands before Galaxsea could find him.

The little wooden boathouse was so consumed by moss, grass, and tendrils of vines that, at first, Ivan didn't even see it slouching next to the water. At its feet, the restless waves lapped at a small, concrete ramp.

Brilliant, Ivan thought. He was about to say the same to Winston when the latter ordered: "Get out."

Ivan started, stung. "What?"

"Get out and guide me," Winston clarified. "Both our rearview mirrors got knocked off on the way here."

Sure enough, they had been. Ivan hopped out of the truck, shivering at the wind on his wet clothes and hair. The concrete platform didn't look wide enough, not by a long shot. The thing was designed to launch personal boats, not a vehicle of this size.

"Winst—we're gonna have to find another way," he shouted.

"There's no time," Winston said. "He can't stay in there much longer."

Ivan looked back at the wrecked pavement behind them. There really was no going back, either. Even this truck's specialty tires, designed to hold the weight of such a huge animal, would be damaged after rolling through so many jagged pieces of pavement and splintered tree trunks. He hoped the storm wouldn't delay Barney or Katie in picking them up, because even if recognition wasn't an issue, this truck wouldn't be able to get them home.

"Alright. You have zero inches on either side. Just go straight."

The truck beeped loudly as Winston put it in reverse, and the trailer wobbled dangerously on the too-small ramp. Water lapped at the back tires.

"Okay, stop."

Winston put on the emergency break and stepped out to meet Ivan behind the trailer, sloshing through icy, knee deep water to stand opposite him. The artist's curls were the only bit of warmth amongst the darkening sea and woods.

"Okay," Winston said, sounding admirably calm, "when we lower this ramp, there won't be a lot of time. He's gonna come rolling out really fucking fast, and he'll kill us if we're caught behind him."

Ivan nodded. He could imagine that five tons of sea life would be lethal, rolling towards you on an incline.

Winston took a deep breath, steadying himself. "Okay, on three." He reached up for the ramp's release lever. "One."

"Two," Ivan said.

"Three."

With a screech, the ramp fell down, clamoring to the ground. Winston and Ivan leapt out of the way as a truck-full of metal pipes rolled into the sea, each bobbing on the waves until one end dipped down and their weight pulled them under. As the last one disappeared, Seymour still sat motionless at the dark end of the trailer.

Ivan wasn't sure if looking at the whale or looking at Winston was worse. Even the birds had hushed their anticipatory chatter. In that moment, there was only a terrible word, echoing endlessly in both of their minds, a word that would forever be laced with dread following that day:

Stuck.

The whale almost looked like he knew, or maybe that was just Ivan projecting on the pathetic image in front of him. Dorsal fin collapsed, onyx skin slathered with crusting lotion—it was a criminal state for such an animal to be in.

And Winston…heartbreak could not begin to describe the expression on his face.

"No." He shook his head. He climbed into the trailer, and Ivan watched him, frozen. "Oh, God no." Winston rushed over to where Seymour lay, flat on the sheet, surrounded by folds of net. "No, we're so close, please be okay."

Ivan climbed out of the water and met Winston at the back of the trailer, unable to breathe, unable to think. He almost didn't dare to check if the whale was still breathing, but he did, and he was. However, Seymour's skin didn't feel cool enough to belong to a whale. Despite all their efforts, he was about to overheat.

"He's gonna die soon if we don't move," Ivan said, unsure where his sudden calm had come from.

Winston was sobbing, holding onto Seymour like the whale was his lifeline. "I killed him," he said. "You were right. I shouldn't have intervened. He would have had a terrible life at Galaxsea, but he wouldn't have been—"

"Don't say it," Ivan said, hatching a plan. "I know what we're going to do. Can orcas swim backwards?"

Winston sniffed. "Yeah."

"Then help me," Ivan ordered, turning around to untangle the net from Seymour's right flipper. "Make sure the net's only underneath him, not around him."

Winston didn't need to be told twice. He immediately set to work, and when that was done, they stood at the same time.

"Do you know what we're doing?" Ivan asked.

"Backing into the ocean?"

Ivan didn't confirm, just slid out of the trailer while Winston rounded it and threw himself into the driver's seat. The engine roared to life again, sounding oddly small in the coming storm, and the trailer was lowered into the sea until only the truck itself was still dry, poking out of the surf like a beached whale.

Don't think beached whale, Ivan thought as Winston put on the emergency brake and jumped out again.

"Let's go!" Winston shouted, barreling into the freezing water without a second thought. He made it look far easier than it actually was. Ivan's calves were already numb from wading out the first time, but the cold was far more acute the more of himself he exposed to it, and it took willpower to inch forward past his knees. When Ivan reached the almost-submerged back of the trailer, the water was deep enough to swim, and he kept pace easier with Winston.

"Come on," Winston called. His voice was trembling; the cold, it would seem, affected them both equally. Against his better instincts, Ivan obeyed, swimming towards where the apex predator was floating in the dark.

"Grab his tail," Winston commanded. "Guide him out."

Though Ivan was nearly certain it was achieving nothing, he grabbed Seymour's massive flukes and, praying that the whale didn't try to hit him in the head with them, did his best to pull. Winston, meanwhile, braced his legs against the back of the trailer and began to push at Seymour's snout.

The whale clicked, and it occurred to Ivan that the water was still rising.

"Winst!" he called. "The seabed!" Soon the entrance would be underwater, and if that happened, they were done for. They'd slowly drown as the sand swallowed them.

"I know!" Winston snarled, immediately going back to cooing to Seymour. "It's alright, you're home, now. You can go…" Ivan was just beginning to think that they might end up dying for this whale when, miraculously, he felt himself pushed backwards by several feet, clear from the trailer's entrance.

"Winst, get out!" Ivan got a mouthful of seawater, which he immediately retched up. He heard a splash as Winston dived, and, relieved for the time being, put a few more feet between himself and the trailer. He was horrified both by how dark it had gotten and how far they were from shore. Though the waves made it hard to tell at first, within a few seconds, the entire back of the trailer was completely submerged.

For a painful half-minute, Ivan completely forgot about Seymour. Eyes burning from salt, delirious with cold and terror, he called wildly for Winston while straining to maintain control over his numb limbs.

With a gasp, Winston surfaced beside Ivan. "Don't stop," he said, swimming back towards the whale, who appeared aware he was free of the trailer. "Help me guide him." Ideally, they would have done just that, and kept backing him up until they were in deep enough water to safely turn around, but Seymour was eager to leave. With one flap of his flippers, he moved so far so quickly that Ivan could swear he glimpsed fear in Winston's eyes.

"Help me guide him!" Winston repeated, trying in vain to grab for his tail. "He could beach himself." He swallowed a mouthful of water, and Ivan, his muscles screaming, swam to his side, knowing full well they wouldn't be getting close to the whale again.

"Winst."

"We have to help him!"

"Winston."

"He—"

"He knows what he's doing!" Ivan said, eyeing the blueish tint of Winston's lips with worry. "He remembers."

They looked back out to the Sound just in time to see Seymour's collapsed dorsal fin disappear beneath the waves.

&❧

They barely made it to shore.

Ivan and Winston didn't bother trying to hide themselves or check the front seat of the truck for hair or other giveaways. They only filled their fists with handfuls of tangled, wet grass and dragged themselves out of the water, collapsing amongst the gravel, and dirt, and wildflowers, their aching muscles seizing and their skin too numb to notice the prick of splinters from destroyed trees and woody shrubs. He and Winston pulled whatever grass was in reach around themselves, desperate for the warmth of something dry. Somewhere, the sun was rising, but the storm above them kept it shrouded in heavy grey.

"How old was he?" Ivan asked, his voice hoarse from shouting and, ironically, dehydration. A vein of lightning flashed, joining the cliffsides cradling the bay like a tightrope.

"Thirty-five," Winston said, still out of breath.

Ivan's heart sank. "So he was old. I mean, I'd heard they live for fifteen."

"Did Galaxsea teach you that?" There was a grin in his voice.

"I don't remember."

Behind them, the trees they couldn't topple groaned under the beginning of the storm's force.

"Captive is 15. On average."

Ivan looked at him. "And in the wild?"

Winston turned his eyes to the sky. "Fifty."

Ivan exhaled. The wind stilled, and it began to rain.

Epilogue

Chicago rain was not the same as Seattle rain, that was for certain. For one thing, it always came with the thunder that was so rare back home, loud cracks in-between flashes of lightning that added to the already-chaotic lights and sounds of the metropolis at night. Winston had been in no hurry to pull out his umbrella when the first hesitant drops fell, and had gotten poured on as a result, Barney and Katie pawing at his bag and cursing. Tonight was the first time Winston had seen her since she'd moved last year, and he swore she'd grown even more impatient than she'd been before.

Finally, the giant umbrella sprung up like a mushroom, and the three friends were spared from the water pouring down its sides (or, mostly spared...poor Barney still had an arm exposed to the November downpour, though Winston knew he'd sooner die than complain).

"Married life is turning you into a lightweight," Barney said to Winston, just as Katie tripped on a crack in the sidewalk. To her, he added, "And teacher life, for you."

Winston rolled his eyes, but if Ivan hadn't been sleeping off the fever he'd picked up a few days ago, they might have shared a look. Judging from the events of their honeymoon, there was little possibility either of them would be turning into lightweights anytime soon. The amount of wine and cheese they'd consumed in Italy had prepared their livers for all but the most nuclear of indulgences.

"At least mine is intentional," Katie said, bringing their leftover pasta to eye-level and frowning. "Do you think this is leaking? I'm smelling a lot of garlic."

"That's just Barney's breath," Winston said, and when Barney grabbed for him, he pulled the umbrella away, exposing his friend completely to the elements. Immediately soaked, Barney went around Katie and grabbed Winston, and the two of them scuffled until she crossed the street without them, continuing to walk parallel to them with the hood of her jacket up until they made such a show that she rejoined them.

"Umbrella privileges revoked." She took it from Winston, who didn't protest.

"Do you ever wish you'd kept doing it?" he asked Katie, referring to her singing, or rather, her singing for performance.

The cancellation of her debut album had been the primary topic of discussion at dinner, and had lasted all the way from breadsticks to entrees. Katie had gotten a chance most people never did. Though it had been years ago, he still remembered how just weeks after uploading her first EP, she'd started to get attention. Indie song charts, emails from both scam and legitimate agents, more streams than she ever had hoped for and, it so happened, an offer to sign with a label to produce a proper debut.

After years of tumult, she'd ended up teaching music classes here, instead, and not to kids who, for the most part, needed or wanted them. Katie's students were on a rotating schedule of frequent absences, with several having already disappeared before her first semester ended. She'd had to buy pretzels from the vending machine for a student whose stomach kept growling during a private conference and whom, she found out, had not eaten for over a day, because her parents hadn't fed her. And yet, Katie maintained that there were many in the class, including the ones who were suffering, who were unquestioningly brilliant, hardworking, earnest, or some mixture of the three, and they lifted the rest of the group into liveliness on all but the worst days.

"I don't know," she said finally. They stood at a crosswalk, waiting for the hand (halt) to turn to a man (walk). When it did, she continued, "I guess I do. But it's more of an impulse than anything else, if that makes sense. I know it wouldn't make me happy, even if most people think it would."

Winston supposed he understood what she meant. Ivan had helped him put his art on exhibit for a few shows, but the truth was, he felt strange advertising it. It ruined it a little, to have to put on a suit and mingle with a glass of wine and justify to everyone the uniqueness of what he was doing. In fact, his and Ivan's biggest fight since they'd married had been over the last of the showings, and Winston's asocial attitude throughout the entire thing.

Thunder cracked, and Barney and Winston jumped. The latter wondered how Katie was able to sleep through rain here, when it came at night. Hopefully it didn't wake Ivan up. The last time Seattle had gotten thunder had been over a year ago, and before that, it had been the morning of Seymour's release. Speaking of which, it had been some time since he'd gone out to visit the most infamous whale in L Pod. Maybe once Ivan was well again, they'd head out.

"I think it helps to have it not be about a brand," Katie said. "I'm writing more again, since I've started keeping it private. Or for them. It's nice not having to worry about making something worthy of public discourse."

"Do you ever sing for them?" Barney asked.

"Mostly," Katie said, "they sing for me."

"I'm glad you're happy," Winston said, "even though we miss you like hell."

They said goodbye on the front steps of the hotel where Barney, Winston, and Ivan were staying, and Katie requested Winston tell Ivan she'd missed him, though of course, this was not the same kind of missing that Winston had mentioned moments earlier. Tomorrow, they would grab brunch together before the boys headed back to the train station to chug back across the country. Winston teared up a little just thinking about it, and he knew Katie could See the redness of his eyes when he pulled away from their hug, even in the rain.

After he said goodnight to Barney in the lobby, Winston pondered what Katie had said. He supposed making art for the private eye was a beautiful thing, but then again, although he didn't like the politics of the high art world, he liked his paintings because they reached outwards and drew people in. Hell, that had been how he'd met his Soulmate, after all. Even if it had been through a portrait of a bigot (which, having no sentimentality towards, he and Ivan had thrown into the trash long ago). Winston had always associated personal art with shame—i.e. Ivan's photographs, which he still showed to no one but Winston, Alli, and his mother—but perhaps there were some cases in which there was power in privacy. Perhaps everyone progressed in different ways, in different directions, and it mattered less that they arrived at the same destination if they were always ready to pack their bags and continue onwards.

Winston was about ready to pack his bags himself. When he swiped his keycard to his and Ivan's room, which smelled of Kleenex and Nyquil and rain, he nearly fell flat on his face tripping over their suitcases, and made such a racket that he woke Ivan up.

"Sorry!" Winston whispered, after his husband rolled over and groaned. "Are you feeling better?"

"Not really."

Winston shrugged off his jacket and boots, propped his umbrella by the doorway, and set the leftover fettuccini in the minifridge. After, he crawled into bed with Ivan, despite the latter's protests, and pulled his lover's too-hot body closer, knowing he'd be sitting next to him on the train tomorrow anyway.

Their hotel was nice, but at the end of the day, it still had the degree of coldness characteristic of any temporary space. The pillows had too much give, and the comforter was thicker than the quilts at home, but Winston was looking forward to leaving this artificial softness for the hardy little house just outside of town that he and Ivan called theirs, including the salt water that sometimes ran from the faucets and the crows that made a racket every time they wanted to sleep in. Tonight, they had the crash of thunder instead of the crash of the waves, and the blaring of traffic horns instead of the conversations of corvids, to keep them awake. And yet, the muted glow of red and green traffic signals, which Winston could See out the window, brought the warm reminder that the world at large was becoming more a home each day under the guiding hands of those that loved it.

Acknowledgements

When I originally set out to write Saving Seymour, it was with the intention of doing it in secret, and then one day pulling the published novel out of some hidden pocket and plopping it down in front of someone. "See?" The shiny new cover would say. Ha. That would show them.

Through the process of writing, revising, and getting to know rejection uncomfortably well, I realized just how important people are to the process of producing a book. I could not have done this without the people in my life, whether they are still in it or not, and I want to honor them properly here.

Thank you to Cade, the first person I dared speak this concept to. You were a good friend in a strange place and I hope you're very happy, wherever you are.

Thank you to Lynn, Lukas, Sunny, and Hannah for being betas, and to Lynn again for always understanding what I meant when I said it was an Ivan kind of day.

Steph, you gave me even more extensive feedback than this last group, and I don't think this novel could have been what it now is without your advice. My undergraduate professors Parker, Nazar, and Nafziger also gave wonderful advice, but somehow it lacked the spice of your declaration that Ivan "sounds like a Capricorn."

Thank you to Thomas, my copyeditor, and Tricia, who illustrated and formatted the cover. You were both wonderful to work with, and you did your jobs with such apparent ease that you made me miss freelancing. I could not have done this without you.

Thank you to my mother, who named the whale, and to my grandmothers, who taught me the stubbornness necessary for publishing.

To Query Shark, for helping me adjust my query, and to the agents who took the time to read my manuscript.

To my favorite author, for showing me that women can wear suits and oxfords.

Finally, to the indigenous tribes, activists, and scientists doing all they can to save the Rezzies, thank you for helping keep this wide world full of things worth writing about.

9 781736 174111